BADRIA A

A NOVEL

Crossing Embers

TRANSLATED BY SAWAD HUSSAIN

daab

Badria Al Shihhi

Crossing Embers (Novel)

Translated by: Sawad Hussain

© 2021 Dar Arab For Publishing and Translation LTD.

United Kingdom
60 Blakes Quay
Gas Works Road
RG3 1EN
Reading
United Kingdom
info@dararab.co.uk
www.dararab.co.uk

First Edition 2021
ISBN 978-1-78871-082-4

Copyrights © dararab 2021

All rights reserved. No part of this publication may be reproduced, stored in a retrieval system or transmitted in any form or by any means, electronic, mechanical, photocopying, recording or otherwise without the prior permision of the publisher, except in the case of brief quotations embodied in reviews and other non-commercial uses permitted by copyright law.

This is a work of fiction. Unless otherwise indicated, all the names, characters, businesses, places, events and incidents in this book are either the product of the author's imagination or used in a fictitious manner. Any resemblance to actual persons, living or dead, or actual events is purely coincidental.

The views and opinions expressed in this book are those of the author(s) and do not reflect or represent the opinions of the publisher.

Text Edited by: Marcia Lynx Qualey
Text Design by: Nasser Al Badri
Cover Design by: Hassan Almohtasib

Dedication

To my parents: I love you from the depths of my being.

(1)

For the soul goes from me to return to you
Day after day and my eyes shed tears that they
Cannot look over to where you are
And see you clearly ever again

- Friedrich Hölderlin (From Selected Poems by David Constantine)

To hell with the lot of you, you white-hairs, this wretched life. To hell with Salim and everything. My life's been wasted for nothing, lost in a mirage full of empty promises. And for what? It's all out of my hands. Um Qais's crowing rooster wrenched me from my heavy nightmare, my body shaking and drenched with sweat. 'Oh God, protect me.' The black woman, in her translucent white clothes, clings to the vestiges of my restless sleep; this time she's smirking, then she winks before disappearing once more.

The rooster didn't let up its mad crowing; he's known for his off-kilter timing. How many times had I cursed him for intentionally crowing right at my window! But this time I was thankful; that dream had been suffocating me, and I didn't have it in me to drive it away.

I shook off the rest of my restlessness and took a moment to look around at my surroundings. Darkness still gently blanketed the room. My wooden body refused to respond to me. I sat catatonic for a long time, until Mohammed bin Nasser's voice rang out with the call for the dawn prayer. Alarmed, the ungrateful jinn in my body slipped out and went on its way. Finally, I could get up and move freely. I wiped my brow with my palm; it felt strange to be so sweaty on such a chilly night.

I should have known that the rebellious, stubborn boy who used to play with me in my bygone childhood wouldn't be satisfied with me, and that he'd chase after the impossible, as usual—after another kind of woman, one cut from a completely different cloth. If only I'd rejected him from the start.

I should have married a Sayf or Yaqub, to show him how all the young men in our extended family desired me.

'Zahra, get up, *ibnati*. Go pray and bake the bread.'

Dismayed, I pounded the clay wall with my fist. This was what all my mornings were about: praying and baking bread. Sluggishly, I went and kindled the oil lantern. *What had Salim wanted with me?*

While I had spent my days in a never-ending cycle of nothing new, nothing to live for, that arrogant cad had been chasing another woman.

Vexed, I stuffed the lantern in a small opening in the wall. Its feeble, flickering light allowed me to find the pot of dough that I had prepared the day before, just before I'd gone to sleep.

Other than death, what had that black woman brought him? He drowned after his boat sank to the bottom of ocean, even though he used to swim like a fish in our local falaj, the manmade irrigation channel. What a dark destiny....

And here I had sat, waiting: a fool.

The dry grass didn't catch fire despite my repeated attempts, the matchsticks burning my fingers each time. Impatiently and fuelled by my growing anger, I poured out all the kerosene left in the house, and only then did the flame catch. The fire cast a giant shadow of my crumpled body: flickering, then growing darker, shifting and staying still, bubbling with anger like its old owner.

He had refused to stay on the mountain, demanding to travel after the war broke out in the village. He left before the defeated rebels sought shelter on the mountain. That's when I knew he wasn't coming back.

'I want to see the world, Zahra. What's beyond the mountain? They say it's the ocean; do you know the ocean?'

I was at a loss to respond. He'd shot me a frosty glance and took off. Stuck-up, crazy man! Didn't he know there was war raging everywhere?

'Zahra.' My mother's voice cut short my train of thought. 'Fill the *kharas* up with water.'

'Yes mother.' Once again, the chore of filling up the clay pot. The ocean. What was the ocean that Salim would talk about for hours on end when we were young? When I finally asked my father, he calmly looked at me, his *misbaha* prayer beads slipping between his fingers. 'Endless salty water, full of fish.'

Was that it? Then I could have filled the falaj *with salt to keep Salim from leaving!*

The aroma of *rukhal* wafted through the courtyard that sprawled in front of the house. Yesterday, the aroma of the flatbread had whetted my appetite, but today not so much. Something inside me was wriggling and bubbling up. I placed the tray of bread on the reed mat and covered it with the palm frond *shat*. Next up was the second stage of my repetitive days. Placing the *handuwwa* atop my head, I walked to the lonely well, in silence, nothing except for my yawning and the grasshopper's song announcing a new day.

What was it that didn't make me enough of a wife for Salim? I was beautiful; I baked and cooked, and my tanjeem *patterns were the most intricate skullcap embroidery on the mountain.*

What was I missing?

I was tidy, obedient, and I worked like a donkey. Why had he left me for someone else? What did she have?

My steps grew heavy, and the full metal vessel on my head sloshed, raining refreshing drops on me. He had always been a charmer; all the girls had envied me because I was his cousin, betrothed to him from a young age. Even my other uncles' daughters had been jealous, because I had been his father's first choice.

A storm of blood raged in my ears. The mountain made me a laughingstock, and soon enough I'd be the punchline of jokes, the tasty morsel of gossip shared over snacks of dates and coffee during breaks on journeys.

I can't keep myself hidden any longer. That vain man made me his plaything, keeping me hanging in limbo on a string, neither belonging to him nor to anyone else. How I hated him, and hated myself for believing his lies for so long. What did she have that he'd give me up?

I poured the water into the *kharas*, my reflection on the silvery water hazy and obscure. But in the mirror, I was an old maid over thirty, even though my face was still radiant, as rosy as fresh henna, my piercing jade eyes undeniable. So why'd he leave?

What did that black, snub-nosed woman have over me?

Had he meant to insult me and hurt the family's pride by doing what he did? Perhaps not, since he'd never been the reckless type, and that's what made me even more miserable. He'd been rational, composed. Why didn't you come back? How could you prefer to die far away in the arms of a strange woman from a foreign land? I wish I'd died before finding out you had someone else that you'd touched, that you'd caressed. Weren't those intimate moments meant to be mine and mine alone?

Had another womb other than mine carried your child?

Silence stretched like a shadow pursued by the hesitant rising of the sun. I felt a lump squeezing my breath. How miserable I am!

I heard the clamour of my father and brothers coming back from *fajr* prayer, having their breakfast and then setting off for the field. A monotonous, vicious, unchanging cycle; is that why he left?

'He'll come back when all he can see is the mountain,' his father had said. Yet see how he'd been so bold to disappoint his father and dash peoples' hopes. He'd always dared to challenge what was accepted. Hadn't he gone his own way to join the rebels, while we were stuck in rooms and cellars with our men as British aircraft pelted the mountain with fiery bolts of lightning? While he had gone on thinking his was a worthy cause, hadn't he fallen, riddled with wounds, men fervently murmuring the *shahada* at his impending death?

At this, my heart fell between my hands, plunging further when his sisters yowled, announcing the imminent period of mourning. But despite everything, he hadn't fled with the fugitives. He had remained, awaiting his destiny, as my uncle hid him from the Sultan's men, plunging him into a well and declaring him dead. His body was ravaged by illness and infection, and he stared Death in the face.

My heart could die from the pain I feel for him, not being able to run to him or take him in my arms.

I learned about his condition from my uncle's gossipy daughters, tolerating the sting of their tongues for his sake.

He had been sick for so long that I lost hope.

But he came back alive and kicking and, as usual, asking for the impossible. He asked to leave and, without waiting for permission, picked up his cloth bundle and left. He didn't come back, and now he never would; my beloved was dead, taking my life with his.

'Spawn of the devil! I must have forgotten to say bismillah when he was in the womb.'

Poor uncle, I wonder how the mourning gathering you held for your disobedient son went. Did you cry? Or did you pretend, as is your wont, to be an impenetrable dam, stony-eyed, looking forever resolute, feigning indifference and blanketing yourself in masculinity?

'I won't forgive him for being away for so long. He's forgotten his family and friends, and no one will cry for him even if a wave does swallow him up.'

At that time, I hadn't known what a wave was. But that night, I cried at the spectre of my marriage crumbling. There was no turning back the clock.

My uncle's prayer must have leaked out and found its way to the sky, because a wave did in fact swallow up Salim, and sucked him down to the depths.

My being among the women caused sorrow; all of them had been married since they were thirteen, while I was gnawing my fingers, furious at a husband the sea had swallowed up, leaving me ravaged by the years.

I chuckled to myself once more.

'Mohammed, Ali, Saeed! Breakfast!'

As if they had been waiting for that very call, they rushed toward the spread on the reed mat in the courtyard. I retreated to my room to wait for them to finish so I could then wash the dishes; non-stop service without a single word of thanks breathed my way, even in secret.

'They say she's the daughter of a man from Ibra, that he married from there.'

Ali cackled. 'African women…no man's gone there without marrying one.'

'The trip to Africa doesn't seem very pleasant. A tiring journey, the dangers of the sea, and all for the sake of marrying a slave that will sully your lineage.' Ali snickered at Mohammed's comment, and my father cut them off, the *misbaha* beads never leaving his fingers. 'There's no difference among people except for how pious they are. But a slave girl? He left a free woman for the sake of a slave!'

It was like night and day between the start of his sentence and the end of it. What a chasm between his turquoise prayer beads from Mecca and the disdain in his voice! Suddenly, the booming voices from the courtyard softened, and they started whispering about something else.

It must be about me.

It was all about me: meaningless mourning, repulsive sly sorrow. I didn't want to answer my father's call, because what good would his pity do me? I heard my mother say my name as she quietly confronted my father. He raised his voice, cutting their conversation short. 'She'll do whatever I say.

Since when do daughters say no? She's become the talk of the mountain.'

My father left the courtyard, his brows knitted, not making eye contact with me. I noticed the blue prayer beads coiled tightly around his fingers, suffocating them.

*   *   *

There would be no shower of affection unless whatever my mother wanted was bound to infuriate me; she stroked my head while tenderly patting my hand, which she hadn't done in such a long time. She had been preoccupied with less emotional yet more beneficial matters: she had a green thumb for mountain flower buds and green qat *stalks, and she was much more affectionate with them than when she stroked my head or caressed my sweaty hand. Whatever was compelling her sudden tenderness was sure to upset me.*

'Zuhaira,' she said, using a nickname I loved, which I hadn't heard for an age. She had used it when telling me how I'd have to wait for Salim, when I reached puberty and she told me about boys and the courtyard. She forbade me to play and run in the alleyways, teaching me how to hide 'it' with the utmost secrecy. We spoke as if plunged into a shameful lifestyle. I had been terrified, telling her with tears wetting my cheeks, 'Ummi, I'm bleeding.' I thought I was going to die, but she smiled as calmly as she was doing now and said, 'Don't you worry. Don't tell anyone. Put a clean cloth down there and tie it round your waist.'

'I'm scared I'm going to die.'

'You won't die if you stay away from boys. Your father will kill you if he sees you playing with them!'

'Won't I die first from all this blood?'

'Go and clip the *qat*, Zuhaira. You're a woman now.'

Only much later did I come to know that it happened to every girl. I learnt why I had grown up, and how I knew more when my mother wasn't with me, and how it wasn't as shameful or lethal as she had made it out to be. Her strong voice jolted me from my thoughts, reproach streaming toward me through her slit eyes. 'Zuhaira, you're a woman now!'

Would you look at that! The same words from when I was seventeen, the same intimidation mingled with scorn. The equivalent expression, 'You're a man now,' didn't instil the same fear in my brothers when they hit puberty. Instead, it was laced with pride and accompanied by trilling calls of joy. My brothers' heads weren't bent as mine had been. They were confident. Men, my father would slap proudly on the back. Men, my mother would receive with love and a warm smile.

'Zuhaira, stay focused. A woman whose mind wanders needs a husband!'

I didn't mean to laugh; it just slipped out, cynical and bitter. My pent-up fury was coming unbound, as if the cowardice I had drunk from her breast had all but evaporated.

'Listen here, your father will hear you and come over to slap you. Shhhh.'

'What about you, Ummi?'

You can never forget that first slap, humiliating and hot. You kept on scratching Mohammed with your nails. Then he pulled your hair and called you a sheep. 'I'm not a sheep ... I'm not!'

'Sheep are slaughtered and billy goats survive. A billy goat like me is worth a thousand sheep.'

I hadn't responded, resentment and rage boiling. I had instead scratched him with all my might, drawing blood. That's why the slap had been hot, and the talebearing to my father humiliating.

Even now, I don't dare look into my brothers' faces. I imagine myself in their eyes as a sheep being led to slaughter each and every day. When I do catch a glimpse, I see them smirking.

My mother muttered softly, reluctance and confusion written on her face, her dark green eyes flashing a warning, 'Your father and your uncle ...'

'What about them?'

'You know Abdallah?'

'There are dozens of Abdallahs in our family!'

'Your uncle Saeed's son.'

'What about him?'

'You're to marry him.'

I felt my heart stop, overcome by an eerie paralysis. I repeated what she said over and over, tasting it in my mouth. Abud? Did she mean the child I carried when he was still in swaddling clothes? The eighteen-year-old boy? She must be kidding. Maybe she got the wrong Abdallah. It must be one of my other uncles' sons; if he was already married, no worries, but not Abud. Since when did she make mistakes when it came to marriage? Mother was only good at relaying bad news.

Only last year I had been making fun of Riya, Shuhab's daughter, because they had married her off to Musa. He was five years younger than her. I told her to suckle him well and sing him a sweet huwwa. *I kept on teasing her till she'd had enough and kept her distance. Now I had to accept the child that I'd played with when he was an infant, to whom I had slipped sweet* mabsil *and* nuql. *Marry Abud?*

'Who again, Ummi?'

'Abdallah, Saeed's son.'

'Why? Marry me off to any other cousin. How about Rashid or Fahm... do you want women to laugh at me? Abud's just a child and doesn't know anything. I won't marry him even if hell freezes over!' My voice grew hoarse. Was I crazy for asking for a sliver of mercy? My heart roared in my ears like rain beating down on a palm-frond shack. The soil on Salim's grave hadn't even settled. I felt completely hollow; how could I expect mercy here? Why was I such a fool?

'That's what your father said. Now don't cause us any headaches, Zahra. You know how our family works. Don't wear me out!'

'I won't marry Abud even if they kill me.'

My mother tilted her head, as if contemplating a sharp riposte, but she shook it slightly instead and said, 'Your father's going to discuss it with you this evening.'

'I won't marry anyone ... I don't want Abud.' My voice choked, and my body trembled under the weight of a sudden fever, draining me completely.

A familiar smile from my mother made me quiet down enough to forget my wild outburst. The pigeon in Um Qais's cage had been freed, and it took off, soaring high into the sky.

'Yes, Zuhaira, like this you're more rational. Trust in God, my girl....'

* * *

The news of my engagement to Abdallah spread like wildfire. I didn't dare venture out except early in the morning, to fetch water and other household necessities. I grew to despair of everything. I harboured a persistent desire to end it all.

There was no mourning ceremony held for Salim, since they had been utterly furious with him. I wondered if they would forget me as easily if I continued to refuse?

Salim had been beloved, but love did him no good in the face of such anger. They forgot him, easily erased him, and quickly decided to set right what had been ruined.

I should have screamed, should have torn up their faces, should have held the *qat* shears and sliced open the belly of whomever brought it up, should have ... how powerless I felt, how crushed.

What sort of game were they playing with me? After all my obedience, I was to be rewarded with ... Abud? And Salim, to whom I'd given my heart for almost twenty years, was gone. Poof—just like that! Were they asking me to clean my arteries of my love for Salim to make way for Abud?

'Zahra, you've got to get ready for the wedding.' It had been forty days since Salim's death, exactly forty. 'You'll go to Nizwa to choose gold jewellery for the wedding—now, which of the mountain women gets to do that? It's never happened before and probably won't happen again. How lucky you are, my girl!'

Luck? You conniving old woman, you only know how to take orders and brag.

'For Abdallah, they'll buy a golden dagger, and he'll be the envy of all.'

I wish I could slice open his belly with that dagger.

'Abdallah is a good match for you. Our God doesn't forget anyone.'

If you'd just shut up, Ummi. I'm not so stupid that I can't see how anxious you are about being humiliated. Those two narrow eyes that turn to stone when it comes to me.

'After tomorrow, Friday, you'll all go to Nizwa. You don't know Nizwa; you only know the mountain. You'll see the ivory souk with all the beautiful clothing. You'll be dazzled by all of it. I've gone two or three times with your father to sell honey and rosewater. Back when you were kids....'

I can't stand your chatter, Ummi. I wish I could just zip your mouth shut!

(2)

O, distant compelling fulfilled hour,
Which once enveloped even the lost

- Gottfried Benn

Only now do I understand why Salim preferred that black woman to me.

I can't, even once, do as I like; it's out of my hands.

Like any woman deprived of her rights, my beauty has run cold, and it's shrouded in humiliation. Here I am, prisoner to a marriage I can't even wrap my head around. I'm forced to walk the path charted for me. No different today as a thirty-something than I was as a three-year-old child. Nothing has changed for me except for the handful of bitter pills I swallow every day, disregarding my ulcer-ridden, languishing body.

It's Friday. My mother lays out my clothes and perfumes them with incense, then pats them with homemade rosewater. She chatters on about Nizwa, gold, conspiring against my uncle's daughters, ascribing to them the traits of a wasteland.

'Come on now my girl, your father and uncle are waiting for you. They've been back from dawn prayers for a while.'

'Uncle?' I searched her face. Maybe she was playing a joke on me, a bad joke, but she raised her index finger to her mouth and whispered, 'Your uncle is going to go sell some gold and goats. Your wedding isn't going to be cheap, *habibati*. You'll all have lunch in Nizwa, and I think you'll spend the night there too, because it's a long, tiring journey.'

'You said it'd just be only Ali and Baba.'

'Is your uncle a stranger?'

'As always, I'm the last to know!'

'Oh Zahra, you're grumbling too much these days. Shame on you; a woman of your standing shouldn't object to men's decisions.'

My uncle towered over my father's slight frame, and even though he was four years older than my father, he looked younger. His puffy jugular veins were a symbol of rude health, and his radiant smooth skin and dark hair dye, which he got monthly from Nizwa, made him look the picture of relative youth. Poor Baba on the other hand wasn't good at taking care of his wrinkled brown skin, and the inferior henna that he used to chase away the specks of grey in his hair, as well as his hunched-over body, made him look older than he should.

My uncle calmly smiled at me, the first time since I'd seen him that morning. He cleared this throat before pronouncing emphatically in his customary cadence, 'I'm sure you'll be comfortable with us, Zahra. You won't have an aunt who harasses you like all mountain girls complain. May she rest in peace. My daughters are still young, as you know; you can't imagine how happy they were when I told them you'd be joining our home. You haven't visited us since you were engaged to Salim. Why is that?'

'Young? Said will marry Maryam while all of you marry me off. Your girls could have visited me if they wanted. Maryam is excused, we can say, but the rest aren't engaged yet.'

He furrowed his eyebrows, but kept quiet. Then he threw a cursory, commanding glance in my father's direction and, as usual, Baba hurried to oblige.

'Zahra, shame on you! Is that how you speak to your uncle?' In a fit of reluctant, affected anger, he made as if to slap me until my uncle forced a smile. 'Don't hit the bride...spoil her a bit.' He stared at me coldly and turned away.

Oh God, what's happened to me? Why can't I keep my temper in check? Why can't I just keep quiet? What made me say something as silly as that? My father kept grovelling to his brother while I turned my head and kicked the lazy mule in anger. If I walked, I'd be moving quicker than this stupid creature. It was all about keeping up appearances out here; at home, just a few hours ago, I was toing and froing like a mule myself: waking up at dawn, on the go till dusk. What a joke to pamper me with this false coddling! I know for sure that the third day after the wedding will be the beginning of my life of servitude, forever working like a donkey in my uncle's house.

Our path sloped downhill and became more rugged. The mule hesitated, cautiously stepping to avoid the sharp stones and the thorny bushes springing up from the uneven ground.

The farms dotting the foot of the mountain looked much smaller than what their owners had gone on bragging about, and the clay houses with their palm-frond roofs looked like they were piled up, one top of the other. I could clearly make out the clothes spread out on the roofs, next to the lemon trees and clusters of dates swaying in the sun. *How beautiful you are, mountain. Beautiful in your elegant pride and your towering height but, sadly, heir to generation after generation of an unmerciful way of life that's lived on your peak.*

My father and uncle rode graceful horses. They slowed down, finding it difficult to drag my stubborn mule over the jagged rocks.

Oh, my poor brother Ali, your fair forehead inked with dark discontent. But at least it's the first time I've come out better off than you. You and the rest of my brothers had complete freedom, wandering freely, flirting at the falaj, getting together with friends and coming home whenever you pleased, napping every day while I fought off sleepiness as I washed up the dishes from lunch, the sun my only companion. Even in the field, you barely lifted a finger to harvest ripe dates or clip the qat *grass for the livestock. Mother and I handled it all; mother, who never complained, who pushed you to go have a rest, leaving the two of us miserable till sunset. You might as well be a royal heir, with us women your slave girls worked to the bone.*

The men encountered some farmers at the foot of the mountain facing us; they too were on their way to Nizwa, to sell goats and honey. Quickly, their chatter grew distant, and I struggled to follow the thread of their conversation.

'This new gas is going to ruin all our businesses. I wonder if there's going to be any need for cattle and lemon fields?'

'They say it's much more valuable than gold. That's what they say, but God knows best.'

'Is that so? You think we'll find any in our fields?'

'They're digging wells, that's what I heard. Really deep ones. Using these huge machines borrowed from the Europeans.'

'How kind of them!'

'Hush! It's not as if they're doing it for free. They're obviously taking a cut.'

'Criminals. In any case, do you think we'll find some in our fields? If we find some, we won't need anything else. We'll be kings. We'll have it all,' my uncle said in a near-whisper that dripped with hope and unfettered greed. But what the farmer said next made his face drop with disappointment.

'This gas isn't for anyone to extract; it belongs to the earth.'

I heaved a deep sigh, and silence prevailed once more. The only sounds were the clip-clop of hooves meeting pebbles and the bleats of goats injured by the difficult terrain. The men exchanged curious looks, taking in each other's herd of goats. My uncle looked enviously at his neighbour's plump, strong sheep. I braced myself to hear one of them recite *Al-Falaq* to ward off the evil eye. Tension hung in the air for a moment until one of them picked up the thread of conversation once again, talking casually about how young men down the foot of the mountain were leaving for Africa. I thought I'd hear some new piece of information about Salim or his alleged wife, but the talk was about something entirely different.

'Did he come back again?'

'That *zutti* would sell his own father to make a quick profit.'

'He still has some merchandise he needs to move. He's close to sailing again, and people say he needs the money to fix his boat. Like all the mountains of money he makes from selling slaves and weapons isn't enough!'

'People of his kind never change their ways. It's in their Indian blood.'

Ali half-smiled as he followed the conversation, resisting the urge to jump in with his own commentary. What came after was so dull that I stopped paying attention.

The sun was high in the sky and the road seemed to stretch on forever.

Cold sweat zigzagged down my back, making my *thawb* stick to me, making me itch. *This cheapskate; I wonder if he knows Salim and his wife? Is he the one who dragged him to Africa? And does he know what happened next?*

'Ali, why aren't you talking?'

'About what?'

'Anything ... about Africa, for instance.'

He looked at me sharply, knowing what I was getting at. Reluctantly, he said, 'Salim is dead. *Yarhamuhu* Allah. Let him rest in peace.'

'How did he die?'

'You heard us that night, don't play dumb.'

'But wasn't he a good swimmer?'

'It's called a storm. Strong winds and water from every direction, you get what I'm saying?'

He was drawing out his words, scoffing at me. Once again, he was making me feel less than him, from another world, simplifying his language to make it easier for me to understand, as if I was a stupid child. Arrogant.

'His wife?'

'What about her? Why are you asking all these questions all of a sudden?'

'Will she come here to the mountain?'

'I heard that her father's paralyzed and that her mother is sick. She wouldn't come even if she had the guts to do it. She's working there to support her parents and her child.'

'We all have to work. Nothing for her to brag about.'

He bit his tongue and smacked the mule to get a move on.

'She farms, harvests, sells in the market, cooks and travels. Do you do all that?'

'I do all of that as well as milking cows and taking care of the house. Okay, maybe I don't travel or sell in the market, but if I was allowed to, I would.'

'She's smarter, more aware. Your brain is small.'

'*Your* brain is small. I'm not stupid.'

He breathed out heavily, gnashing his teeth. 'I don't want to fight with you today, you're the bride-to-be!'

'Are you making fun of me?'

He arched his eyebrows.

'It's a done deal, Sister. We're on our way to buy your wedding jewellery.'

I was speechless. The pitying looks of mousy Abdallah's sisters and their wickedness were the last things I wanted. *How sick this life makes me! I'm going to have to wait hand and foot on my uncle's spoilt daughters, preparing everything for them. And when they burn me with their barbed tongues, I won't have a strong husband or father to keep them in check. Instead, I'll have an uncle like a dagger plunged into my heart, stubborn and merciless. Marrying that Abdallah? Over my dead body!*

'Ali, who's that miser the men were talking about?'

'A Nakhuda from Sur; he's got a bad reputation.'

'Why would you hate a sea captain who's far away from you?'

'He's full of himself, bragging all the time, like he owns the world or something. They say he's of low origins, a bastard.'

'But you all buy slaves and other things from him. He's doing what you all want.'

'Selling slaves is haram. He kidnaps people and sells them all over, carrying them to Dhofar, Aden, and Sur. Everywhere, everywhere.'

'Do you know him?'

'He's the one who told us about Salim. We came across him in the field. He was looking for our uncle, to tell him about Salim's death, and about his wife and child.'

I started, surprised. I was seeing Salim in a different light. No doubt this reviled captain had some close connection with him. 'When does this Nakhuda take off again?'

'What do you care? I won't tell you. Pulling your weight on this lazy mule has worn out my arms.'

'Do you want me to get off?'

'No ... no.'

Even when I'm rational and well-balanced before him, he's still as arrogant as the rest. Let him die of exhaustion. I won't get down from this mule and give up my only comfort.

Buck thorn and *ghaf* trees scattered along the way provided shelter from the sun, the shade a welcome canopy while we prayed. Ali was fed up and in a bad way when Uncle demanded that we keep going. In my most patronising voice, I said to Ali, 'Keep your chin up! It can't be much further to Nizwa. Take it easy, Brother.'

His face grew even more crimson at my mockery. 'If you don't shut up, I'll split your head open with this rock.'

How delightful it would be, even if only for once, to get one over on one of my brothers. How many times they'd soiled clothing that I'd just hung out in the morning for me to have to rewash it numerous times, all without a single word of thanks sent my way.

'I'll shut up, but tell me about Abdallah.' I said this as if the matter at hand concerned not me, but someone else altogether. He thinks he's manipulating me, but I'm the one with the reins here. He needed to calm down.

'He's the best match for you in all respects,' he said excitedly, his scorn tinging every word. 'Salim died to save himself from you. And Allah sent Abdallah to you, a powerless boy who never says no, so you can make him do your bidding with some candy. Oh God, how much Abud loves candy!'

'Are you trying to belittle me?'

My defeated tone moved him, and he quickly responded, 'Oh Zahra, all the other girls are happy with their lot, why are you grumbling?'

'Because Salim told me that he felt the world closing in on him and that he would die early.'

'If he really could see the future, then he would've avoided his own death. Salim was only good for idiotic rebellions. He almost died because of this stupidity. Don't you remember the war? I still think he did it so that he could brag to others, to tell them he was a fearless adventurer. Let him rest in peace, let's not dig up graves, Zahra.'

'At least he wasn't a coward. He didn't sneak into cellars like the others. You're just jealous because Maymouna was in love with him.'

'Shut up. You don't know anything. My God, how stupid you are! Ah, there are the hills of Nizwa on the horizon. It's late. I think we'll stop at an inn.'

The idea of running away exploded in my head. I tried to think about my inevitable wedding with something like pleasure, but the devil sat in his place for a long time, leaving no space to think about anything else.

The room was crammed, with a smell that was neither offensive nor pleasing, and the ground was covered with a straw mat—old, but clean.

My uncle talked at length with the young black slave, whose anxious eyes, for no obvious reason, caught my attention. He wrung his hands when he was unable to answer my uncle's simple question about the owner of the inn, as if feeble-minded. The men wolfed down the food I had prepared that dawn, and in no time fell into deep sleep.

I stayed in my own room, mulling over my thoughts, trying to move past this idea. Al-Shaytan, that old devil, brought the idea of leaving back to the fore, and why not? But I hadn't stepped out of such bounds before. I didn't dare for a moment even think about resisting; what was happening to me? I sought refuge from God once more.

Without realising it, my eyes drifted to the confused movements of the slave in the hallway that faced my window. *One chance to give myself an entirely new life, a new heartbeat, one less terrified than mine right now. No ... no*

... wayhi, they'll kill me, butcher me with the daggers that I buff every morning at home. It's better not to think about such things.

I trailed the annoying fly that had followed me in from the inn entrance. It had a strange, annoying buzz. The atmosphere in the room made one feel sick, the silence looming like a dreadful creature, and the fly accosted me through my damp burqa. I was burning up, and time slipped away, roaring as it departed. I tossed the burqa to one side and lay down on the couch. The fly kept crashing into the wall, searching for an exit. As soon as it despaired, it returned angrily to me. *Dumb animal.* The small window overlooking the hall was open and nearby, but the fly kept bumping into my face. *All roads lead to hell.*

Afternoon was nearly over; the food in front of me had grown cold. I felt a strange heat course through my sweaty body, and Abdallah's sonorous laughter crashed into my ears. *What has he done wrong to end up with me? What have I done wrong to live full of resentment for my so-called great family?*

The fly traipsed across my dry lips, but this time I didn't chase it away, letting it play with the prominent dry flakes of skin. It had delicate legs, it tickled my lips, its body trembled, it sensed everything–except the nearby opening in the wall.

'We're going for prayer...are you okay? Lock the door with the bolt till we get back.'

I nodded as if struck mute, my throat dry and my chest tight. Ali's eyes quickly took in the untouched food, and he forced a smile before mumbling, 'Worried about the wedding?'

I noticed that the fly had gone through the window, making its way outside at last.

* * *

The slave was deep in sleep when I shook him awake. He straightened up and yelped. I scolded him, though half-frightened by his massive frame. 'Shhh ... shhh. Calm down, I won't tell your master you were sleeping.'

'Oh God, madam, what is it? I swear I wasn't looking at you through the window, believe me. I haven't said anything about your appearance to the innkeeper. What, you don't believe me?'

He seemed naïve, his stupidity making me all the more uneasy.

'No worries. But if you don't want me to say anything about you nodding off, then do me a small favour.'

His mouth dropped open, and he looked around as furtively as a thief. His foolishness grated on me, because time was ticking away quicker than a panicked heartbeat. 'Don't be scared, I'll pay you well.'

He stayed quiet.

'Do you know the Nakhuda from Sur?'

His expression changed instantly, from absentmindedness to a sly, piercing stare. 'Does your father know you're asking after this captain?'

'I'm the one asking the questions here, so answer me quickly, there isn't much time!'

'He's got a bad reputation, and you're from a good family. Your family are well-regarded among the best and most powerful people.'

'*Now* you know how to talk? Tell me what I want to know and I'll give you ten rupees.'

'Madam, that man is the one who brought me here. I was so young, still drinking from my mother's breast. And this stupidity that you see in me was brought on by his beatings and torture. If I had stayed there, it would have been a different story.'

I cut him off abruptly, my fear growing like a giant djinn. 'I know, I know. Will you take me to him or should I ask someone else?' I was drawn to the inn's entrance. I didn't know anything about the area outside, so I added as a final plea, 'I'm sure that, if I go missing, my family's men will tear you from limb to limb for letting me go out on my own.' My breaths quickened as I stepped feebly outside the inn. This was the first time such madness had seeped into my humdrum life. I felt destruction and death lurking in the shadows, waiting for me at every turn. A potent mix of horror and anticipation scorched my face with a peculiar thrill. Finally, I dared to face being shamed, but it amazed me how much of my life had slipped away already, victim to delusion. Now I found myself stubbornly clinging to false hope. That day, right then, I'd reclaimed the right to do as I saw fit, although in any case, all possible paths before me led to death.

'*Sayyadati*, madam, you want to get me in trouble. No, that isn't the right way to get to that scoundrel.' The slave followed and then overtook me, as I had hoped, walking in front of me and looking around. He popped into a side alley. I followed him without daring to look at my surroundings. What if one of the men from the mountain saw me now? What if I heard my uncle's furious cry? My legs grew weak as I imagined the menace of the daggers slung around the waist of every man. Ah ... what madness was this? What was happening to me?'

'That's the shack that Sultan lives in. You'll find him cooped up like a chicken in there; he and his men all sleep in the same place. If only you'd change your mind so we could go back to the inn.'

'Are you scared?'

'You go over to him. I'll wait for you here.'

'No ... no. You go and tell him first that I want to speak with him. Then stay until I finish speaking to him, got it?'

'Why should I go to him? I'm not the one who wants to speak to him.'

'Go on, before the men find out that we're missing.' In the light of his increasing hesitance, I realised how dangerous this man must be, but he quickly returned to grumbling. I stood, not brave enough to look around him. *The men must be on their way back to the inn by now. I've got to go back. I'm not strong enough for such a rebellion, and a clumsy one at that. Yes ... I've got to go back.* Before I could succumb to the wave of cowardice washing over me, I heard a husky voice call out to me.

'This slave told me you want to speak to me.'

My entire body trembled as my eyes fell on the strange man before me. His figure made me stiff and confused. Nothing could have prepared me for this beautiful brown man.

'Am I wrong? Why are you looking so scared, woman?' He turned to the slave behind him and asked, 'This is her, right?'

I wished I had gone back, or that the ground would open up and swallow me whole.

'Green-eyed daughter of the mountain ...,' he started, staring shamelessly at my bare feet, '... with feet radiant like silver, what do you want? As far as I know we haven't met before.' Then he quickly turned to the slave and chuckled, 'Lucky man, aren't you? Walking around with this one here at night.'

Turning to me, he went on, 'Come on, my sweet, why are you shaking? If I had known you were coming, I would have sprinkled rose water.'

My throat was parched. This man was danger incarnate. I followed him skittishly to a dark clearing shaded by trees, far from prying eyes. I made sure the slave was nearby and then whispered haltingly, 'I don't have ... much time. I need a favour.'

'That's why you're trembling ... I don't usually do favours.'

'I'll give you new gold.'

He circled me deliberately, taking me in afresh. 'A runaway bride ... running from shame?'

'God forbid! I'm the daughter of Salim, the son of Sheikh Saeed bin Salim, the son of ...'

His eyes suddenly grew bloodshot. 'A sheikh's daughter! What do you want with me, woman?'

I felt dizzy and leaned against the tree next to me. 'I want to get out of here.' I saw the anger in his eyes and added, 'I also have some money that I've saved up. I'll pay you well.'

'What are you running away from, a respectable bride like yourself? From shame that will be uncovered on the wedding night?'

'No ... nothing like that.'

'Are you crazy? Gambling with your life like this?'

'He's much too young for me. Please stop yelling.'

'Look how you're shaking. You're terrified, and yet you're ready to risk your life. Do you know what it means for a sheikh to be angry?'

'Please answer me. I don't have time.'

'Take you? Do I look crazy enough to bring death upon myself?'

I was leaning my full weight against the tree, my legs betraying me. 'Look, I'll pay whatever you want, the gold earrings I have on and these two rings. I'll even give you the wedding dress they're buying for me.'

He burst out laughing, and the peals shook me to the core. I looked at him, my eyes supplicatory. He gave a nonchalant sneer. I felt again how despicable I must look to this superior gender, a speck of dust. My looming regret plunged me deep into despair. I cursed all those sick thoughts of taking revenge on my family, and of my powerlessness and how embarrassed I felt.

'Are you chasing a ghost?'

I didn't say anything.

'Let's say I accept, where would you go? Who would protect you, sweet thing that you are, and the daughter of a respectable family. Yes, sure, I love money, but I don't mess with getting on the wrong side of the sheikhs.' He beckoned to the slave and ordered, 'Take madam to the inn.'

'Okay, I'll go. But please don't tell anyone about me. It's as if you never saw me.'

'Coward.' He sighed as he shook his head. 'Take her before her family knows she was here.' He ignored my final pleading look and muttered, 'I swear this sheikh's daughter is going to bring us to ruin.'

(3)

He who determines his destiny by winning or death,
seldom faces death.

- Unknown

Oh God, I'm shaking all over! A sharp shudder pummelled me, and now my whole body feels as if the Shaytan that had been inside me slipped out, only to return, so that I'm wasting away yet again.

In my head a hundred pent-up ideas roused themselves from forgotten graves: a child in a far-off corner; shame; tottering ghosts that swarmed in from all sides.

For a moment, I felt alive again. I was born again a thirty-year-old, the past thirty years a wasted whiff, and this newly arrived dream of disobedience beckoned a renewal from behind all those borders and dismal fences. I didn't want to return to the house where my wedding party was being planned, but before long the dream broke apart, abruptly announcing its end as it ran aground once more, on the jagged rocks of reality.

Oh Salim, if only you could've seen me a few moments ago! Despite my anxiety, which you know well, I am walking in your footsteps so I can experience the real side of life, behind all those horizons, where you told me people are living a different way, one that might be better for us than what we've inherited. As for now, I've gone back to the same girl I was. Who knows, after a few hours maybe I'll go back to the mountain, to bury my fleeting rebellion in the embrace of the cows or use it—this yen to thumb my nose at tradition—as fertilizer for the qat *garden.*

'Do you believe me now? Didn't I tell you that he's downright rude? They say that yesterday, a woman visited him and spent the night, so he drove away his friends and made them sleep outside.'

'I wish I hadn't gone.' My sense of time came back to me. 'Do you think they're back?'

'Maghreb prayers ended a while ago. I think you're in for some trouble.'

I sighed sorrowfully and said, exasperated, 'Here's the inn, take your money and shut your mouth. If we come across them, let me do the talking, don't you dare let a thing slip out.' My heart pounded as we stood at the threshold. *Will we find them with their daggers in hand, roaring? What will they do to me and the poor slave?* I managed—barely—to keep myself together. In any case, the dagger would spare me a miserable life at Abud's side and the mockery of others.

I closed my eyes in fear and said bismillah, walking inside one step at a time. The inn was quiet. Were they spying on me? I stopped suddenly midway; what a coward I was!

'Go and check out the area,' I ordered the slave.

'Eh? Why me? *You* should go.'

'I said you go.'

'You do it!'

My heart leapt out of my chest when I heard footsteps near the entrance and a strange voice calling for the slave. I dashed for my room and, before I opened the door, I thought I heard movement inside. *Are they waiting for me in there?* Hearing nothing after a further pause, I slowly pushed the door and looked around fearfully. *Is someone breathing behind the door? Or is my own heavy breathing confusing me?*

I put my hand on my chest to calm my racing heart. I was soaked in sweat, my face hot and inflamed. *Here I am again, a cowardly study in contradictions. I'll go in. Whatever happens, happens.*

Nothing happened. There was no one crouching behind the door and the room welcomed me in silence.

I let out a lengthy sigh. I removed my burqa and sat staring at my face, dark with terror. My crazy adventure had ended in failure. Did they go out looking for me?

What I desperately needed right then was cool water streaming over my body to wash away thoughts of what I had done.

Raised voices outside made my guts twist. The owner of the inn was swearing at his slave and asking him where he'd been for so long. The slave responded with his customary, simple-minded babble. *I wonder if he'll spill the beans. Oh God, the man is a distant relation. I paid him very well, so he shouldn't say anything.* As soon as the quarrel between the slave and his master died down, I decided to take a cold shower, hoping to wash my head free of all this fear and stiffness.

God, please protect me from the accursed devil. Why can't I calm down? Why do I like chasing down death and the impossible all of a sudden? What power do I really have to change my position? Should I just pick up my bundle of clothes and take off for somewhere else? Where? Do I want shame in this age of dignity? I'm sure that I don't want Abud as my husband; I can't bear to have that child next to me. To pant next to my ear and plant a kiss on my neck; just thinking about it makes me sick! If only he had an intensity in his eyes like that despicable man, a muscular body like his... I shook my head furiously. *This day has been a disaster, I'm sure I'm going senile.*

I sat in the room gnawing at my fingernails, something I'd done since childhood, though there was nothing much left to gnaw at. The silence blanketing the place made it tense. Where had the men been all this time?

'Zahra?'

The answer came quickly, in Ali's worried voice. I hesitated momentarily, and refrained from opening the door. 'Who is it?'

'Your brother, you fool.'

I stared at his pale face for a long time, and his grimace and the redness of his eyes prepared me for what was coming. 'Did you sleep?'

Was he going to interrogate me to catch me in a lie?

'Me? No...I couldn't, I'm not used to this place. Where were all of you?' His eyes glanced around the room, taking it all in until they stopped at the mirror, which reflected his weary face. 'We were late, right?'

He's testing me again, playing this dirty game that ends only one way: with death.

'We went to finish what we'd come for. You know they brought you for a change of scenery, that's it.' When he saw the ease now draped across my face, he added, 'We bought gold, silver, and wedding outfits for you. Most of it is very expensive. *Wallah,* by God, you've begun to acquire a taste for the expensive, Zahra!'

'I've always worn such things on celebrations like Eid. It's nothing new for me.'

This time, I won't get annoyed by his sarcasm; all the fear I had left was chased off after my crazy outing.

'Oh, Abud's sweet bride, I'm so tired, here's your dinner. We ate out with one of the sheikhs of Nizwa, and there's still another banquet in a little while. I'm exhausted. The innkeeper has brought his daughter here in case you need anything.'

Quickly, I asked, 'So they brought me here for a change of scenery, then?' I ignored what he said about the innkeeper's daughter. I didn't need anyone else to notice my coming absence.

'Let's say it's so the friends harassing you wouldn't make you change your mind.'

'Change my mind? Would that stop the marriage from happening?'

'Of course not, but you'd be irritated and upset our mother.'

'I see.' Truth was, I wasn't annoyed by his observation one bit. No doubt I had exaggerated a lot about how my brother had mistreated me. I couldn't fathom why I felt guilty about what I was about to do.

'Actually, Uncle bought you two slaves. What a gift! Slaves will hem you in from every side.'

'Slaves? Didn't you tell me that buying slaves has been banned? Didn't our father say that we're all God's slaves?'

'There are differences. I don't want to fight with you right now, Zahra. I'll come back after the dinner, if you're not already asleep. I think Uncle wants to speak with you. You should see that gold he bought for you! You're very lucky, Zahra.'

He left me with those words choking me once more. I fail to pinpoint, for my own understanding, even one explanation for why they'd brought me here to Nizwa: heightened anxiety perhaps, or showing the world how well they're treating me, or maybe my uncle intended to torment me before owning me. Thoughts flew around in my head, one after the other, hundreds of them killed by the terror that had rapidly taken up residence inside me, ever since I'd set out on my crazy, failed sortie. Out of my forgetfulness, and without warning, there emerged the face of the scornful captain. I don't know what had stopped me from spitting in his face when he said those final shameless words to me. Maybe I reeked of weakness, which made people underestimate me without a second thought. I stood in front of the mirror in my damp black burqa. Maybe this submissiveness was written on my forehead. Did I get it from my father?

'Zahra.'

My uncle's voice at the door snapped me back to the present. 'Yes,' I whispered as the door opened and my uncle's puffy face shot in through the crack. He filled the cramped room and sucked out all the cool air.

How I dread you—how I wish you were never on the mountain! Then I'd be a calm woman now instead, preparing for her daughter's wedding rather than her own.

'Couldn't you tell it was me?'

I wonder if the mountain would be better off if you didn't exist. Sorcerers pass their magic down to people like you, and sorcerers die knowing that those who remain will inherit their magic, even if reluctantly. That's what grandmother used to tell me.

'Zahra, my son Abdallah is motherless.' He drew closer to pat my head. 'You'll be everything to him: his wife and his mother.'

Exactly the words that any magician worth his salt would say. Uncle, my uncle, this tenderness you draw on your face and carry in your voice is an unnecessary drug. I've already realised I'm utterly powerless.

'Take care of him and show him the right path.'

Are you afraid that I'll overpower your only son? I swear I'll make him humiliate you just as you've humiliated me.

'Abdallah is shy but he's like sugar.'

Sure, he melts quickly with nothing left on the tongue but sweetness.

'Why so quiet? Shy, my girl? As it should be; good girls don't talk in the presence of elders. God bless you. *Barik Allah feek.*' He stood by the mirror to look at my reflection. 'You know that Salim was ungrateful and didn't know your worth, but Abdallah's not Salim. He'll cherish you and treat you like a queen.'

When will this sermon end? How far are you going to take it?

'And my girls love you. They'll help you in everything. Forgive them for not visiting; they so rarely go out.'

That's why I always bump into them when I'm out buying fava beans.

'This is the least you deserve. I've made sure to hand it over to the bride instead of her parents, so you'll be satisfied, my daughter.' He handed me a big bundle with stiff politeness. He hadn't been forced to make this grand yet hilarious speech, but he'd come to guarantee my silence and give me a headache. This was how he bought obedience from his whole tribe, and at such a low price: with sweet-talk.

'Open it and see how much I value you. Look at this *ghaws* and *shambar* golden headdress, and these ten rings, one for each finger, and this silver jewellery for your head and feet. There's something to adorn every part of your body. You deserve it and more. Aren't you pleased, Zahra?'

I nodded mechanically. The sight of the gold was enough to suppress any rebellion, enough to make any woman to give in. Now, with this bundle in my hands, I lost all hope of cancelling the marriage. This was the price of my misery.

Salim's face, hazy in my memory, became clearer in my head: 'Don't let them exploit you, you've got the strength to fight back, if you want it,' he said. God rest his soul, but what power was he talking about? And wasn't this timeless, inherited weakness stronger than all my desires to rise up?

Why did you leave me? Why didn't you say no then when they told you that I'd be waiting for you? If only you'd taken me with you, we could have travelled together. We'd live far way and create our own traditions to be handed down, and our children would have a completely different life. But you decided, stubbornly, idiotically, to go all on your own.

'Zahra, are you dreaming?'

I snapped back to reality. He let out a violent laugh. 'I said we're going to go visit one of the vendors now, one who sells silk. We've chosen a few fabrics for you and your sisters. We'll pay him and then go back, and by God's grace we'll get home to the mountain right after the dawn prayer. Don't worry, even the innkeeper is from our family.'

I nodded, signalling my satisfaction, and he left with a smile plastered across his lips. *Various reactions wage war in my chest; I'm miserable and des-*

tined for bad luck. Maybe I'm being unfair, maybe it will all be better than what I've imagined. The voice of guilt again.

*   *   *

Are you angry with me, God? Is that why you're doing this to me? I've been treated unfairly. My teacher Ahmed, who taught me the Fatiha, used to say that God helped the oppressed. But if you have mercy for me, then why throw me into such sorrow?

Teacher Ahmed ... what reminded me of him at that moment, and of the large *ghaf* tree next to our farm?

My cousins and I had sheltered from the sun under its thick branches, stricken by fear of the elderly teacher's whip and his wife Zeyana's trachoma-infected, bloodshot eyes. The *juz 'amma* of the Quran had been in our laps. We followed the teacher's reading attentively, lest we get reacquainted with the stinging of his whip. As for Salim, he was the best, as usual, his recitation charismatic, with a memory that never failed, saving him from the taste of the whip, while my feet were lashed hundreds of times. But I was never resentful of my teacher; I loved reading the Quran under the *ghaf* tree, and I loved Zeyana's scolding at the end of the day. That's why they didn't leave me for too long under the tree; my father came to collect me midway through my lessons, saying that my mother needed me to help with the dough, that I'd had enough. But my uncle's daughters stayed on, and all the boys, too. Didn't they celebrate *al-toymeena*, when the women of the family could boast of them finishing the Quran?

My mother never seemed concerned, or maybe she just let all her suppressed fury loose on me that time the hot metal peel stung me. She had grabbed my hand and made it drink in the heat above the burning iron, saying–despite my yelps of pain–that this way I'd get used to the heat. With this, she was telling me how jealous she was of my cousin Maryam, who had finished reading the Quran that morning.

I never saw Teacher Ahmed after that, but I'd still grip the holy book after the dawn prayer and read what I could, crying when a word was incomprehensible, or a whole surah even.

I always took less than my uncle's daughters—less luck, for instance—and I learnt later on that my uncle had had a hand in all this. I didn't know why he hated me in particular; did he see hatred in my eyes? Today, this bundle before me might as well be a deed of sale. He'd bought me in one fell swoop.

There was a light knock on the door. *I wonder who's knocking and pulling me out of my sorrow? Could it be the inn's slave?*

'Who's there?'

No answer came, so I thought it was the wind.

'Open up.' The voice was just above a whisper, and familiar. Worried, I asked, 'What do you want? Didn't you dismiss me, gentleman that you are?'

'Don't arouse suspicion. Open the door, woman.'

'I don't usually let men into my...'

'I'll tell them you were with me.'

I couldn't have that. Carefully, I opened the door.

'Show me the money.' Just like that, without any pleasantries. He was wearing a short-sleeved white shirt and a short embroidered *izar* that revealed his long legs.

'You need to leave. My family will come and kill us both.'

'Don't worry, no one saw me. The inn's empty, except for that man dozing at the door.'

In the lamp's pale glow, his bare arms were coffee-black. I pinched myself in secret disbelief. He took in the room with hungry eyes.

'Are you still scared? Am I that hateful to you?'

'I'm not used to men in my...'

He threw a quick glance at his reflection in the mirror, then cut me off. 'I think you have something of mine. Where is the gold?'

'What changed your mind? Do you need money all of a sudden?'

'Yes, I have a pressing need for money.'

'Leave now, my family will come and...' He turned to face me, staring at me, taking me in from head to toe, his gaze lingering when his eyes locked on my burqa. He lingered so long that I felt the blood erupting in my veins, my heartbeat roaring. This man evoked a tangible unrest in me, an ugly tension.

'Have you changed your mind, woman? I can leave if you really want.' He made for the door with heavy steps. I stayed rooted to my spot. I guessed he was playing some dirty game to humiliate me. He stopped at the door, chuckled and said, 'Damned girl! In just one day, you've understood what I'm after... But I really do need the money.'

I still couldn't believe that I was alone, for the first time, with a male stranger in a narrow room like this—a man concerned about a woman like me, inexperienced in such situations. I couldn't believe that I was back to planning my escape, even though I was convinced it would be an adventure that carried only death and shame in its folds.

'Aren't you scared of my family?'

'My boat needs fixing up. Tomorrow we set off. The sailors didn't make much profit today, as people aren't buying anything from me. I don't have enough money to fix the boat and pay the sailors' wages, and delaying the trip isn't an option.'

'But people say you're rolling in money.'

He stepped away from the door and paced around in a circle. 'All rumours, my dear girl. I can't escape envy.' Then he looked up and scrutinised me. 'You want to go or not? Don't stall, I don't want such issues from the start.'

'I don't want to die alone here, but I'm not sure if I'll be safe with you.'

'Good grief, this really is the talk of noble daughters. Don't worry, the deceased was my friend.'

I felt a lump in my throat when he described Salim as deceased. 'How can I trust what you're saying?'

He shrugged and said in a sharp voice, 'The money! Money!'

'And what's to say you won't steal my gold and abandon me?'

'I can't deal with the revenge of sheikhs. They know where I work. I don't want people badmouthing me. I'm a respectable man, you know. Show me the money.'

Carefully, I took out and untied the bundle that had the gold wrapped inside. His eyes widened at the sight of the glow in front of him. '*Poor you! This is more than any bride deserves.* Are you crazy enough to leave such comfort behind? Don't change your mind now, though. Your eyes are running over with fear.'

'They're coming, get out while you can.'

'You're such a scaredy-cat. Just know it won't be a walk in the park—there are men and the journey's exhausting, I don't want any tears of hesitation or longing. Do you know anyone along As-Sawahil?'

'You're complicating things. I need some time to think.'

'Are you still here tomorrow?'

'No,' I said.

'So then, tell me now. Don't worry, everything will be done well, just give me the gold.'

'No.'

'Half?'

'Do you take me for a fool? Everyone calls you a cheat.'

'The subdued lamb has become a wolf.' He laughed so suddenly that my fear came flooding back.

'Go, go. You're going to expose me. I don't want to leave anymore.'

'You said 'everyone.' Did you dare ask about me?'

'Shhh, keep it down, I can hear steps outside.'

He drew closer and whispered, 'My reputation precedes me, yes, it does. Is that why you came to me? In spite of my low name? Do you think you'll be safe with a thief like me?'

My bones rattled under his piercing gaze. He had long, perfectly tapered fingers, and everything he did had a hint of panache. But his was a strange, narcotic danger. I swallowed nervously and became more hesitant as time passed. I smelled burning flesh. Where was it coming from?

'Don't panic so much, woman. Sure, it's full of men, but I'll tell the sailors that you're one of my relatives, going to visit your sister in…umm…where do you want to go?'

'I don't know.'

'You can decide later. So, should I come by again tonight?'

'But…'

'Now is not the time to hesitate. I don't like child's play. You were pushy before when you spoke to me. Did the gold change your mind? I'll come by.' He slipped away quietly.

What's happening to me? The burning smell grew stronger. *I'm really scared. Scared of myself.*

* * *

Ali was really chatty this time, very unlike himself. He sat down next to me and spoke at length about how sad he was that I would be going to my uncle's. I was fairly certain he was making fun of me in his own special way.

The night crawled along with each breath I took. I felt afraid and guilty, feelings that lasted a while. Here I was, crawling with them, yet Ali couldn't stop talking about the clothes he had bought for the wedding.

What if the sailor had lied to me? What if he found money elsewhere and so wouldn't need me anymore? Would he leave me to take my final journey to the mountain? If only he hadn't come by! I had started to make peace with it all, and now here I was back to feeling sick to my stomach, the devil inhabiting me, messing with my head and making my hands quake. I went back and forth from looking closely at the door to the small window. The only thing I could feel was the shaking of my bones to their core.

'What's with you, Zahra? Are you scared of something?'

'No.'

I shot out of the room like a bullet. I had exposed myself; why couldn't I control my body? *I wonder if he'll abandon me. I wish he hadn't come. I really am starting to lose it.*

The night settled over the daylight, shadows announcing its sovereign power. *I wonder why Ali decided to talk to me now? Why was he quiet all these years, only speaking now?*

'Do you want me to sleep here? Are you worried about the inn?'

'No ... not at all.' *I wish you will just leave now - soon I'll burst out sobbing, I'm so nervous with anticipation. Go on your way, I can't hold it together. I'm shaking! Why is that pirate so late?*

Finally, Ali decided to head for bed. He patted me on the head and looked at me as if it would be the last time. 'I'll miss you Zahra. You must be anxious about how far apart we'll be, being in different households.'

Ah ... such feelings, feelings that I don't want to deal with right now, and this vulnerability that I had always wanted... Where had such words as these been hiding all this time? Everything quaked around me; had I decided to give up on the stupid, dangerous trip?

What will your "I'll miss you" do for me? What will come of such declarations? I'm going to marry Abud whether I like it or not, leaving desire on a forgotten shelf in my memory. What would I reap if I gave in? But now, I'm more determined than before, so go on Ali, and let destiny take its course.

*   *   *

I have barely any hope left. Most of the night's precious hours have passed.

I was tricked twice into hoping for a getaway by the cunning whispers of that devil Sultan. *The coming evening carries the ululations that will accompany my coffin as it approaches my uncle's house. My eyes grow heavy slowly, slowly. The older I get, the crazier I get, it seems. I think it's better to do what they want—no risks and monotonous sleep.*

Was that Ali's jab waking me? 'Damn those who trust women. Are you sleeping?'

I rubbed my eyes to make out the face of the one speaking in the dark.

'Oh God!'

'Shhh ... shhh.' He muzzled me with his paw. 'Didn't I tell you to wait? Why are you sleeping?' His lips were right next to my ear.

'Get away from me.' After I remembered, I added, 'You're the one who's late! I thought you wouldn't come, and then you barge in here like this!'

'I still need money. How easy it is for you to change your tune. Come on now, get your things together and don't forget the gold.'

'What are you going to do?'

'The slave is bound and gagged. I don't think he'll be able to break free. As for the innkeeper, he's asleep in his room. His daughter's there, too.'

I stopped myself from screaming. *He's a real bandit, just like the ones in my grandmother's bedtime tales. How could I have thought I would feel safe with him?*

'Scared? I told you there's no time to hesitate.'

'And my family?'

'They're all fast asleep. I checked on them right before I came here. So come on now, *bint al-halaal*, get a move on.'

He suddenly yanked me by the arm with his steely fingers, pulling the bundle of gold next to me. I went half of the way outside with him while trying to silence the drone of growing danger.

'What's with you? Why did you stop—have you lost it?'

'I don't want to go.'

His eyes flashed as he dug his fingernails into my upper arm. 'I said there is no room for weakness. I'm here for the money, and you'll come along, even with your legs over your head.'

'No.' I wrenched my arm from his grip. He handed me the bundle and walked ahead of me without looking back.

'God damn you! May Death tear you to pieces. You're as good as dead when they find out.'

I swallowed my fear and silently began walking behind him. I tiptoed around the trussed-up slave. The darkness was a heavy blanket on the rooftops and alleyways. My heart ached from fear, and my head was just about splitting into two.

He led me into a narrow, frightening alley. I stood at the entrance, hesitant. 'Come on, you idiot.' I followed him mechanically, reached and then went past the point of no return. The alley seemed endless. My head was heavy, and I walked with faltering steps. I crashed into tin cans strewn across the ground, and my companion grew annoyed at the din.

'Keep it down!' he hissed, before the rest of his words dissolved into a secret dialect of cursing verse.

Oh God, what have I done? Where will my madness take me after these thirty years? Maybe it's all just a nightmare, and if I pinch myself, I'll find myself a child far from all these worries. But the pinch woke me up to a nightmare, and the man in front of me in the meagre starlight turned back to me again and again. What if he attacked me and stole the gold? How would I face my family? Everyone?

He stopped and signalled for me to do the same. I clutched the bundle tightly. He glanced furtively to the left and then the right. The darkness was mute, except for the crowing of some distant roosters.

He walked lightly, and I followed him, my whole being fearful that a face of one of my family's men would jump out in front of me, putting an end to this whole adventure. But nothing of the sort happened. Our path was free of any movement. We were creeping along in the dark, exactly like thieves. We walked a long, level path, uninterrupted by any creature. My companion started to slow down; his caution had vanished. I started to succumb to the emptiness, thinking of the end.

'We're nearly there. They're waiting for me in the car.'

'And me?'

'And you?'

I jumped suddenly when I heard a sound next to me.

'What's with you? It's a cat.'

'*Auzubillah min as-shaytan ar-rajeem*. It's a djinn.'

'A djinn?'

'Yes, they walk round at night in disguise.'

'Dressed as cats?'

'As anything, even humans.'

'So, you could be a djinn, then?

'Stop laughing, there's nothing funny about it. Where are you taking me?'

'As-Sayh.'

This was enough to cast a shadow of doubt over me again. As-Sayh was a no man's land. but I had crossed the threshold of no return, of reason. There was no escape.

'Will the djinn kidnap us, do you think?'

'Why won't the car come here?'

'So that they don't think you're running away with me.'

'Who's *they*?'

'The djinn,' he said, then doubled over, letting out a rumbling, hateful laugh.

(4)

Ah—if I was truly myself—
If in my declaration—some atoms of the galaxy
In which my vigour swims.

- Shawqi Baghdadi

It was the first time I'd been able to breathe in air as moist as that of this refreshing night, even though I felt shame at finding myself squeezed into a minibus chock full of sleeping sailors, an embarrassment that made my legs quiver. I wasn't used to finding myself among men in this way, especially strangers. I felt alone and dizzy.

I don't know what awakened my fears, as I had been left on my own in the back row of seats without any fuss, but a sinking feeling still engulfed me. I became a sort of observer with half-open eyes, the bodies in front of me having surrendered to sleep. I caught the driver following me with his eyes in the mirror above his head. My hated companion was squeezed in among three huge sailors in the bank of seats in front, lost in a deep sleep.

Nothing could make me have faith in the handful of men in front of me. What if I dozed off? Pirates, as my grandmother would call them, and their faces, their stench made me retch. *I wonder what the men in my family will do when, on returning from dawn prayers, they find the inn slave tied up, and connect it with my disappearance. They'll think I was kidnapped, but the shame will be much worse if the slave talks.*

A strong shudder jolted me. As my grandmother would say, that was death quickly visiting the body. *If the slave talks, humiliation will trail them, and they will bow their heads in shame. I have brought shame upon my people. How is that, when I am the sensible, rational one? I wonder if they will try to chase me down and kill me, wiping the shame away from their eternally upheld heads. Or will they return to the mountain, cutting me out of their lives and forgetting about me?*

Oh, why did I decide to bring such shame upon my noble family, full of such pride? For what reason had I preferred to stay, terrified, under the watch of a suspicious sailor?

I admit that I chose the fastest way to die. Every now and then, the face of a young boy mumbling from a reoccurring dream looked at me. His eyes were drooping, absorbed in the dream. Despite the clear innocence writ large on his small face, I didn't trust him any more than the others. I had learnt not to trust boys–perhaps my mother was justified in this matter. Perhaps, for once, my naiveté had kept me safe.

The strange, novel growl of the car was the only voice amidst the exhausted bodies. I hadn't seen a car since the end of the war, and I hadn't been able to ride in that one. It had seemed terrifying during the time of the war, swallowing up bodies like an ogre of lore.

Oh God, by the truth of these bright stars in your sky, by the dark distant mountains. Oh God, please have mercy on me, save me from this desperate madness.

The snoring of the small sailor in front me cut off my wandering train of thought.

I pinched myself, once, twice, and three times, the pain each time sharper than before.

Is this what I had wanted and aimed for? To be among a band of thieves? Yet, in spite of all that, it was nice that I wouldn't have to be next to Abdallah's fluffy beard ... it was nice that what was to come was unknown. I was eager for it, as if I were a character in the legends of djinn, an unlucky soul searching for happiness. Inevitably, the horsewoman of sleep towered over me. I hugged my expensive bundle and surrendered to the rocking motion of the car.

I almost fell on my face when I woke up in alarm. My heart beat wildly while I looked around, as if my father's and uncle's faces were surrounding me, ruffling my calm.

'Are you okay?' said the sweet, drunk voice of the young, hallucinating sailor. In the sparse dawn light, I could make out a large birthmark on his left cheek, and I nodded to him, exercising great caution. But he went back to sleep after I pulled on Sultan's arm.

'What's with you, woman?'

'Nothing!'

'Did you see a djinn?'

I didn't answer.

'What are you not saying? What are you afraid of?'

'I'm not afraid. No one would dare...'

The astonished, arched curve of his eyebrows shamed me into silence.

'Calm down, *bint al-halaal*, everything is as you wished.'

Dawn was slipping away slowly, the grooves of the clouds on fire, afraid of what the new day would bring. *This morning is different from all the past mornings of the past years; today, I harbour feelings of impending ruin–even the days of war didn't make me feel this way.*

*   *   *

Like all domineering men, this odious captain is unpleasant. I'm tempted by an unruly desire to spit in his eye. Who knows, maybe I'll break through all this radiating power, this arrogance that propels me back to my old way of life.

What makes Abdallah's face come to mind again? Death is upon me; I feel it devilishly pulling out my soul. Will Abud be the dagger that ends my life? Why does his face now lurk in all corners?

My family's faces, eternally clothed in anger and shame, nested in my mind, hemming me in like the web of a poisonous spider in the ancient buckthorn tree at the edge of our courtyard. Home.

The night sees off its tails, the sparks of dawn shining, agitated. Here we are in a new day. My father will arrive home disappointed, and my mother will strike her face as she proclaims the shame that has descended on the family. My uncle and his daughters will brand me a brazen thief, and all who know me will curse me till Judgement Day.

Will Ali be riding uncle's horse now, armed with his new dagger, with which to bury my shame?

I looked behind me. The dust that the vehicle kicked up veiled what was there. *Ali must surely feel disappointed in his well-behaved sister. He would never have believed that she would set out one day to challenge the family and face death. She who was such a coward and used to overflow with honour and purity.*

I trembled like someone possessed. *I don't want to go back to that mountain. I'm now on my way to another world, an unknown world. It may defeat me. It may make me gnaw my nails, regretting that I left my small house in the mountains and the friendship of fat cows in the pen. Or maybe the unknown world will make me happy....*

Where is joy? The world sees me as an old woman now; would I be happy if I saw the woman who stole away my only beloved, or for a king to open his doors and treat me like a princess? As if that would happen!

The sailors started to stir, one after the other, each immediately looking curiously in my direction. They then started doing anything to get my attention. *All men are one and the same, regardless of the stratum of society they're from. I'm the prey, and each one of them possesses a natural tendency to hunt, even if only with their rusty rifles.*

'So, Sultan, you ended up bringing her along?' The man speaking turned to me with great curiosity; he was intimidating, with a long bushy beard. He scratched it a lot and massaged his armpits. I sought refuge behind the back of the chair in front of me and shut my eyes so I wouldn't have to face him.

'She's been here for a while, Saleh. Didn't you see us when we came?'

The man ignored the captain's snide comment.

'So you smuggled her from her family's house? You didn't listen to me and brought her anyway.'

I froze in my seat, startled at his contemptuous tone. I braced myself for Sultan's response.

'None of your business, Saleh.'

'And how will this... How will she come along with us for the journey? She'll be a headache. Did you have to be so chivalrous at our expense?'

Most of the sailors, awakened by the gruff exchange, shot menacing looks my way. My heart flapped, and I squeezed my bundle to calm myself down.

'Stay away from her, Saleh. She's a relative!'

I had expected in that moment for Sultan to abandon his resolve, seize my bundle, and throw me out of the vehicle. But he just looked coldly at Saleh. 'Do I need to say it again?'

Saleh contented himself with mumbling, then grew silent in his seat. *My God, how angrily they are staring at me. Why? I am paying more for this trip than they earn in a season. No man has the right, after today, to look at me like he's got the right to appraise or own me. I'm fed up with this vicious cycle.*

I looked at the young boy in front of me. He was confused, trying to fend off sleep as he stared in my direction. He smiled bashfully, then looked at the captain lying carelessly beside him. 'I swear I didn't mean to look at you, lady!'

He turned to his boss, scared stiff. He responded with his cold back, then relaxed as if nothing had happened.

'I'm Ilyas,' he went on. 'I've been working with boss Sultan since last year.' His accent was strange. I deliberately turned my face away from him to get him to stop talking. He got the hint and retreated into his seat.

After a bit, I grew curious and focused on their colourful tales without seeming too interested. Behind the driver, there were three giant slaves with wide eyes, who barely talked. Behind them were smaller young men with barely-there moustaches trading stories, who glanced at me now and again to make sure I was listening to their repulsive yarns. Next to them, in the separate seat next to the door, sat an old man deeply absorbed in reading what appeared to be the Quran.

Am I to live among these people?

Why didn't I feel cheerful now that I was following in Salim's footsteps, which I had wanted to do for so long? Why was worry eating me alive? Why oh why was I going to As-Sawahil? What else would there be, save for heartache?

The vehicle stopped after a bit at one of the few Christ's thorn trees on either side of the road. The men started to move and yawn. I retreated once more, as if they were primed to pounce on me. But they started filing out, grumbling about the hard seats and the reckless driving.

'God snuff you out, Sultan! Those seats broke us! We were made for boats and donkeys, not cars.'

Sultan stood up suddenly, his movement animated with vigour. He spoke playfully with those lazing around, then looked at me with indifference. 'Stay here till I send for you.' He got out quickly, and I heard the driver with the wandering eyes ask in an exhausted voice, 'Where are we stopping? We'll reach Manah in a bit, so should we stay there overnight?'

'No, keep going to Al-Mudhaibi.'

'But they'll die of hunger and keep complaining about their backs.'

'We'll stop in Manah to buy provisions and fill up on water from Wadi Bahla. We won't stop often, and we'll keep going like I said.'

'But...'

'Discussion over.'

The driver threw a dirty look at Sultan's back and whispered to one of the boys next to him, each word more final than the one before it. 'I don't know why he's in such a hurry. He divorced his wife before coming to Nizwa!'

'There's always another!'

Young Ilyas turned to me, smiling wickedly. 'Boss told me to sit next to you to chase away any men.' I turned to face the young man with the birthmark, fear etched on my face.

'I don't mean any harm, believe me. You're like my sister Sumaiyya.' Silence fell between us, and I stole a look at him. I found him looking out the window and amusing himself. I thought for a long time before starting to talk with him. *I don't think he's someone who would inform my family.*

'How long have you been working with this captain?'

He was taken aback by my initiative, but answered, smiling innocently, 'I told you already, maybe you forgot. I've been here since last year.' Silence fell once more before he interrupted it. 'Do you have kids?' His seemingly innocent question made me laugh.

'I'm not married.'

'My cousin didn't have kids after marriage. She was meant to be for me, but they married her off to a sheikh who had money and status. Really old. It's six years and still no kids—seems like they're paying for what they did to me.'

Even though his comments were dropped into the conversation without much connection or reason, they were amusing. 'I'm poor, my whole family is poor, my father's been dead since I was young, and my mom was pregnant with Hashem. A shark ate my dad while he was at sea. He was fishing alone in an old boat. Even so, the lot of us could only find work at sea, except for my brother Aziz, who was different. My mother sent him to study in Saidia. It's super expensive, and that's why I work with Sultan.'

He was like someone entranced by a surah, fearful of it being interrupted. He was simple, free of the usual male complications, with a spontaneous laugh when he talked about innocent peculiarities. I liked his style, so I whispered hesitantly, 'There will be girls better than your cousin!'

'Better than her?'

'The African girls ...'

'I don't think there's anyone better than her: she's beautiful, her hair is black and soft, and she has full legs.'

'You should be embarrassed by what you've just said.'

He caught himself, turning red. 'I haven't seen her like that. It's just—that's how she looked as a child. Where I'm from, girls who are free don't go out much.'

I felt the need to add: 'And if they did, you still shouldn't look!'

He laughed, then was silent for a while. I gazed at what was happening outside the vehicle. Men in threadbare clothes and their brown bodies growing blacker, with curly chest hair like a beard. Why were they eating like they hadn't done so in a month?

The spittle of their food flies among them, and they're not concerned in the slightest, as if they're trying to get in as much as possible before death. Damn the disgusting pigs.

Feeling out of place bit into me, deepening my sadness. I waited for a few moments before asking him, 'Have you visited all of As-Sawahil?'

'Yes, yes. I've been to all of East Africa. We went to Pemba, Kilwa, Mombasa, Zanzibar, beautiful green places. Africa is beautiful.'

I dared to go further. 'And the African women?'

'Patient, work without complaining.' He heaved a sigh and continued, 'But they've become westernized.'

'But some of them are married to Europeans.'

'I like the girls of Sur better.'

He was still a novice. After a year, he would have–like the rest of them–a secret wife on the African continent, birthing him a caravan of coffee-coloured children, and his legitimate wife in Sur. *All of them, including Sultan the captain, must have a woman or two along the African coast. Liars if they say otherwise.*

My heart tightened once more. *Where is my family now? And what are they doing? Let them go wherever they wish, because now I'm too far out of their reach.*

*   *   *

I wondered how this devilish desire to flee came around so suddenly, in the blink of an eye. After such a life of obedience, had I blown up all trust in this one moment of stupidity? Was it stupidity, or was it madness?

Yes ... yes ... yes....

*   *   *

I finally got out under the captain's orders, after he had taken the sailors far away.

I ate some of the stale rice that Ilyas brought me. It was salty. Which hand had cooked this shoddy repast? Didn't the men taste how salty it was? They swallowed it with delight. Their faces, despite the filth, shone with health and vim. *Hasn't the salt sapped their strength and arrogance yet?*

Sweat covered a good part of my face. The weather was a bit cold, and the burqa constrained me with its dampness and the smell of my successive breaths. *Do I wear it because I am free and beautiful? Or because I am afraid of eyes undressing me? My cousin Alia wears it even though she's hideous.*

I wished I could lift it the way I secretly used to in the field. How sweet the air had been, brushing my face and freshening it with its direct embrace. But I was yet to forget how I came to wear it. I didn't wear it because I was afraid of other's looks. The truth was that I liked when it wasn't just my mirror taking in my beautiful face. I remember many a time, while walking in my uncles' fields with the veil lifted, catching their sons' attention, stopping them dead in the tracks of their daily work. I wore it before I knew that I had a beautiful face.

I was eleven at the time, or actually younger, and my father had been in the field clipping *qat* to sell to travelling salesmen. That day, I was leading little Mohammed with my right hand and in my left was the coffee pot my mother prepared every morning. I recall I wasn't myself that day: I had punched my brother in the head while we walked. My father had never looked at me the way he kept on looking at Mohammed; he had never carried me even once the way he always did with Mohammed. He never placed me under the ancient *sidr* tree, he never patted my head tenderly or kissed me affectionately. Suddenly, the stranger showed up, shook hands with my father, and stared at me for a while. My father caught his lingering stare and, as soon as the man left, my father's face clouded over. Without saying as much as a word, he started to drag me toward the house.

My father didn't pay attention to the scattered thorns along the path, nor to my bare feet trickling blood. I felt I had committed an unforgivable sin, without knowing what it was. I gasped. Maybe he had seen me punch his beloved son. I swore on his head to the contrary, but he kept up his wild pace, agitated, going on angrily about something I couldn't understand.

His teeth glimmered in the sun, making me more terrified and silent. Under the sun, his teeth looked like the edges of a sickle, like the blade of a knife. After that episode, I no longer went out with my face exposed to the sun. My mother put this on my face and forbade me to take it off under any circumstances. So I didn't.

I never saw my father drag any of my brothers the way he did me, and in his flash of anger, I'll never forget how he had the clarity of mind to keep Mohammed safely away from the thorns, and to pat his flowing hair to comfort him.

I groaned once. Twice. *This musty dampness beneath this repulsive burqa! What is it other than drops of blood drawn out by an old thorn, a malicious, patriarchal thorn stinging my face and making me bleed? Damn the past, damn this burqa.*

The image of Mohammed rolling in my father's lap, playful and giggling, hardly left me, walking in my memory alongside the image of my bloody, torn-up feet. I shuddered at the image. If only the earth had swallowed me up after that man arrived.

'Are you ready?'

For a moment, I forgot that my face was exposed and turned to the familiar voice behind me. Long moments passed before I decided to put the burqa back in place over my refreshed face. He stared at my face, at my features, its structure, while I stared at him, waiting for his reaction to my uncovered face. He didn't show much surprise, and his eyes hungrily explored my face.

'Why did you take off your burqa?'

That's all he said, indignation written on his face, his forehead wrinkled.

'I swear, I forgot.'

'Don't remove it again.'

His voice was terrifying, his pupils dark, and his hands were balled up, as if he too were about to drag me. This familiar reaction violently shook me, crushing me underfoot, and I sought comfort in my bundle.

He took a step back, breathing heavily, his tightened features growing slack. 'You're a good-looking woman, you know that, and my sailors will harass you if you show your face. Stay out of such trouble. Let's get back to the vehicle.'

I grudgingly walked behind him. All the others were waiting for me to enter before them, their scornful eyes taking me in. Without a doubt, they thought I was a fallen woman.

The growl of the engine pierced the air as the distant palm-tree farms approached bit by bit. My body trembled in stops and starts, as if I'd been zapped by a bolt of lightning.

He had followed me into the vehicle and sat in the same seat, far from me, beside the opposite window. The vein in his forehead bulged rhythmically, furiously, like that of my father's. The sailors whispered to each other and chuckled amongst themselves. The sun kept rising higher and higher, warming the sides of the vehicle, raising the temperature inside. The sun seemed angry with me, too.

He suddenly leaned toward me and muttered, 'If I see you take it off again, I'll take you back to the mountains.' And then, in a sterner tone, 'I don't want your money if it causes endless fighting among my men. I'd sooner let your money fall into the sea than allow that.'

My head felt even hotter, and as the sun rose higher and the vehicle roared, the man beside me kept cursing, laying bare his anger.

This captain didn't differ much from any other man. The man who had been different had been for someone else, and he'd left. My great man had left, leaving me to face melancholy and grief all by myself.

I had run away, and yet the shackles felt even tighter than before, and this hateful man beside me had become the new dictator in my life.

(5)

'Oh skies, by your beautiful azure, and by your scattered stars
by your great galaxies, your sun and moon
guide me up the path to your exquisite city.'

- Younis Al-Akzami

Oh God, what have I done?

*   *   *

Sultan never let me out of his sight.

It's as if he was waiting for any whiff of rebellion to pounce on me. As soon as we reached Manah, which was thronged with people rushing to the mosques, he looked at me and sharply ordered, 'Come with me.'

'Me? Why?'

'I'll tell you later.'

I didn't dare disobey him because I sensed the undeniable hint of a threat in his tone. I followed him and overtook the sailors, who were devouring me with their eyes as I passed right through the middle of them. It was only when I left the vehicle that I felt my cheeks burning.

Their eyes searched in a way I wasn't used to: my head, my body, my clothes and even the tips of my toes; undressing me with their eyes, as if I were a brazen woman, a target for everything but their respect. Sultan stole a look at the bundle between my clenched hands and chuckled, 'Your family's quite tight-fisted!'

'Pardon?'

'You look like a mouse. Why are you so scared of me?'

'I'm not scared.' My heart quaked. He had an inscrutable expression. How harsh his features were, the colour of his eyes in the dazzling daylight closer to the colour of mountain honey, and his nose straighter than it should be. Despite the distance I'd put between us, I felt his exhalations pierce the burqa, brushing my face. This man really was the pirate of my grandmother's tales, the thief unafraid of death and who didn't die! Forcefully, I asked him, 'Can my family's men reach us here?'

'Of course. Your fat, rich uncle has thoroughbred horses.'

I whispered to him softly, in a strangled voice, 'So why don't we keep going, then? They'll kill us all.'

'No, I think they'll just kill you. We'll just say that you paid us to take you to Africa.'

I stood trembling.

'You'd just betray me so easily? You want ...' The lump in my throat prevented me from going on.

He looked at my trembling, limp fingers and gave a hearty laugh. 'You're so scared of them that you'd be dead in seconds if you saw them. Take it easy. They don't know where we've gone, and we haven't taken our usual route. Also, we're not stopping for long here. We'll buy some food and keep moving.'

'Why did you make me get out with you?'

'To buy you some necessary things.'

'What things?'

'Medicine, clothes, a sponge, and soap. Got a towel? *Ghusl* to wash your hair?'

I looked at him coldly. 'I don't have money to buy all that.'

'Why, you've got Karun's treasure.'

'I'm going back to the bus.'

'If you do that, I'll take you back to your family.'

'I don't want any medicines or soap. Why should I buy what I don't want?'

'I like you. You just say what's on your mind.'

'I'm not trying to be stubborn. I want to keep the gold for more important things.'

'Is there anything more important than being clean? Didn't your mother teach you how to bathe and remove sweat? You'll be more beautiful that way.' His eyes took me in once more. I went utterly red. I wasn't that young anymore, to feign ignorance of the meaning of his thinly veiled innuendo. Such a bold statement shoved me into a world where I felt overwhelmed with darkness, by that which was forbidden, which had fermented for years inside me. It seemed my body was trembling and my pulse racing, betraying the forbidden thoughts I was having. I didn't dare to meet his insolent eyes. He forced me to remember how I'd fallen into Salim's arms with the excuse of having tripped, and how his warm hands felt my head, lingering, comforting me, and how he'd whispered hoarsely, 'You smell wonderful.' It was the first time I'd experienced the feeling of bodily pleasure.

'I'll make sure you pay me back,' Sultan said.

But then Salim had turned to stone, leaving me to fall to the ground. He had known it was a ruse and left. That day, I stayed at the well and loosened my braids and touched them. I had grown aware of the charms of my body and its need for a partner.

I felt myself numbly returning to my hated station—the captain's husky voice was enough to end my reverie as quickly as it had begun. 'I don't want anything.'

He scoffed and spat in disgust, 'Stingy and dirty. Fine, I'll pay for you.'

'I said no.'

'Eish. If only you'd stay quiet the way you were.' *Why is he doing this for me? Is he really trying to be courteous? He'll inevitably deceive me–there's no such thing as a chivalrous* zutti. The place we were right then was breath-taking, and it took me far from the fear and anger camping within me. Palm trees everywhere, clusters of dates of all colours dangling, glowing in the sun. Men entered the compact clay mosque, indifferent to the heat. A group of farmers passed by with beautifully crafted empty beehives in hand, greeting Sultan, who swiftly responded. I saw only two women, scurrying away and steering clear of everyone as they made their way to the mosque.

Sultan stopped at the men's section of the falaj and hastily performed his ablution. 'Stay here till I get back. I'll only pray what's necessary in the mosque, and I won't be late.'

'Should I stay at the part of the falaj where men are doing their ablutions?'

'They're doing it over there by the door. No one is doing their ablutions here, as you can see. Women are washing their dishes over there. Don't leave this spot. Go and pray under that tree.'

'What's it to you? Just go.' He looked at me, taken aback. I turned away angrily. 'You're not my father, my brother, you're nothing to me. Stop ordering me around.'

'Hah, what set a fire under you now? You were quiet up until now.'

'Once I pay you your gold, I won't see you again, so why are you my master all of a sudden?'

'Oh God! I didn't think you'd be difficult. God damn y- ... the devil! Keep your voice down.'

'You've broken your ablution. You swore at me.'

'I swore at the devil.' He turned and left.

How I hate this man; how I fear him. I can't understand him, and I can't keep fighting with him, for my fate is in his hands.

* * *

He stopped at the perfume stall in the middle of the souk, but didn't linger for long. 'Why did you buy *Sanamaki*?'

'Who knows, maybe it'll come in handy.'

'It's bitter and dangerous.'

He walked on to buy some fabric, ignoring what I had said. As soon as we left the souk, he whispered, 'Once, I slipped some *Sanamaki* to one of the slaves when I was sick and tired of how arrogant he was being. Slaves should know their place. They were made to do what they're told, and that's it.'

'That's haram,' I objected. He furrowed his brow.

'Haram, you say? Isn't it haram how you've run away with strangers? Slaves will always be slaves, no matter how hard you try to lift them up. They'll always be less important than us. God made them slaves, after all.'

'That's nonsense. You're just saying that because you make a living kidnapping and selling them.'

'And your father? The *Mutawwa* religious type? The preacher at the mosque encouraging tribal politics—didn't he buy two slaves from me last year? Listen here, woman, you yourself don't live without slaves, right? Who cooks at your weddings? Who does all the work you grumble about? They're pleased with how things work; they know why they were made.' A cunning smile flashed across his face. He carried all the malice of this world, all its ills, and he revealed them openly, frankly, unlike me. Within me was the seed from the mountain that embraced hypocrisy.

*   *   *

Why can't I pick up the banner that Salim left behind? Why am I ordinary, and why can't I be as open as Salim was? Why can't I be who I need to be in order to win him over again? A vagabond inheriting the sick tradition of enslaving others.

* * *

When we got back to the vehicle, the men had changed seats, except the elderly man, who hadn't moved an inch. *He must be a guest of theirs.*

I was surprised to find someone sitting on the seat behind me, staring at us. He was the same man who had started the fight last night.

'Go back to your seat, Saleh.'

'I'm tired. I want to sit here now.'

'Saleh.'

'I won't move, Sultan, whatever you do.'

He was massive. It seemed like he was spoiling for a fight. I expected a prelude to Judgment Day to play out between him and Sultan, but nothing of the sort happened. Instead, Sultan pulled me to sit in the chair Ilyas had been in, while he sat in front of Saleh without comment. The monotonous drone of the vehicle started up after that, and I went back to being scared and worried. The hostility in the eyes of all those around me made me feel weak. Ilyas leaned toward me and said softly, 'He was talking about you two.'

'Who?'

'Saleh. He said Sultan kidnapped you from your family and...' Ilyas kept on going without looking at my face, '...he said Sultan stormed your house when your family was out, and you welcomed him.'

My tongue froze at the stinging insinuation.

'He said that Sultan told him about how he'd invaded a woman's house in Nizwa when her husband was out.'

'What?!' I had to respond to this insult, which a man from the mountain would never have dared breathe to a woman from a good family. Ilyas grew nervous at the consternation in my voice, and hastened, 'Calm down *sayyadati*, calm down, my lady. Saleh will kill me if he knows I told you.'

'What? Am I meant to keep quiet about lies told about me?'

Everyone turned to look at me, and before I could go on, Sultan spluttered furiously, 'Shut up. God damn y- ... the devil!'

I stayed still in my place, terrified; it was clear that I would be the victim of any fight here.

The atmosphere was charged, and no one dared to speak, even quietly. I was speechless, my ears ringing with the curses of my family from afar, my body in pain, like that of someone who had been stoned for a crime. I needed to have a long talk with myself, a sort of airing-out session. I needed to go back to the mountain and get married, even if it was to one of our slaves. I couldn't keep quiet, the pressure of my regret was too much, and that was the one feeling I couldn't stomach right now.

'Is Saleh crazy? Why can't your captain keep him on a tighter leash?'

'He knows a lot about the ways of sailors and the sea. The captain wants Saleh to work with his crew because he's smart and knows the sea better than he knows his own father.'

'So? Isn't there someone else who knows how to navigate the sea?'

'Of course, I myself don't know how he puts up with Saleh. You must know about Sultan's rich wife from Sur?'

'What about her?'

Ilya saw the change in my demeanour. 'The poor woman. She just found out that Sultan is married to someone else in Zanzibar, and that he has a daughter with her. Someone told her, and we think it's Saleh.'

'Also married to an African woman, you say? Damn the ....' I swallowed my words, afraid someone might hear me.

Ilya gave a wry smile. 'There's probably a European, too, who knows.'

'Why did he leave the woman from Sur?'

'She was a real looker. I saw her once by chance. But she was the jealous type, and he has two, three, four wives.'

I turned my face away, overcome by my hated sense of inferiority. What could she have done? When she got angry and fed up with the lies and longing, he divorced her like a mad dog, forever tied to scandal and children that would always remind her of her naiveté. *How easy it is to get a divorce, men reducing us to a bunch of flies that you can swat away once you're done enjoying their company.*

'Are you mad at me? Honestly, that wasn't my intention.'

'What about you? Didn't the sea teach you to marry from every coast?'

'I'm not rich enough to provide for more than one wife.'

'If you had the money, nothing would stop you.'

'Not more than four, *sayyadati*, that's haram.'

'But let's say you were allowed more. Would you marry more?'

'Of course.'

I shouldn't be surprised—even this nobody has inherited the absolute power of men.

'Actually maybe, maybe not. They're so tiring, and I wouldn't have any peace.'

His desire to correct himself, despite his visible streak of male swagger, made me smile.

My whole situation is nothing more than a joke.

* * *

Why am I so outgoing all of a sudden? Why am I no longer as I once was, happy with my fate and living in my house? Aren't I tired of analysing everything? Why can't I just be simpleminded, thinking about my day, pleasing my family? Why are my veins straining in my body, and why did my heartbeat gallop when I discovered how I'd been exploited all those years?

Oh God, it's so exhausting to live differently from how I did in the past, facing down the spectre of possible shame after thirty long years of being submissive, believing everything I was told? What would've happened if I'd been happy with my destiny? What's new about a middle-aged woman marrying a young buck? Hundreds of other women have had to do so, grinning and bear-

ing it. How can I run away when I've criticized that my whole life? What's so different now?

*   *   *

I heard them grumbling when Sultan ordered the driver to head past Al-Mudhaibi and stop at Wadi Al-Fahal. They were fed up with sitting for so long and tired of the dust that was settling on their lashes and in their hungry mouths.

'We'll carry on to Al-Mudayrib, stay the night there, then get up in the morning to go to Bidiyah, and from there to Sur.'

'That's too much for us, we're not used to it. The boats won't leave for Africa for another two weeks, so what's the rush?'

'Ah, Nasser, are you tired of sleeping? You never objected to a journey where you slept the whole time before. What's bugging you now?'

Everyone held their tongue, and all their fatigued, growling eyes fell on me, blaming me for the breakneck pace of this journey.

Once we finally reached the rest stop, their faces relaxed, and they crowded the door to get out, to unfurl their crumpled bodies, the fatigue washing off of them.

'Do I know you from somewhere?'

I froze. I looked at who was speaking; maybe he was one of the men who visited the mountain from time to time, but he looked a complete stranger.

'Don't you know me?'

I kept silent.

'I know you have a brother called Mohammed, and that your family is from the mountain.'

At these words, every muscle in my body tensed. I shrank in my seat without daring to look up.

'Your brother didn't tell me about your close relationship with Sultan. He seemed to look down on Sultan when I met him, calling him *zutti*.'

Silence.

'I saw you in the field; you were working, and one of my relatives told me that you were his sister. It was last Wednesday. I remember very well.'

'You're mistaken, I'm from Nizwa.'

He looked at me, confused. 'But ...'

'You're mistaken, I don't have any family on the mountain.'

'God be praised, what a resemblance! I guess you're not her. Her name was also Zahra, though.'

For a moment, it seemed as if he believed me, but then he kept on going. 'She's the daughter of a noble family, real rich folks. My relative said she's a widow, and they don't want her marrying someone outside the family. I guess I'm wrong. You look younger than what they described, though.'

Sultan appeared in front of us, glaring at the young man. '*Wallah*, Juma', since when are strangers allowed to be alone with our women?'

The young man disappeared as quickly as he had come, and I stayed where I was, gathering up the broken pieces of myself. I dabbed at the sweat under my burqa, craving a cellar to swallow me up.

'Zahra, I told you not to speak to them. Those young men are such flirts.'

'He told me he knew my family from the mountain.'

'You told him?' he said, shocked.

'No, no. He said he'd seen me there a few days before, and that he knows Mohammed, my brother.'

'And what did you say?'

'I denied it, but he didn't seem convinced. He kept talking and insulted me.'

'Stay calm. He can't confirm it no matter how hard he tries. Maybe now you can see the benefit of wearing the burqa?'

'He'll go back to the mountain and tell them where I am.'

'No, he won't. I'll make sure to never take him back to Nizwa.'

For the first time, I sensed purity in his intentions.

*   *   *

I touched the water flowing over the shiny pebbles, some larger and some smaller. The water was cold, despite the eternal abundance of sunlight on this land, this wadi cleaving the land, crawling like a never-ending snake, like the *falaj* running by our house in the mountains, where I would wash clothes and dishes, crying and complaining.

Oh, my lovely house and sweet falaj, how are you now? Who is caressing your waters now, oh falaj of my sorrows? Will I ever get another chance to fill my throat with your pure, sweet water?

'I want to marry you, Zahra,' Sultan said.

I looked at him, thunderstruck, unsure of what to do. *Sure. I should probably expect many such casual offers from every man here, no matter their stature or background, but not this fast.* He was taking advantage of the situation, as they say. I saw the man before me just as they had described him: a thief of humble origins.

How easy it must be to add a stray vagrant to the goats in his pen. To nibble her on the wedding night and then throw the bones away with the rubbish, leaving her to be wracked by loneliness.. And who do I have to defend me, after all? A homeless woman, cut off from all family, with no way out, fleeing the frying pan for the deceptive comfort of fire.

'What about the one who waits for you, and what about your child on the distant coast?'

When I had confronted him before, he had always been shocked by my audacity, but his face this time was tinged with something closer to fury.

'What is it to you, Zahra?'

'Have you gotten bored of storming people's homes? Of your problems with that rich woman?'

He was no longer surprised at how complicated I was. He skipped pebbles across the clear water of the wadi as he looked at me, smiling, ignoring my insult and provocation. I faced him, deeply resentful of his ability to run after different women, his ease of movement, his ease at sharing his body with them, a man able to disguise himself under many different masks, a man who could ruin any woman, comfortable in his sense of superiority and in his contempt for his prey.

'Go on now, Sultan. You must be joking.'

'I'm not kidding.'

'So then, look at me at least.'

'I've never once looked at something without making it mine, even what seemed out of reach.'

'Except for the daughters of noble families.'

'Even daughters of noble families. I've had them, Zahra.'

I didn't know how to respond. I was, after all, talking for the first time about something forbidden.

* * *

Why such looks of a predator about to swoop on its prey? Why do I feel like a piece of meat sacrificed at Eid? I feel as though I'm naked while I'm still clothed. I feel afraid, although I'm strong enough.

Allah … Allah. Oh God of men and women. Oh God of the weak and strong. Take me where you want me to go. Keep me honourable. Take me to the home where I feel safe and respected.

(6)

'O travelling pigeon,
Undulate ... and hover in the safe vast blue
A peaceful pigeon
And tweet from your new nest

- Kamal Nashat

So what if I was satisfied and stayed here?

So what if I stayed serving and labouring like a donkey and ...

But you, my beloved mountain, I can't believe that I won't see you after today; I can't believe I won't get to speak to my sweet childhood friends; that I'll no longer be resentful of my uncle and my brothers.

So what if I become the butt of the midday fava bean sellers' jokes, if I were to laugh instead at all this frustration, exhaustion, and fear. Why have I become like this? Why am I thinking like this, and putting myself in situations that I can do without?

Sur came into view, and I thought it embodied one of my grandmother's spells, one of those nightly hallucinations that I used to inhabit, where a sorceress would chase me to eat me up. This vast blue expanse, stretched out before me, whipped up fear and anticipation.

No, by God, it really wasn't my grandmother's magic. I rubbed my eyes for some time while perched on the back of a seemingly always-smiling she-camel. So *that* was the sea, and *those* huge floating houses were the boats that Salim had spoken about before he left. And *there* was the enormous white sail.

Oh God, I wished I could get down from the uninspiring vantage point atop this camel. I was exhausted, and the way my legs were bent had made me lose feeling in them. The vehicle was more comfortable than this torture, but it had broken down shortly before Al-Mudhaibi and Sultan, faced with a choice of walking all that way, had to accept proceeding by camel, an animal I'd never ridden before and won't be riding again.

The rugged terrain was why the vehicle broke down. The driver couldn't repair it, so he gave in and came along with us to Al-Mudhaibi to take someone back to fix it.

'Do you like Sur?'

'It's all sea. Look at how this place is swallowed up by the sea. Beautiful.'

'Do you want to live here in Sur?'

'I think your secret Zanzibari wife is more deserving of that, Sultan.'

A look of disapproval flashed across his face, fool that he was. I preferred to take in the sparkling town under the sun.

'You're a liar. Sometimes you say they're equal, and other times you reveal the truth.'

'I'm a free woman.'

'Oho! God forgive us for such things, then.'

'You'd better pray for that, because you're on your way to hell. Look over there—women and children have started to gather, and they're running and telling everyone to come see us. Go and greet your children. Who knows, maybe all of them are yours.'

'Your tongue has run away with you, daughter of the mountain. Whoever saw you trembling with your bundle when you first arrived wouldn't recognise you now, with that poisonous tongue of yours.'

'That must be your mother, the one with the salt-and-pepper hair. How scary she looks.'

'How can you see her face from here? My mother is of high birth, she's a very good woman.'

'All mothers are hard on their children, but maybe she's good to you because you're a man. Men here are crowns on their mothers' heads, even if they're thieves and fornicators.'

'You're crazy, but you've got to live with her for two whole weeks while the men get ready and repair the boat.'

'*Your* mother? What's she got to do with me? Do you want to disgrace me? She'll think I'm your mistress. God forbid!'

'Don't worry about what she says. I think keeping the people of Sur on our side is more important than my mother's opinion.'

'What I care about is that you get me as far away from my family as possible.'

'They'll come after you when they get word that a beautiful fair woman came to Sur accompanied by Sultan, a stranger ...'

I didn't pay much attention to this drawn-out speech that he, naturally, made convoluted. The sea was more appealing to look at, the land before me wide and blue. For this marvellous creation travelling in all directions, Salim sacrificed his life. It gave him youth, aspirations, happiness. It gave him satisfaction, or something like it. I wondered if it gave him a beautiful life, plunging him into ecstasy, yearning for its secrets.

He left me to dream of my almost tomorrow, of a hazy wedding night, time spent sitting as I embroidered stars on *kumma* for my husband's head, and the tasting of saffron-infused halwa. How stingy he had been when he forbade me the delight of knowing the sea, the delight of imagining this beautiful expanse, and how foolish I'd been to believe that the sea was a well full of salty water that sardines swam in.

'I wish the water would just crash over me. If only I could take an endless bath in it,' one of the men chimed in.

'The wadi was right in front of you, but you turned your nose up at it, as if you've never taken a bath in water full of dead cockroaches,' Saleh countered.

'I've never bathed with cockroaches, Saleh.'

'But they were there. You were carefully picking them out.'

'At least cockroaches are better than mosquitoes or your lice.'

What surprised me was that in the middle of this wicked exchange of words, and amidst all that resentment, there still existed a strange unity binding them together. A strange friendship forged from time spent in each other's company and something else I couldn't put my finger on. *They love this town of theirs, and God damn whoever dares criticise any part of it, or scowls in disapproval. They love this blueness and these small floating houses that look out onto the sea, and the gleaming white fizz on its calm surface, like daytime stars showering the place with light. Oh, the wind coming from the sea, the cool moisture slipping into arteries congested with sun, stiffness, and dust.*

The women devoured me with their looks, while Ilyas tried to force the camel to kneel so that I could alight, lightheaded as I was.

I dreamt of my own room and a straw mat to sleep on, but curiosity made me a tasty morsel for their eyes and mouths, even though not a single one dared approach me, the woman who dared to be part of this gang of thieves. I turned to look for Sultan, but I didn't find him. As for Ilyas, he apologised and ran off toward the group that had gathered, waiting for him.

I stood beside the kneeling camel, looking at the joy drawn on their faces, their warm reunions with their sons and daughters. Those warm looks and promises sent to the eyes behind the burqas. As for Saleh, there was no one waiting for him; like me he was alone and estranged, irritated with himself. Each of us felt like a fraud, an orphan. Such joy didn't include us, pariahs that we were, created on a different planet without a God to love us.

I got hold of my disappointment at watching all of them—those who had been impatient yesterday to speak with me, even just a word—as they had now fanned out, ignoring me like any other passing thing: unremarkable, a forgettable moment in their lives.

I felt a lump in my throat. A crushing remorse descended on me, so I turned on it with the greatest condescension. In the mountains I was well known, and faces would radiate with welcome and joy when they caught sight of me. From now on, no one would know me. Everyone in every place I went would be a stranger.

'Are you feeling out of place? Poor thing,' Saleh said, stretching out his last word so as to carry his sarcasm. I knew, at that moment, that he felt exactly as I did, or maybe even more so, since this was his birthplace. 'God knows,' I replied, not knowing how to feel in that moment.

He looked at me, searching my eyes for the meaning of my placid expression. His face was full of pain and chagrin. Even though the others couldn't stand him, I didn't hate him in that moment. He was only good at going on the offensive to hide his own pain.

'Are you really part of his family? I'm sure the two of you are lying, for I've never heard of him having any relative called Zahra. Come to think of it, I've never heard of him having relatives from the mountains,' Saleh said.

'I'm not from the mountains.'

He scrutinized what he could of my niqab-covered face, then turned his gaze to the teeming crowd, which had started to disperse.

'They'll go home, have a bath, eat clean food, then find a bed and sleep like a baby. Don't you think they're lucky?'

'All of us will bathe, eat, and sleep.'

'Like babies? You might think that, and maybe you'll sleep well, but I've never slept soundly.'

'You keep thinking of people and how they treat you. If you left them alone, then you'd sleep better.'

'If I were so good and let them be, they would bite me.'

'You just don't want to change. Get away from me before someone thinks something's going on between us.'

He laughed bitterly. 'Lucky bastard.'

He walked alone to the undulating sea.

*   *   *

'Hey, you fallen woman found by the wayside, you've got a lot of nerve coming here.'

God have mercy on me. Save me from this furious woman charged with resentment, looking at me with all the hatred in the universe. She was a young woman, wearing a sheer black abaya over her clothes.

'What's with you? Are you talking to me?'

'Is there any other fallen woman around here? You man-thief, you despicable woman.'

Anxious, I wasn't responding how I'd have liked to. I was weak, with no one to back me up. Women gathered around us to get a look. An old woman grabbled my attacker and told her to go back to her house, but she shook off the old woman and almost grabbed me, full of fury and hatred.

'Hey, you fornicator, this depraved man has never lived without a slut at hand, even when he's at sea.'

The shock of hearing Sultan's name in the mouths of the women around me jolted me. I recovered from my confusion. *This must be his ex-wife, then; what had I done for her to spit such poison at me?*

'You better watch yourself,' I finally responded.

'Oh, so you speak! You've got some nerve, you depraved woman.'

'You're the depraved one. I swear, if you don't shut up, I'll hurt you. You don't know who you're talking to, uncouth daughter of a seafarer.'

'You immoral woman, you bitch.'

I couldn't stomach such language. My body was shaking, and my heart beat so fast I felt my blood fizzing in my head. No one had ever spoken to me like that before. I'd been more cherished at home than this. Everyone knew I was a sheikh's daughter. But my precarious position here, reinforced by the group surrounding us and backing her up, made me swallow all these insults. I didn't want to create an opening that would reveal what was really happening; that would be the real scandal.

The women pulled my attacker back as she reached for me with furious paws. Her vulgar insults continued to rain down, but I kept swatting them away with my silence. My head was exploding. How did I end up here? I wished I'd been happy and stayed put where I had been.

At that moment, Sultan suddenly appeared, panting heavily. He looked at me leaning against the kneeling camel, and at my raging attacker. 'Ghania, God damn the devil, what are you doing here? Why aren't you staying indoors during your waiting period?'

'Waiting period after our divorce? Hah, my darling, you brought her with you, eh Sultan? Like this, in front of everyone? God damn you, you unreasonable man.'

'Ghania, go back to your father's house. Cut it out, woman.'

'Of course, she's fair, and beautiful, and she's from Nizwa. Why wouldn't you go for her instead, you roving-eyed sinner?'

'Ghania.'

She wasn't deterred by his severe look. She was really fuming. *Whoever trusts a man like Sultan is crazy. And whichever woman gives herself to him is the loser, no matter how long or short they're together.* A face appeared; it was of a man about my father's age. Infuriated, he looked at the fiery Ghania snapping away and rebuked her sternly. Coldly, she looked at him. 'You've come to see me, eh *Abi*? Congratulations! Mabrouk! The man you married me to has divorced me. They told you that Sultan's a rogue, but you didn't listen. Go on and celebrate now. He's come with his Nizwa mistress, and he's kicked your daughter out like a stray dog.'

She was raving; I felt for her and her lost youth, despite my anger and my unpleasant situation. The father grabbed his rebellious daughter and dragged her behind him, with her swearing the whole way, since she didn't have anyone else to turn to. In that moment, Sultan looked at the ring of women and children. They were staring at him with barely concealed resentment and a mélange of a hundred other emotions. Once he barked at them, they scattered, leaving me to catch my breath.

He looked at me, brows knitted, at a loss for how to respond. As if he knew what was going through my head already, he didn't comment on what had just happened. He just offered a meaningless look and said quietly, 'My mother is waiting for you.'

'I'll never go with you. Isn't it enough what that catty woman just said?'

'Leave it alone. It's just words. Well, unless she and her friends come and murder you in your bed, where you'll be alone.'

'That doesn't scare me. Let me be.'

'You don't know her. Ghania is a vicious woman when she holds a grudge.

You won't be spared. Come with me and at least avoid people's wagging tongues until we get on the boat.'

'No.'

'If you won't come, then I'll just leave you here, waiting for your family.'

I shot him a look pregnant with hatred. As always, he was able to manipulate everyone, to make them live on his terms. Deflated, I followed him, dragging my heavy bundle.

* * *

This deceitful old woman is as evil as her son. She only takes me into her arms in front of her gathered friends to pretend she knows me. In a silky, charming voice she said, 'Oh God, Zahra, how much you've grown, may your mother rest in peace.'

Her affected accent was so convincing that the women in attendance started to retreat, to give us some space for our overdue reunion, to share what was on our minds. As soon as the last of them slipped away, his mother released me from her embrace with a shocking revulsion and exchanged contemptuous looks with her son. '*Wallah,* if you do that again I'll disown you,' she hissed. 'Why are you making me lie at this age, Sultan?'

'It's okay, Mother. Zahra is a sheikh's daughter. It's okay if we help her.'

'You're a misguided girl, and you have to go back home.'

'I wouldn't have made it this far if you didn't need the money.'

She wasn't impressed by my impertinence, and she kept on about parents' rights and the decency of daughters until her harangue wore me out. At the peak of her dispensation of virtue, there was a sudden knock on the door. She suddenly changed tack and started talking about my father, as if she knew him, and his extended absence since he had married a Nizwa woman. 'Your father angered our people when he insisted on marrying outside of Sur. Ah, *ahlan* my dear Maryam, welcome, let me introduce you to Zahra, my father's cousin's daughter. You've heard of her. Her mother died, so she decided to go to her sister in Zanzibar. You definitely know her. She lived here for such a long time. Alia—do you remember her?'

'Alia is her sister? What a wonderful coincidence!'

At this, Sultan took his leave, but not without looking at me and chuckling. As for the new arrival, she had removed her burqa and started to stare at me as if she were interrogating my features. She was outrageously beautiful, with wide black kohl-lined eyes hemmed in by two tidy, rich, arched eyebrows. Her nose had a slight upward tip to it, and her lips were full, as if stained with henna. When she smiled, her gleaming white teeth came into view, making her even more beautiful.

'Zahra, meet Maryam. She's Sultan's cousin. She was destined to marry Sultan's brother, but he died shortly before the marriage. Out of loyalty, she's refused to marry any other man to this day.'

I swiftly removed my burqa. I was suffocating, as if I'd been locked in a wolf's den, with Sultan's mother the mercurial she-wolf, changing the hue of her coat from one moment to the next.

'Ah, *mashallah*! God be praised, aunty. Zahra is very beautiful. Just look at her: she's fair, her eyes are green, she has dimples. You don't look like Alia, Zahra, you look nothing alike.'

'Alia takes after my father, and I take after my mother's side.' I glanced furtively at the old woman and found her swallowing her half-frozen smile. The truth was that I really liked Maryam; she was far from the type that was concerned about the shallow, quotidian affairs people talked about in the *fuala* coffee afternoons. She spoke like someone who had studied and learnt a lot. Next to her, I felt shallow. I was happy just to look at her while she talked at length about the death of Sultan's brother, Umar, two days before their wedding.

'I was waiting for him to come to our house, and they brought his corpse, celebrating as if he were still the groom. Imagine! I had only known him from behind a veil. At first, I'd rejected him, but he coaxed me into rethinking my decision. He really wanted me.' She looked at Sultan's mother, who came and went, busying herself with housework.

'He died. I'd been hoping to live with him. He wasn't your normal man. He believed in romance and equality. Afterwards, there was a rumour that Sultan would marry me, but I refused him. He wasn't a good match for me. It's not just because I was being loyal to the one man I respected, but because there's no one else like him.'

She went back to looking at me, smiling. 'Strange how you broke tradition and preferred to travel to Africa. Not so long ago, I felt like I was the only stranger in this place. You talk like those from the mountains. Didn't you take anything from your father?'

In that moment, I didn't want to lie to her. I seized hold of myself and said, 'I was brought up more by my aunts.'

'Oh? But you still seem so reserved. Sorry that I'm such a chatterbox when I find someone to listen to me. Are you usually so quiet?'

'No, it's just that I like to listen to what you have to say. You seem like someone who has learnt a lot. Did you study?'

She laughed heartily and whispered so Sultan's mother wouldn't hear. 'They didn't let me finish the Quran. They said it was disgraceful to do it among boys, and this sly old lady here was the first to support the idea.'

How wonderful it is for a person to have someone on their side, encouraging them, to take them by the hand and let them know they're not unnatural, not sick, but rather a creation that refuses to die, that has the resolve to pull down mountains.

* * *

She grabbed my hand at the door and whispered in my ear, 'Don't let Sultan get to you. He's got a wife in Africa and another one here, and they say there's another one in Nizwa. He caused your sister Alia pain. Your sister Alia left on the first boat for Africa after he discarded her and her children.'

My face went pale.

'That day, one of the captains on the coast married her. Did you know that? I get the sense you don't even know Alia!'

With her last words, it became clear that she wasn't stupid enough to believe that I was related to this town or its people. She was clever and had a heart of gold. She promised that she'd come back and then left. As soon as I went back inside the house, the old woman met me, her face screwed up. 'Had enough of your empty chatter? Found someone to support you in your escape and outright disgrace?'

'It's none of your business.'

'Ah, so she also taught you to be rude.'

'No one taught me. Get out of my way.'

Her features were an older version of Sultan's.

'The daughter who challenges tradition is a rotten good-for-nothing.'

'Tell that to your son, the slaver.'

She grimaced, a red mist descending over her eyes.

'You talk as if you own us. If not for the inevitable scandal, I would throw you out.'

'You've said it all now. Now leave me in peace,' I said. Her slight body crumpled to the floor, making me feel guilty. I heard her mumble in an unexpectedly faint voice, 'I seek refuge from God's anger. There's neither decency nor propriety with elders anymore. This is a time of tyranny and injustice.'

I was torn between ignoring her and apologising. As I studied her in that strange, humiliating, balled-up position, the latter more like what I wanted. 'Forgive me, I'm tired and I didn't mean it. Where did your son go?'

'He went to the boat. What do you want with him? Wasn't Ghania and that foreigner in Africa enough for him? I wonder what he sees in you.'

'I don't need him for anything. Your son is the last person I want.'

'But he said that you're running away from the mountains?'

'Does he always tell you everything?'

'I don't make him.' She shifted a little. 'Except when a woman like you comes along out of nowhere, and he asks me for help.'

'So, it's a usual thing for him to bring a woman along with him?'

The old woman considered my question carefully. 'Three before you. One of them got married and is in Zanzibar now, and another was a slave freed by her master who decided to go back to her homeland.'

So he buys and then returns, used merchandise. What else does this bastard get up to?

'And the third, aunty?'

'I don't know, I don't know...'

'Isn't your son scared of playing with people's lives? Buying and selling? Doesn't he fear God?'

'They're slaves, just slaves. What about it?'

'And you?'

'We aren't sold. We're Arabs.'

'But I heard that you're *zutti*, lower than slaves.'

Her eyes became slits as she launched her riposte with astonishing speed, 'Ask anyone in Sur about us! We're no less than you, sheikh's daughter.'

'But admit it, aren't *zutti* inferior?'

The woman shuddered at my rudeness. She stood up in front of me, all her weakness gone. 'What do you take yourself for? *Wallah*, may your death be at the hand of a slave.' She left for her room.

What are Sultan and his crazy mother other than cunning, greedy thieves, bound by rotten blood? A short while later, Sultan came in.

'Why did you fight back? The woman isn't asking anything in return for you staying here, except for some respect. What's with you? What do you know about the *zutti* people? These are thorny issues; they'll only make your head hurt.'

I kept my silence.

'And don't you dare raise your voice to my mother, Zahra. Who do you think you are?' He sat opposite me, close to my face, his breaths as hot as summer. Reflexively, I recoiled. 'Do you want to make sure we're not *zutti*, like you heard? What difference would it make?'

'Get your ugly face away from me. Don't test me, Sultan.' He quietly looked at me, studying my naked face for a while, his eyes travelling over every part of my face and the locks of hair that strayed from under my headscarf.

'What moron would leave you to marry someone else?'

'What a cliché! Get away from me.'

'If only you'd give me a chance and marry me.'

'Get out of here.' My shrillness astounded him, and he left laughing, without another word.

* * *

I stood in front of the boat, as I did every morning. It seemed in better condition now, shining in the chuckling sea. *Your open sails soar in the cool breeze, the winds favourable for travel, boats big and small preparing to leave, the sailors arriving together like a swarm of ants, brown like the wood of the boats they are boarding.* Merchandise in their boxes was strewn across the port or slung across the sailors' shoulders. The women were few, bringing the most vital necessities and then scurrying away. Or else, like me, they stood at a distance to watch what was going on, while the children were constant guests of the port, running around the boxes and on the planks for boarding ships on the warm, majestic sea.

Sultan arrived, carrying a huge crate. He had just shaved his head of thick hair, and it was bare. As usual, Ilyas was whistling, carrying a rope made of palm fibres, waving hastily my way. The breeze that stole into my nose was cool and fresh; I wished I could remove my burqa and breathe it in properly.

'Sultan said we'll leave tomorrow, *inshallah*.' Ilyas's face was hard to make out, as the sun behind him cast a shadow over it.

'Why don't we set off today if the boat is ready?'

'We're still not done buying stuff. There's a race to buy fish, which means the sellers have jacked up the prices. The boats planning to set off soon are buying fish even at such high prices.'

'Don't tell me that Sultan wants to wait until the prices come back down.'

'No, Sultan got himself sorted out some months ago when he agreed with some fishermen to buy their fish every day on the condition that the price was reasonable when the boats set off.'

'Buy fish every day? What does he do with them?'

'Don't think he's a fool. He'd buy them at dawn and then head off to sell them fresh in far-off areas that don't have fish. So, you see, he won then, and he's winning today. We have large families, and some of us have more than one family. There are blessings in taking the initiative.'

'More than one family?' *Poor and destructive.*

'I bet always having a woman at your side brings peace of mind.'

A bunch of sailors, as usual, started to harass me, but I paid them no mind. One of them drew closer and chuckled, 'Can't keep away even after you spent the whole night together, eh?'

His friend added, 'You're welcome to come with us. We know how to treat women right, too!'

I had heard enough. I took off my sandal. They dispersed, guffawing. *Such narrow-mindedness from these men every morning. We're only good for bed and the kitchen.*

I swallowed my saliva—I couldn't let such things get to me anymore. *I'm a free woman now.*

And here comes Sultan, exploding at me for going against his strict orders. 'Did they tease you? You deserve to be killed and more! How many times have I told you to stay inside? A woman's place is in the house. Where are you going?'

'No need to tell me this all over again.' I ignored the rest of what he had to say and just kept on looking at what was happening around me.

'Why are your eyes wandering like this? Do you insist on coming here to find a husband?'

'What is it to you? I think I'll go back to the house even though I can't stand your mother.' His drawn-out laughter irked me.

'Truly, you're more daring than all the men I know. If only you'd give me a chance.'

* * *

'They said that you're godless, and a thief.'

'Is that the worst you've heard? Come now, beautiful, wash up and pray. Don't forget to pray for me. These days I really need genuine prayer.'

Nothing seems to shake him. Sultan is the one person I envy. How amazing it is to be a man. He takes off, without the bother of a burqa, with no shame, and no one looking down on him.

* * *

'Why don't you marry a slave from Africa, then?' The words of the livid old woman in her daily rants against me stirred in me, once more, a deep sense of loss. *Here I am before myself, a weak heroine. Like others, I carry hundreds of compassionate expressions of people taking pity, but they're all just words, none of them actually came to anything. And when there's no action, feelings of inadequacy and frustration fill the void, masked by sweet phrases. Meanwhile, within us there is a cavity the size of the universe that can never be filled. A cavity growing bigger and bigger ever since I was nourished with such fears in the forgotten days of my sojourn in my mother's womb.*

Why was my answer silence? Why did I contradict myself now, wanting my freedom but still unsure how to feel about slaves having it? I curled into a ball, unable to respond. I, a pretender among the loudmouths talking of equality, a mob that was just as hypocritical.

*   *   *

The only person I was sad to leave behind was Maryam. She stayed despite her rebellious spirit, unable to cut ties with her people. *She'll stay back, waiting and waiting for a long time, and if she finds that perfect man (and that's if!), it'll be too late. All she'll have in hand are brilliant ideas that haven't been achieved.* As for the old woman, leaving her behind was a blessing like no other. She enthusiastically gathered up my things and helped me wash my clothes. Her joy went so far that she wafted my clothes with incense and gifted me a heavy bottle of expensive perfume. She didn't want to see me anymore, and I excused her for that. The boat, brimming with its large crew, announced its obedience to the captain and his order for departure. Among those bidding farewell, I saw Maryam and her mother. As for Ghania, I couldn't make her out; I hadn't seen her since our brawl.

Here I was, bidding farewell to land, my final overwhelming worry. I had spent my last nights on land, all of them without sleeping a wink, not beckoning sleep to come. I twitched at night, my clothes damp with sweat. Darkness and fear were all around me, and the annoying devil possessed me, his hand caressing a poisoned dagger, which it plunged it into my body over and over. I had become intoxicated and didn't care about death.

Even though the idea of death seemed horrible, and not at all acceptable, sometimes when the thought of it occurred over and over, it became strangely normal; all that was left was the initial shock.

White birds bless the journey, their cries mingling with the crash of the waves. Today, I leave behind Abdallah, my uncle, and my angry family. Really and truly, today I'm going far away where there's no nonsense and no hand can usurp my rights anymore. Before me is a blurry path and behind me everything is hateful. The waves rise, drowning out the voices of those bidding farewell at the port, and the eyes under burqas are blurred by tears, while other eyes are full of bitterness and anger.

Poor crying, complaining woman. She knows that, far from home, there is another woman on some other coast, using magic and potent potions that keep men under their spell, even when in their original marriage bed at home.

You poor woman, carrying distress in your chest for a moment, your obsession with him haunting you, burning you, destroying you. You're unable to declare it; rather your tears are hidden in the darkness of night, motionless under your blanket, far from the light of the moon.

What if I were these women, saying farewell to their husbands, one belonging to their caravan? A woman boiling and melting down, melting out of sadness and jealousy, with only impatience in her hand, seeking succour from a charlatan who sells her a fake potion to charm her man back home. Just one look at these pushy morons reveals their exaggerated enthusiasm, their yearning for women on other shores. They were destined to have everything in their hands.

It seems God chose them to make customs before promptly preferring to uphold the ones that suited their own arrogant, revered gender. Damn the joy that flashes in their eyes at leaving their families, their lips singing ballads and whistling. Damn the rights that they come up with on the spot to suit themselves.

A final look at the receding port, where the women the only ones to remain until the last moment, bidding farewell, their eyes and their children hanging onto the phantom of the boat tossing to the tune of the peaceful white wave.

They might come back–they've got to come back, even if after a long time, to murmur lies of desire and longing, to talk about how much they missed their families. Lies of torment and alienation, with only a woman's belly on some far-off coast to reveal them. Such women smile, remembering a night of hot love and a brown sailor conquering the storms.

* * *

Damn you and your superior selves. And maybe, for the thousandth time, I pinched myself. *Am I really the Zahra of old who washed utensils at the falaj and took care of the house and the cows? Was that me chatting at the well? And carrying the water pot? And the bowl of dough?*

* * *

'So … are you happy now? After today, the shame that you ran from won't follow you. Look, land is getting further and further away.'

'I swear, I'm not in the mood for a fight.'

'My name is Saleh. Saleh bin Qasim bin Abdallah …'

'Enough, enough. What do you want?'

He stood in front of me while I lay crumpled on the deck, a prisoner to seasickness and dizziness. The boat was to-ing and fro-ing, and the man in front of me made me want to throw up even more.

'I know you're not related to Sultan.'

'And?'

'There's no need to lie. You ran away from scandal because of Sultan.'

'Mind your own business.'

'He'll sell you and your family out. He's done it many times before with other women. Ah, I see what you're feeling, it's clear in your eyes. Go and lie down in your cabin. It's seasickness, it'll stop soon, don't worry. '

'Leave me alone. Don't stick your nose where it doesn't belong, understood?' A vein in his temple throbbed, revealing how disagreeable he found my aggressive tone. He shrugged his shoulders, stood in place, then murmured, 'Do you see the white sails? They're new. Also, the boat has a new coat of paint, and the mast has been repaired. Sultan's hit the jackpot, for you are the munificent Laylat al-Qadr.

Obviously, all of this has been paid for by my money.

I couldn't keep it in any longer. I ran to the railing and emptied what was left inside me, and I instantly felt better. I looked at a beautiful white bird in the sky, its call melancholic. Despite everything, on that day I was able to fly far from the hell that was on land.

Today, I'll fly with you, bird of sorrow, and no uncle or Sultan will stop me. No Saleh, and not even my disgusting vomit.

(7)

I saw my father
but he didn't see me stepping toward him
We were estranged: me and the tenderness of his hands
Birds of suspicion and the illusion of deserts

- Ahmed Fadil Shablool

They regarded me with the contempt reserved for a mangy puppy. No sooner had I left the suffocating, narrow room than their condemnation and dreadful mockery tore me to pieces. Their twisted mouths and hostile eyes were repulsive. Ever since my youth, I'd been surrounded by mouths and eyes like these, draping me in shame regardless of my complete innocence. They blanketed me in the utmost embarrassment, and I stumbled whenever I chanced on them. I'd be scared and my face would grow hot, as if I were shame personified, as if I had committed a sin that merited nothing short of death.

'What do you do on the boat, Ilyas?'

'I'm just a simple sailor, someone who keeps a lookout and carries stuff.'

'Do you find my presence here strange?'

All kinds of embarrassment swirled across his face, and he whispered,

'Truth be told, a woman's place is at home.'

'But I had no choice. Why are they treating me this way? Just because I'm a woman?'

'I don't know about that, but I get what you're saying. Have a look at this huge mast. I climb it to look out for land in the distance. Or sometimes I look at other ships, or how high waves are.'

Another ignoramus, only good for patronising and making himself seem the best there is. 'And what do the rest of them do? Look at how they're staring at me because I'm talking to you so openly.'

Ilyas laughed as he caught sight of the sailors getting back to work. 'It's fine, let them think what they want. Men don't take well to having women in rough places like this. Do you see that fat, dark man over there, next to the small kitchen? That's Essa the cook, and that skinny short one next to him is his assistant Nasser, who's really not needed. He's only good at nodding off. If it wasn't for his mother's tears, or the fact that he's related to Sultan, he would've gone on hitting on girls, nearly causing another scandal like the one last season, when he hit on a tribal sheikh's wife on the coasts. Do you know him? He seemed very chatty with you on the bus, but you didn't give him much attention.'

Who could forget that filthy face, those rotting teeth?

Ilyas went on, stealthily gesturing towards the obnoxious beast of a man. 'That's Saleh, of course. He's foul, as you know, but he's one of the most brilliant sailors I've ever seen. That one following him like his shadow is Ismail, Khalifa the bookkeeper's son. He knows the stars like the back of his hand. Khalifa was the silent old man on the bus. His son is nothing like him—he's only good for opposing everything, and for keeping up with Saleh.' He fell silent for a moment, his eyes searching until they found their target. 'That one's Eid. He's really nice and barely speaks. Those guys over there are my friends and do what I do. Do you see Juma' Ghabish, the one Sultan told off when he spoke to you? He's a sailor who rows the boat when the winds die down, like most of them there. They've got arms of steel.'

They worked more purposefully, their voices growing louder, when I looked in their direction. *It's the peculiar male problem of chest-beating, which appears from time to time.*

'It must cost Sultan a fortune to pay the sailors and maintain the boat.'

'Sure, but this boat is much smaller than the ones others inherit. Sultan bought the boat when he was poor. They say he started off with an arrangement where sailors would get a certain percentage of the profits, and that he got fed up with that arrangement, since so few people were ever happy with their take of the profits. It started out with just a few people and now look at how many there are.'

'*Poor* him, then. Are you trying to convince me that he's some great survivor? Where did he get the money to buy the boat if he was so poor?'

Ilyas grinned and looked around. 'Shh, someone might hear you. My mother told me that he kidnapped people from Africa during his time there as a sailor. Another time, a slave owner was in a tight spot and sold his people to Sultan dirt cheap. He always knows how to make the best of any opportunity.'

'On that point, I agree with you. This captain of yours is a great thief.'

'Don't say that! Sultan's had a really hard life. My mother said he's done whatever it took for him and his mother to survive: washed dishes, washed clothes, fixed up anything, anything for a few rupees.'

'What about his father? Was he sick?'

'He left Sultan and his mom, travelling to no one knows where.'

'Serves him right.'

The port had now become something of a memory, the azure sea swallowing us up from all sides. Its mischievous waves spoke to me through its translucent foam, telling me tales from the deep: of sunken ships, and of Salim down below, in its glittering waters, its deep waters, its salty waters. A delicate breeze sent a sweet tremor through my body.

I wonder how you are right now, Mother.

The winds were just right for the sails, with their wide-open arms and happy smiles.

Would you slap me, or cry from missing me?

This dream of freedom and the sea is what killed you, my poor runaway Salim. You said that the impossible was merely one of the thoughts of the powerless, and that where there's a will there's a way, even if it's twisted and long. If only you had shackled your imagination and kept your soul on land.

Ah, how sweet the freedom that rushes through my veins!

Now, after thirty years or more, I feel the superior sex is here to serve me, toiling away, beads of sweat dripping down while I'm over here, just looking on and smiling. Quite the princess I am! Nothing like the mountains at all.

I feel my unsettled belly clear up before this magical blue and these towering, flapping sails.

How are you, my poor mother?

'Get off the deck and go to your room. They're just gawking at you. We don't want any of the shenanigans that usually come when they see a woman. Especially when they see your very fair fingertips.'

I didn't say a word.

'Fine, pretend you can't hear me. I said go to your room, Zahra. Soon you'll get motion sickness again, and you'll throw up everywhere.'

The breeze was mildly cool, and I yearned to fly in the wide, open sky, a beautiful bird free of any fence or cage, a bird unbound, singing a melodious tune, announcing its joy with the breeze.

The waves swallowed the land, the sea and sky coming together to create a world for the bird, a dream world far from reality. *How sweet the sound of this wonderful boat on the sea. I wonder, why doesn't it sink to the depths of the sea?*

I am happy, Mother.

I like this life. I'd love to fly without stopping, hovering and taking in the whole universe below. For the first and last time I'm on top, nothing to grab me, my wings never tiring. With no hesitation, I pulled up my burqa and, with terrifying speed, threw it into the ocean. I didn't look at him or those stupid, contradictory men around me, who were eager to take in the sight of their coastal women while keeping their women back home under wraps. What captured my attention above all was that despised burqa, which I saw calling for help. In that moment, I saw a girl running, her father dragging her over lotus-tree thorns. She was yelling and crying out for help. She was in shock, fear draining the life out of her. *God damn you, burqa, sink to the bottom. I remember my father's red eyes at the stranger's appreciation of my beauty, and Mohammed laughing under the tree. God damn you, burqa, and damn those lifeless thirty years.* The breeze made me quiver all over. It grazed the tiny beads of sweat off my face. Sultan's hands tugged at me once more.

'I swear to God, Zahra, you're crazier than crazy!' I hadn't been aware of Sultan standing beside me, his smile racing hard against his anger. An odd smile, like that of a poor lost beloved.

'Are you sure you're not possessed by a djinn?'

'Get away from me.'

'Like you didn't do anything.'

I faced him squarely. 'No need for all this phony anger. It's none of your business what I do. You like it when people curse you, calling you the foulest words. You seem to find endless pleasure in someone else swearing at you.'

He feigned seriousness as he challenged me. 'You're here as my relative, and what you've done will give our women a bad name.'

'Get out of here! Don't you worry about what people say about me, since we're headed in different directions.'

He stood quietly, scrutinising me. His eyes glistened with mischief. I couldn't ignore how he was absorbing every detail of my appearance. 'You're very beautiful. So considering, as you said, that you're a sheikh's daughter, you've got to be modest. I don't want you to be the ruin of this boat, Zahra.' The calm warmth of his tone infuriated me. He whispered, 'Don't get too hung up on money, beautiful. When I toss you off ashore, you'll find yourself without shelter, hunger and poverty snapping at you. That will be the day you mourn your poor burqa, because you'll be easy prey for any hungry slave or wild dog.'

'So be it. I'd rather die than run back to you. Also, I won't be on my own. I'll go to Salim's wife.'

'Salim's wife? Do you even know where she is? What if she's moved on? What will you do then?'

Now that he's mentioned it, what am I going to do if I can't find her? I was surprisingly relaxed at the thought. I knew that my curiosity was the driving force behind my desire to see the thief of my dream, but actually befriending her? That was impossible. I couldn't countenance seeing her, and she would just be a reminder of how she'd stolen Salim, a reminder that my whole life had been a lie, and if I was being honest with myself, I'd only come to this boat after giving up on my now-mutilated image in the mountains, having grown tired of the tedious routine and pitying looks.

'If it comes to that, Sultan, I'll know where to go.'

'With no money, no relatives, no one to protect you?'

I let out a tense, bitter laugh. 'I'm an old woman now, Sultan. My bones are worn out, so who would want to kidnap me?'

'You're cunning, fishing for compliments.' He knew the exact thoughts going through my head. I started to feel threatened.

'Spit on me if I come running back to you, you slaver.'

'You're annoyed because I didn't compliment you, but yes, sure, you're beautiful. Maybe it's just my luck that your cousin died and you came to me asking for help, just so I could see you and smell the mountain roses on you.'

'You ...'

The sound of a hot dispute outside my cabin cut me off. Sultan shot me a steely look and ordered me to stay put, but I followed him and stood at the threshold to my cabin. I gazed out at the heated fight between Saleh and Ilyas. Ilyas was attempting to protect himself from Saleh's heavy fist, but it struck him on his back and face, and he shrieked in pain, curling up into a ball on the rough deck, motionless. As for Ismail, he kicked Ilyas with his feet, mercilessly, with a strange aggression. 'Saleh, you bas- ... cut it out or I'll throw you overboard!'

Sultan's scathing rebuke stopped the Saleh's brutality short. He stood looking at Sultan, breathlessly panting.

'Why are you out here now, Sultan? Why don't you go on with that slut that you've brought along, as if she's your relative? Since when do you have any family in the mountains? I just heard you talking to her, and she took off her burqa without any shame. Only whores do things like that! Look at her now, do you see her, her face uncovered for everyone to see? Oh, how *proud* you must be of her!'

After that, the only sound was the roar of the waves. Speechless, I saw all of them looking at me the way one does a weevil, one that's got to be stamped out.

Ismail stopped kicking a silent Ilyas and stood perplexed, like me, waiting for the next move between the Sultan and Saleh.

'I'll leave you to calm down. No good will come from more words,' Sultan determined.

Sultan turned his back.

'What a coward! That slutty woman isn't his relative. There's no way,' Saleh said.

Sultan stood for a moment that burned with anticipation. Necks craned to look at him while he stared at me with an empty look. A hundred solutions went through his head but, in a flash, he turned and cuffed Saleh under the chin, sending him hurtling to the ground. Saleh writhed and clasped his neck while Sultan thundered, 'I'm the boss here! Whoever sticks their nose in my business will only have trouble! Don't force me to mess up your lives! Your families in Sur would love to hear of your many secrets dotting the coasts!' He exhaled loudly, seeming to hesitate for a moment before decisively declaring, 'This woman is under my protection, and she is free to do as she wants.' The sound of the latest wave was louder than the one before it, and it was accompanied by the shrieking of hungry seagulls and the flapping of the sail. Silent, ashen faces. Saleh turned his back and walked away, while Ismail stood rooted in place, confused. Sultan ignored him and made his way to me, his withering gaze reprimanding me. Each of the sailors got back to work without comment. I walked to Ilyas, who was very embarrassed as he pulled himself together before me. There was a large bruise under his eye and another by his nose.

'What was that about?'

'Nothing.'

'All those bruises just for fun?'

He lowered his head, and it seemed he was trying not to cry with every fibre of his being. 'Saleh was eavesdropping on you. I tried to stop him, that's all.' When he saw me speechless, he went on, 'You've really caught his eye, but Sultan seems closer to you, as is always the case with all the women. For the Sur women and those from the coast, he's the ultimate dream, despite his suspicious behaviour. Now, Saleh ...'

'Sultan isn't closer to me than anyone else,' I said coldly.

'But he stood up for you. Even when Azza came with us, he didn't put himself out for her like he just did for you.'

'Azza?'

'His wife, who's now in Africa after getting a large inheritance from her father.'

I felt a wave of depression suddenly press down on me. *What's to be found at the end of this crazy adventure? Why did I run? For what? Where will I be in the middle of this angry world, where I can be condemned for anything and everything? And what about this Azza?*

*   *   *

They no longer gave me all their attention as they had in the beginning. Rather, they ignored me, as if I didn't exist. Even though I was more at ease like this, I was filled with resentment at how they treated me like any fallen woman who didn't deserve a second look. For the most part, even Sultan didn't take any notice of me. He scowled when he saw me breaking custom and strolling along the deck without hesitation. But he was occupied with addressing the man at the wheel, or he'd make a point of speaking to Saleh or Khalifa, who I caught scowling at me on more than one occasion.

Here's another day where, once again, I feel unwelcome. I have no family, no one to accept me, as if I've committed some great crime. But I don't care what they say about me, I'll live the way I want from now on. I don't care what happens.

*   *   *

'You can make it taste better with some onions fried in ghee.'

The cook groaned when he saw me in the kitchen. It was more like a small corner designated for cooking, with a rack for pots and a metal tray primed to carry sand and some stones, ballast for keeping the pressure trapped in the covered pots. The large pot on the flame was full of rice, and the aroma reminded me of the courtyard at home.

'Do you want me to help you fry the fish?' In spite of the cool breeze, the smell of fish mingled with the overpowering stench of sweat. He went about his work, ignoring me, so I repeated myself.

'You've got nothing to do here. Go back to your room and your food will be brought soon if you're hungry.'

'I'm not hungry. I just wanted to help.'

He gave me a cold, hard stare. Small beads of sweat dotted his flushed forehead and crawled into his eyes and onto his engorged neck. 'Listen, woman, we don't want any help from someone like you. Now, don't go getting me into trouble with Sultan. Get away from here because I don't need what you're offering. I'm a married and praying man.'

How dare he say such things! His looks were enough to tell me what I already knew: to him, I was a lowlife, only concerned with trapping men. My blood was screaming, announcing its revolt against my silence. Never had anyone ventured to even look at me the way this worthless cook was doing.

'Next time you speak to me, do it with more courtesy. My wrath is worse than Sultan's.'

'I told you, get out!'

I felt insulted all over again. Right then, the cook's assistant entered, whom I recognised right away from the grease collected around his nostrils. 'I see we have beautiful company.'

Everything in that moment was repugnant and stifling.

I don't know why my father's face suddenly appeared before me while, with his head shaking, he sought protection from the devil, turquoise prayer breads passing through his fingers as he praised God.

Pride, my father. You instilled it in me by accident, and here it is melting down before me, and I'm unable to gather it up again. That raised, white forehead of yours, my father, about to bow down. A strange headache arrived in a flash, compelling me muster whatever reserves I had left to make a move.

What if you saw me here? The looks I'm getting, not even your fat cows ready for slaughter would get them. What happened to the God of the skies, father? Why wasn't I happy with my lot, staying there? What if Salim were never born, father? What distances divide us now? And what were the distances before I left?

* * *

'Ilyas, do you know Mia, Salim's wife? Salim bin Masoud from the mountains?'

He looked taken back. 'You know her?'

'Is she beautiful?'

He stroked his bruised arms. 'Mia is a very strong woman. Nothing fazes her.'

'But she isn't beautiful.'

He scratched his temple, a smile on his lips. 'Beautiful, and a workhorse, too. Steadfast. Salim died last year—you know he drowned, right? When she found out about his death, she didn't yell or cry. She took her son and went inside her house, and she didn't come out till the next morning. They say she picked up her hoe, tied her child to her back, and went on tilling her field like any other day.'

'If she didn't cry, maybe she didn't love him.'

'She worshipped him. She didn't annoy him, even once. He would come to us cheerful, and he was wrapped around her little finger.'

'Maybe he hid his unhappiness. Isn't that possible, Ilyas?'

He hesitated before my expectant eyes, which were only waiting for an affirmation.

'I think he was happy, because whenever he caught sight of her bringing him his lunch, he would go out running to her. She'd go back to her field, to taking care of her sick parents, never grumbling.'

'What's new with that? A woman farming, loving her husband, and taking care of her parents. That's the done thing. Don't make her into a saint.'

My outburst and sharp tone made him ask, 'You didn't like her?'

My insides drowned in envy and grief when he described her, since she was exactly what Salim wanted, what he'd discarded me for. 'Have you tasted her cooking? Has she embroidered *kumma* caps with stars? Is her hair long and soft? Of course not, right? She doesn't have everything.'

'I think you're wrong about her,' another voice interjected.

Ah, here he is, interrupting us. What's with Sultan coming here now, after he hasn't spoken to me for all those weeks?

'Isn't that right, Ilyas? Didn't I tell you to stop doing things that would get you into trouble?'

'Forgive me boss, I didn't mean to.' Ilyas backed away without giving me the answer I craved.

'*Poor* you,' Sultan said. 'You oppressed woman. You're going to such extremes searching for an out to give you relief from that thieving woman. What did Salim have that I don't?' He smiled as I looked at him, surprised he was talking to me at all. Charming as usual, with that dark coffee skin, brilliant white teeth, and those sly eyes corrupting the harmony of his mythical face.

'What made you start talking to me again?' I asked. 'I thought you had repented of your flirting ways and had started praying.'

He followed me with his eyes. 'Woman, what have you done with yourself? Why did you do all this, when you were living protected and in comfort? They protected you with guns. I still don't understand what you're getting out of all this.'

'None of your business. Leave me alone.'

'What if you had become a mother, Zahra? Would you have run way from the shackles of motherhood, too? What's wrong with you? What man will accept you like this?'

I spat into the sea and turned away. *Do I hate him this much because his truthful words sting? Why do I hate him, and why do I want to throw my whole self into the sea?* My legs betrayed me. I was looking for a way out, but couldn't find one. If I could just block out his words, make him feel unsettled, even just a little. *I only came this far to know why her and not me, why not me?*

The sea was all around us, the sails aflutter, reaching for the stars and the night with its radiant stars casting serenity. But I couldn't calm down. I dragged myself to my cabin and lit up the oil lamp, its light faint. The room rocked with the boat's movements, the lamp casting its uneven shadow into the dark corners. Shadows danced on the walls, their eyes shining and fading, and then eventually going out completely, a spectre emerging in its wake. It was Mia, with her bright eyes and legendary strength. And there, another spectre was with her, embracing her tenderly. It was Salim! And there I was, hundreds of miles away from them, drowning in delusion and pointless waiting.

How many ghosts are there floundering like me in such a delusion, thwarted, used up? Even Maryam, with her quick and open mind, is on the wall of my room, floundering, with boundaries that she doesn't dare cross, waiting in vain for change.

And I'm the living dead on this boat.

Salim, my beloved, you left me and died. Oh, my handsome cousin who sneered at rules and ran away from them. If only you could see me now! I followed you blindly, like a crazy sightless woman, hoping you would prefer me to the woman who didn't cry for you, and who probably went out the very next day to happily till her land. If I were there, I would have filled the earth with mourning. I would have cried for all eternity.

That is also one of the rules dictated by society: that we shriek, mourn, and cry. But she didn't do any of these, legend that she is, and what am I besides a worthless scarecrow in the field, meant to keep crows away from the dates and mangos, but failing miserably, neither moving nor keeping the crows at bay.

My sweatiness really bothered me after the greasy dinner that Nasser had brought me. I felt the overwhelming need to bathe, meaning I had to go again to that dark place where the four steps led out to sea. I bathed there, forcing myself to hold still on the slippery steps, but the delight of being clean took away my fear of falling into the sea. As soon as the warm salty water touched my body, I felt refreshed and my fear melted away. I wrapped myself in a clean piece of cloth and left my wet hair down to shield me from the heat. Once back in my room, I sat waiting for sleep to come while the sailors outside, their voices all now familiar, traded entertaining tales and sang popular ballads, their voices harmonising with the slapping of the ropes on the mast and the growl of the evening waves. The small opening that overlooked the sea allowed a cool breeze to tickle my damp head, leaving me hazy.

Sweet sleep enticed me, pulling my hand. There were loud voices outside, whether angry, joyful or something in between, and there was a drop of water dripping slowly down my back. I straightened my back and the tingling relaxed. Here were the beats of sleepiness taking me to worlds of magical melodies. I listened to their funny stories, laughing along until I too felt I was there. Slowly, slowly I fell away from myself.

Why today, father, am I remembering you with such bitterness? Hush, you disheartening thoughts, leave me be. What I need now is some hope, far from the cruelty, the contradictions, the neglect.

* * *

The knocking at the door was very light.

'If you're going to sleep, make sure you've locked the door securely.'

It was the same voice with that mischievous tone that I loved and hated equally. My door was locked. Going back to a runaway dream was as good as impossible.

* * *

What's with them? God damn their insolent eyes. Why are they so obsessed with my movements, even the simplest ones? Something as minor as opening the door is enough to spark endless agitation.

I sat in the tight space right outside my room, breathless. No one on this boat was interested in what I was going through. I should have stayed with Maryam, so she could regale me with tales of people, politics, and sadness. Or she could have picked up her bundle and walked with me, leaving all the shackles behind at the Sur port. But she didn't, and anyone else in her place wouldn't have done it either, so what was wrong with me?

'Why are you playing the role of a martyr?'

'Why are you here? Didn't you say I was attracting too much attention and should be ignored? For once, let your word be your bond.'

'I won't get angry. Your words are like honey to me. Why do you upset yourself like this? You know being impatient makes you go grey, or maybe you've already got too much grey hair to care.'

At Saleh's harsh words, I felt a lump clog my throat, as if he had slapped me to shut me up or poured a bucket of cold water over my head. His eyes brightened as they took in how my face fell. He had obviously intended to remind me of my foolish lost years, and the truth was that, even though I knew it was true, hearing it from someone else was humiliating. That was what he wanted, of course.

'Marry me, Zahra, I'll make you happy. I'll buy you some dye for your grey hair. Believe me, I'll really make you happy.'

At that moment, Ilyas's shout echoed from the mast, and the sailors around us shouted gleefully at one another, running to look longingly out into the extended void, out into the distance.

'Mogadishu ... Mogadishu!' They were cheering and applauding wildly in a way I'd never seen before. I withdrew and curled up into a frustrated ball. *I wish I could be a man like them, rejoicing over land, sea, and sky. Not handcuffed by the word shame. Hadn't I always wanted to be a young man, transformed in the blink of an eye?*

I curled tighter into myself as unconcerned feet tapped all around me, nearly trampling me. They were feverish to reach their first coast. Saleh stood before me, his eyes mere slits. He was the only one who felt my presence, his feet careful not to crush me. Instead, he sat down and stared at my face. 'Are you sad to be an outcast here? Embarrassed?'

I remembered the last time I'd felt this way, twenty years ago or more. An innocent young girl at the falaj in clothes covered with slime and urine. Saeed sprinkling me with water, my other brothers following us. That day, at that very moment, the *falaj* was a like a mountain rose garden, but with no thorns.

I had laughed a lot at the sight of muddy Saeed, so much that I peed myself. I was scared that my mother would come at me with her sharp tongue and hands, so I sneaked away to wash my clothes, hoping they would dry in the sun, preventing my mother from picking up on the scent of urine and noticing the slimy smudges. But they pushed me into the *falaj* when I came back, and in that moment all I felt was the joy of friendship. Those were rare moments. We were real siblings, shouting, chatting, having fun, and I flew along, rejoicing, drops flying in the air, intoxicated just to be with them, to be treated as an equal, as a friend. But I made a mistake when I wailed at Saeed for pulling a bit too hard on my hair. I wish I hadn't. Then my mother wouldn't have known where I was. I wish I had swallowed my wail.

Back then, my mother's eyes made me tremble as they widened, announcing Judgement Day. This time, her eyes grew wider than I'd ever seen before.

'You bathed with the boys. What a disgrace you are!' From that moment on, I had to carry a bucket and walk behind the house to the old neem tree, bathing there while trying to tune out the squeals of joy streaming in from the *falaj*, the fun my brothers were having, the hurling of water. If only I'd let them have their way, trampling me, I wouldn't have lost them. I wouldn't have been banished to this solitude, living in fear of what people would say.

'Are you dreaming? Remembering your family and your people? You're like me now. No family, no people.'

'What do you want? Get to the point.'

'Don't believe him. Sultan is a trickster, a smooth talker. I saw him yesterday trying to get into your room, but you'd locked it. Forgive me for thinking ill of you.'

'How is Mogadishu?'

Ease came over him when he noticed how I ignored his previous hostility. Yet he was still slightly cautious, aware of the previous injury caused. 'It's a beautiful place, but it won't be easy to get in.'

'What do you mean? Will they object to me being here?'

A sudden, hateful laugh exploded from his belly. 'No, no. But they've been complaining of a cholera and tuberculosis outbreak. I think they'll force the whole crew to get vaccinated.'

(8)

But oh, where shall I find
when winter comes, the flowers, and where
the sunshine and shade of the earth?

- Friedrich Hölderlin

The last thing I needed was to have a sailor in love with me. Although honestly, I liked the idea. I liked it a lot. I was happy, at least, to have found someone ready to cross the barrier of male superiority for my sake, someone I could trample on, humiliate. Someone who would fall before me without any complaints or grumbling. Even when Ilyas announced the waters of Mogadishu were approaching, he came to me, alert. 'Zahra, they're going to carry out vaccinations. Look at these boats stopping us from entering. For God's sake, I beg you, don't be scared.'

He was crazy about me because he wasn't like the others, those who looked at me like I was an extra appendage. He looked at me with a strange respect. I would feel at ease when I sat front of him, stealing a look at him.

'I won't let them vaccinate me. It's ridiculous. How can I reveal my arm to strange men to prick me with a something like a thorn? No, Suleiman, I won't do it.'

'But it will protect you.'

'Tell them I don't want it.'

At this, he nearly went weak at the knees. I wanted to roar with laughter, but I restrained myself, willing myself to ignore his trembling and the weakness in his legs.

'Okay Zahra, I won't let them touch you. I can hide you over there, in the storeroom. No one will suspect a thing. I'll set you among the provisions. Don't be scared.'

'But I am scared, Suleiman, very scared.'

'No one will dare touch you, I'm here to protect you.'

Despite his low status on the boat, he, like the others of his gender, was trying to make himself seem more important. I nodded submissively, my stupid conscience calling me devious. I wasn't as scared as I was making myself out to be. I just wanted him to serve me as he would the apple of his eye. Running breathless for my sake, resisting his boss for me.

Sultan was busy barking orders at the sailor at the wheel and at Khalifa, while Saleh, who was standing beside them, glanced over from one moment to the next, a strange, stifled look plastered on his face. I stretched out my conversation with the young sailor, paying no attention to his menacing glower. 'Are you married, Suleiman?'

Once more, he trembled. 'No. I would have, but she married my brother after getting tired of waiting for me. My uncle's daughter.'

'Poor you. Did you desire her?'

'No.' He seemed to swallow what he'd wanted to say and changed his train of thought. 'I'll come back in a bit to take you to your hiding place.

Don't you worry.'

I didn't know why I insisted on stretching out my conversation with the young man. From time to time, I'd look at the others around and find them fuming with rage. Sultan, though, wasn't paying attention. He was completely absorbed, or maybe he was just ignoring what was going on.

I liked that no one objected to me speaking to whomever I liked. Euphoria coursed through me. *No one is reproaching me for how I sound. I no longer fear the sting of the whip, and I do as I please. Everyone sees me as having fallen to the very bottom, from which there is no return.*

* * *

From the opening in my room, I saw the African port come into view. A smaller boat approached ours. Aboard it, there was a man dressed in white, waving a rag. Our boat started to slow down, and I heard the sound of the anchor and its chain splashing into the water.

A singular anticipation nearly overwhelmed me. A movement toward the back of the boat had reached its peak, and the voices grew louder, laughing. I heard a knock at the door and felt a sense of victory. It must be Suleiman.

'It's me, should I come in?'

Oh no, why was he *here*? I hesitated in front of the door. This shouldn't be happening. He had completely ignored me this morning. Maybe he'd heard from one of his many spies about my plan with Suleiman.

'Open up! I have much better things to do than play this game with you, Zahra.'

'What do you want?'

He smiled. 'Are you still mad at me? Why are you still mad at me when I'm not angry with you? Even though your beautiful mouth only spews poison.'

'What do you want?'

'So, then you're still angry. Why can't you even look at me?'

'Sultan, leave me alone.'

The sharpness in my voice and my anger made him change tack. 'There are people here to vaccinate us against cholera and smallpox, as you know. Should I bring them here?'

'I won't do it. Go and tell them that I've drowned at sea. I won't get vaccinated.'

'For God's sake Zahra, use your head. Why are you breaking the law? This is for your own good.'

'Immunize yourself—it's enough for you to follow it. Leave me alone.'

'They'll come here, so there's no need to drag it out.'

He didn't give me a chance to object and left me fuming. He wasn't the type I could control. Revolting and arrogant.

By chance, I remembered Khalfan and his simple-minded, unsophisticated treatments. His spells would always fail no matter what he said in front of the mosque. He was called a charlatan, a suspicious character. Some people said he should be imprisoned, dispossessed of all his authority, but the whole village objected. Khalfan's holy hands had healed hundreds of children, as well as those suffering from epilepsy. Even though he didn't do me any good, not even for one day, with all my different illnesses, his treatment was simple and didn't require a sting like this vaccination. I didn't want to remember the hot iron that had been pressed against my neck when it had become swollen. That had been a horrible treatment, completely different.

A knock brought me back to reality. I got up to lock the door with the bolt, but it was already a little bit. I stopped where I was. Today, Sultan would have the last word, and as usual my stubbornness wouldn't help.

'Zahra, it's me, Suleiman. Come quickly. They're completely busy now. Come out and walk to the provisions store on the other side of the boat. Don't run, just act normal and don't look at anyone. I'll follow you there after a little while.'

'But they'll still see me.'

'There are four of them. They're busy with everyone else. Cover your face and walk over from the eastern side. They're on the other side. Don't worry, they won't pick you out in the crowd. As for the sailors, don't worry if they see you. They won't say anything, believe me.'

The walk itself was a sweet risk. I didn't pay attention to the sailors whose gaze trailed me till I reached where Suliman had told me go. They were curious, but as usual refrained from speaking to me.

Once inside, an enormous African slave suddenly obstructed my path when I touched the goods stacked under a black plastic cover. 'What are you doing here?' he boomed.

'Who ... who are you?'

'Go back to your room.'

'What the hell, slave? You dare order around the daughter of your masters?'

'Leave, woman.'

I strung together a hail of curses and saw his face grow dark, his eyes reddening menacingly.

'Leave.'

The difference in size between us was laughable. In a moment, with one finger, he could crush me and drown me in the sea, without any resistance to speak of. But, arrogant as I was, I looked him right in the eye, even though deep down I felt ashamed to insult those who worked in our houses, people we bought dirt cheap.

'Rabea, what are you doing here?'

'I think I should be the one asking you that, Suleiman.'

Beside this hulk of flesh, Suleiman looked like a child. Yet he still went ahead and spoke to Rabea in a quick, hushed voice. Rabea's eyebrows furrowed, clearly not pleased with the idea being proposed. After a short while Rabea left, leaving me to breathe a sigh of relief.

'My God, who's that? I haven't seen him before.'

'He's Sultan's faithful slave. He guards these goods day and night. He doesn't speak much.'

'Why do these goods need constant guarding?'

'Salted fish, spices, and other things.'

'That's it?'

But Suleiman didn't want to keep on talking. He was twitchy, ill at ease. 'Here, I'll make a hole for you in the cover so you can see out. Stay quiet in your place until I come back. Don't move at all. Understand?' I nodded, and he lifted the edge of the heavy plastic tarpaulin. 'Go on now, there are many boxes and a sack full of fish. Don't let the smell bother you, it's better that way.'

The place was really repulsive. I couldn't see anything once he released the edge of the cover. The stench of fish wafted through every cranny. *Maybe I ought to stop being so stubborn and just get vaccinated after all.* 'Does it suit you if I make a hole here?' He poked the cover and I said yes. As he made the hole, I saw the blade of the knife in his trembling hand, and I had a bad feeling. But he made it carefully. I could no longer hear the sound of the sea or the sailors' voices.

Time crawled by. The smell itself was enough to choke me. After a while, I felt my limbs fall asleep. It felt like I would never see the end of this, that I had thrown myself into a foolish situation. I reached out a hand to jostle my leg and hit a box to my right instead. I had to bite my tongue to stop my yelp of pain. I tried to dislodge the box to make more space for myself, but it didn't budge one bit. I pressed my shoulder into the box, but there was still no movement. I tried again. This time, it crashed into its neighbour, making a loud bang. Moving again after that was definitely not a good idea, even if I were stuck here for all eternity. My ears perked up, trying to find out whether anyone else had heard the box crashing, but they were all seemingly deaf. I tried to set the box right, but it was too dark to see what I was doing. I felt something dry. Once it was close enough to my face, I realised it was dried fish. It had a horrible smell. After a heroic effort, I righted the box. I groped the ground to put back the fallen dried fish. The smell was killing me, and the hole in the cover was far from my face now, what with my shifting about. My hand fell on something enormous. It wasn't fish, as I had thought at first.

I brought it closer and felt it from all sides. *This huge thing with a wooden base and a long hollow tube. And oh, here's the trigger.* It felt exactly like the *tafk* rifle at home in the mountain. So *this* was why he needed constant surveillance. This was exactly why that shameless slave had glowered at me. *I've finally got you, Sultan! You dog!*

I pulled myself together and ran my hands through the box again. Maybe I'd find another rifle. Lo and behold, there was one, then another. Many of them, explaining why the fish smelled rusty. They were a cheap cover for a dirty business.

'Come out from under there now.'

I shook when the light momentarily blinded me. 'I said come out!' Sultan's eyes settled on the rifle clasped to my bosom. 'I won't.' He looked sharply at me. Unmoving, silent.

'Now.'

In that moment, there wasn't anything sweeter than using my newfound knowledge against him. 'If you force me, I'll yell at the top of my lungs. Maybe that will make the port patrol happy.' I raised the rifle at him, smiling. He looked at me in shock. Everything in that look spelled death, but he backed away. 'If anyone else had threatened me like this, he'd be at the bottom of the sea. No man has dared to do such a thing before, you bitch.' He then roared, 'Have you lost your mind. Who do you think you are?'

The sharpness of his tone was new to me. Despite how scared I was that he would tear me to shreds, the vaccination party's departure from the boat made me feel in control. 'Again, I'm telling you, you have no right to tell me what to do.'

'What do you know about medicine, having lived your whole life milking cows and taking care of livestock? You know that if you get infected, and everyone knows this, I'll throw you in the sea—alive. I can't lose the whole crew because of a woman like you.

'Can I go out to the port now?'

'To turn me in, you she-devil? You'll never be let out there. From this moment, one of my slaves will follow you wherever you go, even in your sleep.'

'Do as you wish.' I then walked up to him boldly and whispered, 'But our deal is off. After today, I won't pay you a rupee.'

He stood quietly, then spat in my direction and left. I heard him ordering the sailors to let down the smaller boats and load the goods onto them. No one objected to his orders, and his goods weren't searched, despite his reputation. He was carrying a recommendation letter, one easy enough to buy. Whoever opened the door would see Saleh watching it all, chewing on a piece of straw or a fishbone. From the shadows, he was envious of his boss.

* * *

Even men themselves have levels of superiority that separates them, and the same fire that eats them up burns my fingers when I step out into the light. They vary in their sovereignty. Some are at the top, and some are at the bottom. Whereas I, and many other women like me, will always know that we don't have what it takes to lead.

Who would believe that Sultan, who swears and curses like a heathen, does business with people in high places, and could easily obtain a recommendation letter or ten? Meanwhile those crushed on the boat, dozens of them, find every moment difficult. Destiny isn't good at playing the game of recommendation letters with them.

Goodness, I need a nap right now. A sweet nap where I'm in charge of Sultan, a sleep like the one that is making my eyelids heavy.

* * *

All that I want is to fly in the sky...to cast off all my chains in the blue of the ocean and fly solo in the clouds and beyond the sun. All I want is to be completely alone, just me and my free world, a new blue-green world.

All I want is for a white wave to carry me to a world where the fact that I'm a woman isn't important, a place where I'm treated with love and a purity of spirit. A place where my lineage, skin tone, and gender don't matter.

* * *

It goes without saying that, among those who are oppressed on the boat, I'm a hero. Looks of admiration and support trail me openly. And why not? I dared threaten the giant, which they never did themselves. Desiring a livelihood, they turned a blind eye to all they saw, and went against all they had vowed in their prayers to avoid. The truth is that they're simpler than I am. They're waiting for treasure to escape on the shoulders of a genie. They have a patience that the heaviest burdens can't break. Fine. At least the veneration I now suddenly enjoy among them pleases me. I felt that I had done the right thing in leaving the mountain, because they had the same contempt for me on the mountain. Here, the way they look at me has improved, and that would never have happened on the mountain if I'd stayed—no matter what I did.

While such admiration abounded, no one dared say it aloud. I kept to myself, with the familiar guard that Sultan had assigned to monitor me. Sometimes, Suleiman the flirt would come over to speak to me about his feelings, and to remind me in one way or another of the favour he had rendered for my sake. So that I would always see him as valuable, now and forever.

Even so, I asked him to leave, because his repetitive ingratiation and his grovelling voice had begun to grate on my nerves, to throttle me.

'You're meant to be guarding the goods, so why are you guarding me?' My scary bodyguard remained mum. As people said, he was not a man of many words.

'Zahra, I want to tell you something important,' Saleh came over to say. As usual, he was chewing on a piece of straw, chasing away the flies that hovered around him.

'What do you want?'

'I've come to propose to you, as God is my witness.'

This wasn't anything new or surprising. Looking at his flabby body must have made many young brides reconsider marriage. He was a block of flesh, and dirty flesh at that.

'Go and take a bath and clean your teeth. You stink!'

(9)

'My son cannot replace me;
I could not replace myself.
I am the child of Circumstances.'

- Attributed to Napoleon Bonaparte

Am I really so despicable? I guess I am what I am—it's how I've always been. And like any flawed human being, I'm a product of my circumstances, and I can't go and spontaneously change my nature. I can't become a saint overnight, or even in a lifetime. Or many lifetimes. What I've lived up till now is an epoch of frustration. Thirty years, thirty years of weeping, and I'm still the foolish girl pining for her cousin. In spite of his death, and in spite of my family and their daggers at the ready, Salim was my soulmate, and I can't seem to live without him.

Oh, sea! Sea, with your vast surface and strange assurance, why aren't I scared or angry at you? You stole my dreams and my life.

Oh, you poor beloved, you've been gone too long to come back to my thoughts like this. Because of you, I've come to know Sultan, the mirror to my dark self. People with such faces only experience alienation and lies, to the point it makes you sick, which is why they live feeding off one another.

I feel a sort of affinity with the small folds in the outstretched ocean, this dark blue body with white foaming crests, with bubbles that appear before the angry storms.

Will you take revenge on me one day, oh sea, because I brought shame on my family, or because I was delivered from the dagger of honour? No, I don't think these delicate waves know anything but love.

This boat and its crew are a shot of immortal hatred and gunpowder. Where can love be found here?

And me? Do I know love? Was I made full of hatred? I don't think that I'm empty of feeling. Sure, I can be crazy and selfish, but I'm sure that I have known love.

*   *   *

'Do you think you can make me disappear just by closing your eyes?' My guard's face was stony, as it had been every other day. 'Would you follow me if I threw myself in the sea? Don't you have a brain? Cat got your tongue? Why aren't you speaking?' He said nothing, an imbecilic smile plastered to his coal-black face.

At that moment, a war waged inside me: My sermonising to Sultan's mother about her selling slaves fought against the superiority I felt in that moment. I still reasoned like a slave trader, no matter how hard I tried to bend the truth.

I was swept away by the desire to destroy this hulk of a man in front of me.

'Rabea, do you kidnap people to sell?'

He looked apprehensively in my direction. *Finally, he moved.*

'I bet you'd sell your mother and sister into slavery for Sultan. What a traitor!'

His eyes darted to and fro.

'What exactly do you have left to live for? Shame will follow you, and you'll be a slave to a crazy master till you die.'

His reaction made me as happy as it frightened me. He opened his large eyes even wider, and they blazed like two burning embers on the night of a waning moon. His jaw muscles quivered with naked fury.

I made him uneasy. His blind confidence in himself was shaken. And for the first time, my guard left me alone. He didn't comment on what I'd said, not a peep out of him, but at least, for the first time, he went against his master's orders. And this delighted me no end.

* * *

I've grown bored of this place. Now I just want to get to the first port, to live a different life. Time can't pass fast enough; I don't have what it takes.

'Won't you stop pushing my buttons, woman?'

My whole body shook for no apparent reason. I hadn't thought Sultan would actually come in response to what I'd said. I hadn't imagined he would come back and have a go at me, but I'd be lying if I said I wasn't happy to see him.

'What did I do?'

'Don't make eyes at me. I've come to know you well, you she-devil. Are you inciting my slave against me? Biting the hand that feeds you? If it wasn't for me, you'd be licking cow shit in your uncle's sheep pen!'

'With my money, you fool.'

'Don't you dare raise your voice at me like that. You know there's no way back for you now. Why didn't you poison them on the mountain? Your tongue stops blood cold and scares off any suitors.'

'I didn't say anything to get you this angry. I just told him that his mother's soul wouldn't forgive him, since he would sell her for no reason. I just pointed out that his family has lost out, becoming slaves to a thief. Did I say something wrong?'

Sultan balled up his fist and faced me. It was all he could do not to grab me. I took a step back. 'You wild woman, I won't let you destroy the boat I've been building my entire life. I was a vagrant and a thief, only for you to come along and upend my carefree life. I swear, if it wouldn't cause more trouble for me, I would have thrown you in the sea. It wouldn't be the first time that I'd buried a crazy cow like you.'

I thought he was just raving as usual, but he faced me again head-on and continued, 'Don't make me hate you even more than I already do. Keep quiet and keep whatever dignity you have left. You could've had everything, but you've taken a toll on my patience. Know that your death won't bother anyone. Not any more than one of the puppies that I raised and enjoyed shooting at the first sign of disobedience.'

'Drop the act Sultan, you can't touch a hair on my head.'

'You mean that I'm weak before your aged beauty?'

'No, because you know you're not telling the truth. Both of us know what the other holds within.'

'What do you mean? I don't get what you're saying.'

'You more than understand. You like people who go against the grain, like you. You can't harm me.'

'Well in one instance I can, you smart aleck: If you harm me, I'll end you the way I started you.' He forced a smile. 'So that's why you picked a fight with my slave – you missed winding me up.'

He caught sight of the sailors keeping tabs on how long he was spending with me, and he whispered, 'Know that you'll be prey sooner or later.'

'You're all animals. Go away.'

'Do you really want me to go? I know you like talking to me more than Saleh, Suleiman, and all the others. You're the devil's offspring, like Mai. Your father, when he was giving you life, forgot to say "Bismillah" at the right moment, since he was so overcome with desire. And so you, like me, love the forbidden.'

Speechless, I walked off, leaving him where he stood. I walked to my room and was hit in the gut by an overwhelming urge to retch. I was weighed down by a melancholy that I couldn't pin down. I'd left my mother back on the mountain, left my father with his blue prayer beads. How they used to scold me, and how sadly my father would hang his head! *Oh Father, wallah, I didn't mean to tarnish our good name. I just wanted to be in control.* I broke down in tears and wished I could drown in the deep.

* * *

As I wept, Maryam's words came back to me.

'Never be the first woman to rebel and succeed. I'm a coward, so I'm waiting to be the fourth or the fifth. As for the first, no way. I don't have the energy to lose everything.'

Going back home was not an option, nor could I stop this boat. In front of me lay this journey of my choosing. I had to choose the lesser evil, and I'd ended up failing to keep my dignity. I went back to my bitter tears.

* * *

I was weighed down by despair the whole day. Not even when the boat docked at the port that had a beautiful tower overlooking the rocks did my mood lighten. I tried to take delight in observing the people running here and there, with all their activity, but I wasn't able to shake off my lethargy, nor a sinking feeling. Some of the European sailors spread out at the port caught my attention, their small noses reminding me of kittens.

Rabea came back and sat down next to me, with the same blank simpleton's look on his face. I made do with a hasty look in his direction and then went back to observing the hustle and bustle of the port. The sailors started to applaud at the mere lowering of the anchor into the sea, running enthusiastically to tie the sails and lower the goods and luggage. They were thrilled to be here, more than they had been at any other previous stop. And why not? They probably had secret, coffee-coloured wives and children here.

The sailors on the boat ignored my presence, as if I hadn't been the focus of their chatter for all the days before. The only one who was looking at me was Saleh, smiling and yet forlorn. Next to him was Ismail, confused about the attention Saleh was paying me, burning with jealousy. I averted my gaze so I wouldn't be tempted by the crazy idea bubbling in my head at that moment. I caught sight of Khalifa as he calmly collected his maps and books and put them all in a small box that never left his side.

He didn't seem as eager for this port as the others were. Even Sultan had laughed from the depths of his heart as he walked to the port, propelled by a self-satisfied joy. It didn't take long for the boat to be emptied of everyone except me, Rabea, and two grumbling sailors tasked with guarding the boat. My eyes trailed the droves of sailors to the port: here, there, sailors hugging other sailors from other ships, and the beaming Africans jubilant at their arrival. Without a doubt, they were related to them somehow. Probably these were their offspring.

I remained alone, forgotten, an outcast. No one paid attention to me except Saleh, who was sitting under a coconut tree opposite the boat, staring in my direction with a frown.

'Zahra.'

Ah, here's the adoring lover. I forgot about him after not seeing him these past few days.

'Forgive me Zahra, I'm embarrassed because on that day, I couldn't stop Sultan from finding out where you were. Rabea's the one who told him. He never keeps anything from him.'

'I'm not angry. Why didn't you join them? They're all on their way to port ...'

'Malindi. Don't you like it? Look at those beautiful rocks scattered in the sea. Did you see the tall lighthouse? The Europeans built it to guide ships, and that's why they're always strutting around like masters.' Then he quickly added, 'But maybe we should just leave them to do as they please, and we'll do as we please.'

It turned me off that he couldn't stick to one opinion. He was weak.

'Move along. I don't want you standing here next to me. This guard of mine is enough.'

'Don't you want me with you? I could help you.'

'No, no, go on. Please go. They've probably already noticed you're missing at the port.'

'I won't go to the port. I've been tasked with guarding the boat along with these two here.' Saleh gestured to two men, one of whom was Juma' Ghabish. 'We'll go after sunset.'

'Where will you go?'

His temples flushed red in embarrassment, and I got the sense I was about to be lied to. 'We're going to an inn in the middle of town. We'll stay there till late. We're young men, after all.'

'Meaning, you're going to go see women. Then take me with you.'

'Impossible.' He recoiled in shock.

'Why?'

'You're not allowed there.'

'Why not?'

'That's just how it is.'

Next thing I knew, he was gone, leaving distasteful questions pounding in my chest. Without hesitation, I walked toward the plank that had been stretched out, heading down from the boat. It shook under my feet. Rabea followed me without comment. Sailors threw cursory disapproving looks my way, then went on gossiping about me.

'You know, Rabea, I think they've decided to disapprove of everything I do, just me in particular.' I stood for a while in front of the anchored boat, waiting for my so-called guard. 'Come with me. I don't feel the safest walking here on my own. I can't wait to leave.'

I saw Rabea as a much better alternative to Sultan's stinging, obscene tongue. At least, in his presence, I felt safer. When a cool breeze brushed against my face, I admitted to myself, *It's not that I hate Sultan. I wonder if Rabea has a wife here, like the other sailors racing to the shore. I don't know, actually.*

The port was beautiful, with golden sands, swaying coconut trees, and people of different sizes, nationalities and languages. In every direction there were crates of goods and sellers moving from one boat to the next, searching for the best bargains. Gestures and the strange new tongue of Swahili were the modes of communication. *If the people here were to welcome me with cheers, I'd be the happiest woman on earth. But they just stare at me, wide-eyed, and then go back to work in earnest.*

I walked for a bit, now and again commenting to myself on this and that. Rabea still wore his impenetrable smile. He didn't stop trailing me, which he did with a quiet patience. I wished I had a slave like him that would follow me and be willing to sell himself for my sake. *Sultan has everything, even loyalty to the hilt.* One of the foreigners said something in Swahili to me.

'He said that you're very pretty.' That was the only thing Rabea said the whole way. Saying I was tired, I decided to go back to the boat. I was embarrassed by my hungry stomach, which impudently cried out its need for food. As soon as I arrived on the boat, I went to the kitchen and found food prepared. I looked around, but didn't find Essa or his lazy helper.

'Do you want to eat with me?'

Rabea's eyes widened in surprise.

'Don't worry, I'll give you a larger portion than you usually get.' I took a hearty portion of rice and fish and walked far away from the kitchen before anyone saw me. 'Go on, eat quickly. They're all busy today with their stupid secrets. Let's also have our own. You said that foreigner said I was beautiful. What else?' As usual, I didn't expect a response from him. I wolfed down the food that almost formed a lump in my throat, and I didn't look toward my silent companion as he ate quietly.

* * *

The sunset in Malindi had a different flavour. The sun was closer than it should have been, egg-yolk yellow, and around it lay a shy dusk. The men were constantly on the move, whispering to one another, so that their voices wouldn't drown out the muezzin's call to prayer. I didn't feel homesick then, what with the magic coursing through the atmosphere. After prayer, the sailors acted like children, running and playfighting on the cool sand. They took off their clothes and bathed in the cool green water. The young boys like Suleiman, if you could call them that, were in their best clothes, shrouded in a haze of ambergris and musk, whispering secrets to one another. *Everyone has secrets here, even me.*

Sultan himself appeared well groomed and charming, a high-class thief. As soon as he saw me staring at him, he deliberately drew close. His cologne was indescribably heady. 'Why are you staring at me like that, Zahra?'

'I can't see well at night.'

'I'm really happy today and don't want to fight with you. Do you want to come along with me? Or you want me to stay with you two?'

'Why don't you and Rabea get going? You're both so boring.'

He gave a wretched laugh. 'I'm tired of begging White women. I don't want egg whites today. I want clove-and-coffee women, because I'm feeling a bit hot.'

He walked further away and batted his eyelashes. *What a low-life dog, so vulgar, as usual. I really hate him.* The lights of the oil lamps hanging on the boat accentuated Sultan's muscles. He had two other well-groomed men with him.

'God damn him. Why don't you go, too?' I asked Rabea. 'Or you haven't managed to find a lover nearby–maybe you sold her the following dawn.'

He seemed to have gotten used to my provocations. This time, he didn't bat an eyelid and just smiled.

'Okay, okay, we're coming too,' I said.

He stood in front of me, blocking my path.

'We are not going anywhere at night,' Rabea declared.

'I'm going, and let's see who gets the last word.' I walked away from him toward the unsteady plank that Sultan had just worked on a few minutes before. Rabea tried to grab me, but I ran too quickly for him and made for the port.

'Zahra, my dear, stay. Oh, God of the skies!' As usual, Khalifa the astronomer was annoying and, in the moment, I felt possessed and yelled a curse. 'Who does this old man think he is? Just like my uncle on the mountain, with his so-called wisdom.'

I glanced behind me and saw Rabea had given in and was following me.

Towering trunks of coconut trees. Their branches a frenzied night's tale. Each one unique, none resembling the other. They danced and leaned into another, and in the gentle darkness their fruit looked like cautious, fearful black eyes. A wonderful fragrance floated in the atmosphere. Exotic and yet intimidating. Having Rabea by my side made me plunge deep into the dark coconut forest. Within me raged a dark, hateful anger that I hated to think about. The dried leaves crackled violently under my feet. I was afraid of a place like this, full of vermin, snakes, and djinn. I shuddered.

I waited for Rabea to catch up, and then walked on silently. Maybe I would see the end of this ghostly forest.

After a little while, the end came into sight. It was a small village, with straw and clay houses, most of them with a cooking fire burning nearby. The whole place was lit up with a faint light that rose and fell. Barefoot brown boys played in front of the houses, amidst them a laughing pretty girl with her thick, braided tresses. Voices of a quick, rhythmic language grew louder in the luminous yard, exactly like the people back home.

They didn't differ much from people in my country, except for this barelegged girl running free. I couldn't run with abandon like her without people staring. She rolled around in the soil and pulled the others' hair, laughing. I hadn't dared to come across like that. I was a sheikh's daughter, not like other girls.

'I didn't play like that, Rabea. It would have been a disgrace. I only knew the kitchen and the depressing well nearby.'

Unprompted, I wandered toward the houses and rudely looked over the walls of their small courtyards to explore this calm new life I had discovered.

There was a tall woman cooking by the crackling fire, wiping away the beads of sweat dripping into the flames. She wore a tree-patterned dress wrapped around her voluptuous body, her tremendously fat legs visible below the dress.

Her neighbour harvested some vegetables from her compact garden. Next to it stood a calm chicken coop, from which emanated not a sound. The chickens were asleep as usual at this early hour. A child sleeping on her back caught my eye. He was tied to her back and waist, and she was working away without the slightest grumbling. In the house next door, a poor, old woman was cooking in a small pot, naked children crowding around her, yelling out with hunger.

And here, in this house, a beautiful caramel-coloured woman placed pieces of fabric on a sick old man's head and poured out medicine for him with love and patience. A woman was a woman here, whether a child, grown, or elderly. *She makes everything, and all responsibility falls on her shoulders. It seems she doesn't know how to grumble, or how to flee in a boat to free herself from her family, her society, and her past life.*

A woman's voice here means everything.

I looked stealthily at Rabea, his eyes taking in the children huddled around the pot. More than pity, it seemed he was thinking about how much money each of them would fetch.

'Doesn't guarding me take up enough of your time? Do you know that we used to have a dog my brother loved very much? This dog never left my brother's side even for a moment. So many times, he was nearly killed for his attempts to come inside and be next to Ali. You remind me of that dog.'

His face was a vision in pain, but at least he turned his head away from the innocent prey and focused on me instead.

'They found him in the house once and said he was filthy. They tried to shoo him away, but he wouldn't go. He was loyal to my brother to a fault. That's why they got rid of him with a bullet, using the guns you sell. Ali laughed that day, and later he poked at the rotten corpse.' I kept on trying to provoke even the slightest vengeance. 'If my family found you walking behind me the way you do, they'd shoot you. That day, you'd go straight to hell, no questions asked. If I were you, I'd ask for my freedom from that master of yours.'

'You're being unfair to me, *sayyadati*.'

At that point, I felt at ease. Finally, I had been able to unnerve this giant of a man. And here he was, about to cry in front of me, if not for his last dregs of dignity.

'I'm telling the truth. Weren't you just thinking about selling those children for the sake of a handful of rupees? You're a moron, and your master, who was dressed to the nines earlier, doesn't much care for how you feel. He's a smart man to get you to obey him like this, with such extreme sincerity.'

'I'm doing this, *sayyadati*, because they're poor. They're going to have to steal in order to get anything to eat.'

'What garbage! You're just saying that to clear your conscience.'

He bit his tongue, and with startling speed, recomposed himself, as if he knew already that that conversation was a dead end.

'Let's go back.'

He nodded compliantly and walked behind me, head bowed.

Why are we afraid of the night even though it's a delicate, refined creature, not causing any trouble? Why do we fear the rustling of leaves, eyes darting here and there, till we can find peace behind a door with a bolt?

Rabea trailed after me as we went back into the forest of towering coconut trees, searching unconsciously for an evil ghost, which would be looking at us from some vantage point or the other. The trunks of the trees writhed like hissing snakes, the dried-out leaves crunched over and over again under our cautious steps.

I stood listening to what was around me, chaos roaring inside me without reason. I recited verses from the Koran, *Al-Fatiha* and *Al-Nas*, and started to ask for forgiveness using the few formulas I remembered from my father. In one particular patch, the darkness was at its thickest. The distance we had to cover seemed longer than when we'd come this way. *Why do I feel short of breath? There's nothing suspicious so why am I scared, expecting the worst? Why do I feel like prey, like there's someone lurking in the darkness, watching me?* The image of my angry father swirled in my mind, my father intoning 'La hawla wa la quwata illa allah' and shaking his head, lamenting. I shook when my uncle's face came to mind. His double chin, his sneering face, his bulging eyes flashing treason. *Darkness an unknown being, hemming me in. My brothers froth with rage and chase me.*

Darkness is all the same. What's here is just like the darkness on the mountain. But now it has a different smell, a smoky odour. There is a bellowing anger within me, and the feeling that I am prey is a constant companion. An earth-shattering feeling of weakness.

Uninvited, Sultan's face, along with its hateful smile, came to mind. Maybe it was hidden need. I didn't want to say it or feel it.

The sound of a wandering dragonfly and the rumbling of the sea interrupted my thoughts. Rabea was silent as usual. *What tranquillity there is when you hear the sound of a wave, after a long period of silence!*

The fear is gone now. Rabea quickened his steps to catch up with me. Sultan was still out. *Everything about him bothers me. His body, his being, everything about him is wrong. But I still want him around, and this realization bothers me more than Sultan himself.*

A painful truth that, like the others, must die.

*   *   *

The sailors chatted late into the evening, both on the cool sand and on their boats lit up by oil lamps. The lighthouse stood lonely on the rocks, its dazzling lights searching for anyone lost among the waves. *Not a glimpse of light for those far from shore.*

The light of the lanterns reflected off the sea, joining with the lights of the distant lighthouse. The sea was on fire from within and filled the place with awe. The sailors' ugly whispers didn't escape me as I walked among them on my way to the boat.

'She was with that slave in the forest.'

I wonder how the embrace of that slut who hugged you was, Sultan. Does she also smell like cloves and coffee, like this country of hers, simmering with magic, fragrance, cloves, and sandalwood?

I sat in silence while bathing on the slippery, quiet steps. The soap that Sultan had bought for me before departing had no fragrance at all. It seemed this was the simplest soap he could get, and it didn't smell like cloves in the slightest.

(10)

*'Nothing is more damaging
to a new truth than an old error.'*

- Goethe

Insomnia had no mercy on me that night. Chaotic confusion and brutal apprehension roiled my innards. I tried to squeeze my head under the large pillow, but I failed to lure sleep. When I heard a movement on the boat's deck at a late hour, I felt a burst of anger overwhelm me. I looked out from behind my door, trying to find the source of the sound. I saw ghostly figures slip onto the boat, among them one that looked like Sultan. Strange shadows in European clothing.

He led them to the storeroom. At that moment, the slave next to the room suddenly woke. Sultan shushed him with his finger. He forced himself back to sleep. I understood in that moment that those Africans in European clothes had purchased the weapons, and here they were in the dead of night, sneaking around so the local authorities wouldn't catch them.

They carried the crates of stinky fish on their backs and walked with stunning balance toward the shaking plank. Without any hesitation, they made their way to the forest, while Sultan spoke to a man who looked, from a distance, to be their leader. The man then gave him a sack. Money, no doubt.

The whole thing took no more than a few minutes. Everyone then went on their way as if nothing had happened. I closed the door very carefully. I sat where I was, trying to catch my breath. He was a clever thief, like all good thieves, always ready to bribe anyone–friend or foe. Both were one and the same: each of them meant profit to him. The man was a slave to the rupee, and whenever the opportunity for wealth presented itself, he was the first to jump.

Why haven't I slept this whole time? Why am I afraid to ask myself about this dreadful insomnia?

I heard his steps on the deck. I knew it was him from the way his sandals hit the surface. He had an unmistakable gait. I sat for a while, fighting off all kinds of thoughts. His steps faded away, and I thought he must have gone to bed.

For God's sake, what good is there in him? Is there even just one good characteristic? If there was just one good thing, then I could explain my swirl of confusion. *I've got to believe that I have a sensible mind.*

I heard a feather-light knock on the door and thought it was the wind playing with it. But it started up again. I didn't move a finger. I heard the door creak and fear overcame me. Who could it be? Was it my guard? Who else besides him would dare approach my room? I wished I'd remembered to bolt it. I was afraid to breathe.

'I knew you were you still awake.'

Oh God! I couldn't speak. My tongue froze seeing him before me, at a time when all other creatures were fast asleep. It was just us and the roaring of the waves.

'Were you waiting for me, Zahra?'

'Get out of here, Sultan.'

'Shh, keep it down. People will start talking about us. Why are you still awake? Oh, your neck is gleaming in the light from the lighthouse. So fair and beautiful.'

'Leave, now.'

He sat in front of me, close enough for me to see his scary eyes light up. He reeked of alcohol; it was a terribly strong smell. I could almost taste it.

'I want you, Zahra. Ever since that night at the inn. You had sandalwood on. You were glowing. You give the impression of being all virtuous. Why are you alarmed? Come to me, Zahra. I'll marry you, even though you'll never change. Come to me and put me out of my misery.'

He was sozzled. He nearly grabbed me, but he got a hold of himself.

Oh, you beautiful devil. You tickle my quivering heart, calming me and spurring me to do wrong. Leave me alone. How nice it would be to do the forbidden.

'Go away Sultan and seek protection from the devil.'

He took my hand and cradled it in both of his. It was as if I were talking to myself.

'You stayed up for me. The jealous type, I see. Why are you afraid when I'm yours?'

'You've got two wives already, and I won't be the third. Leave such things for a stupid younger woman.'

'Hypocritical, but so beautiful. You have a wonderful, light scent, better than sandalwood. Did you bathe with the soap I bought for you? Come on, just hug me. I want to feel your warmth, like your hands, aflame and trembling.'

He almost flung himself onto my chest. I trembled and swatted him away in terror.

'Get out or ...'

'Stop this foolish modesty. Can't you smell the musk on my clothes? Come, put your nose up against my neck here. Smell the musk. Don't you like it? The pulse in my neck, can you see it? My heart is going crazy, it might just jump out and devour you.'

The path was clear, and the woman within me shook violently, egging me on to accept Sultan's invitation, to embrace the wide chest speaking so passionately. We were miles and miles away. Everything was in her favour, but I still felt scared. The path was clear, but it was deadly.

I wanted to, I swear. *I need that intoxicating smell. I need love.*

'So, you don't want me, then? Are you sure? This is your last chance.'

'Leave ...' I managed to let slip.

If he had insisted on staying, I'm not sure I'd have been able to turn him down.

'As I said, last chance. I won't ask to marry you again.'

My head spun at a premonition of scandal. I'd had a pretty friend, and her mind had always entertained the devil's ways. One day she fell pregnant. At the foot of the neighbouring mountain, I saw them bury her. She had been pulsing with life. Her name was Fadhila.

'You'll regret it, Zahra. I promise you that.'

He stood facing me, his drunkenness now seemingly worn off. He was looking at me with pure anger. 'I'll go, but everything you like about me will end. I know exactly how much you crave my attention. You'll miss it so much you'll kiss my feet. And, at that point, I'll just throw you to Rabea to crunch your bones.'

'Leave!' I roared. I don't know if anyone heard me at that point, and I didn't care. Fadhila was underground, at the base of the mountain, with hundreds of other girls. I knew that she carried the shame of my brothers. She loved them all, and they would take their turns with her. She was just more unassuming prey.

* * *

Oh, Merciful God, what has happened to me? Why don't I know the path you want me to take? I haven't been able to live, believing a delusion and harvesting a mirage. Today, like yesterday, I mow down all those standing in my way. Just as yesterday I lost my family, today I'll lose my old ways of thinking, passed down by my family. I don't have the power to face my old mistakes, and I don't have it in me to create another illusory fantasy.

* * *

The next night, Sultan again made his way off the boat after sunset, a cloud of musk trailing him. A number of the others accompanied him, while the few devoted to their wives remained on the boat, trading stories and telling their secrets to the stars.

As usual, Rabea stayed with me. I wondered if he was also hungry for a night out like the other men, or if he had a woman somewhere already. *A freewoman maybe, one he's hidden from thieves and slave traders, loyal to her for life.*

Fidelity has always been a precious rosebud that struggles to stay alive. The simple sailors barely know this, adoring volatility in emotions, mirroring the manner in which the sea's storms toss them back and forth. Love is like the seafoam, ephemeral.

'I'm missing home and my sheep pen today, Rabea. Before I left, I had a black ewe that gave birth to two radiant white lambs. Today, they're probably more handsome than ever.

'Here and back on the mountain, I had to put up with humiliation to find true happiness. Not long ago, I was happy to chat with my friends, passing some sardonic comment or another if my mother beat me for Ali or Saeed's sake. The concerns we exchanged so derisively once upon a time were laughable.

'Of course, you've never known love. My heart was for Salim, my cousin, but he married someone else from here. How I wish I could spit in her face. I don't ever want to see her. She stole him from me and had a child with him. Your great boss came on to me last night. He found me alone. He came into my room like someone going into a whorehouse.'

The night was still and confused. My silent companion blended into the background even more as the night wore on. My mood darkened.

'I wonder, how many slaves have you kidnapped during this short period I've been on this boat? A hundred? A thousand? My uncle also used to know how to count till a thousand slaves. He was also a clever thief like Sultan. He would get up very early, and they would come to our field. They'd cut roses, pomegranates, harvest honey. The sun still hadn't risen by the time they went to sell it all in Nizwa. When my father arrived, he would be miserable to find his field robbed like that. He would damn the crows and the thieves. That's why we were poor, and my uncle was rich. He bought me, and he also bought my brother for his daughter, Maryam. Do you know why my uncle hates me?

'One day, I caught him in the act, but I didn't tell my father. He idolised my uncle. And who was I but a woman with no brain? But that day, I made sure to tell my uncle that there was a clever thief stealing our harvest during the *fajr* prayer. He was as still as a deep well, as usual. He looked at my face without blinking. Like a falcon ready to strike.

'But why am I telling you this when you're not much different from your master? But I don't hate you, and I don't hate him. You don't speak, only Sultan does, but you're still both thieves, and I'm a sheikh's daughter. The sheikh of thieves,' I chortled with abandon.

That night, I didn't wait for Sultan to come back. I locked the door tight and forced myself to sleep with all my might.

* * *

Two days passed, and I didn't see Sultan at all.

'Did the beautiful woman seduce him? Fool him into thinking he belongs here? Why are you looking at me like that, Rabea? You keep your master's secrets. But his secret is out.'

'No, this isn't like him at all. Sultan's never gone for this long. He must be in trouble.'

That Rabea spoke didn't surprise me, no matter how rare it was. 'You mean to say that the woman forced him to marry her at gunpoint? How noble of her! He must be lost in her love.' Before he could speak again, Ilyas came in, loudly declaring, 'This isn't normal, Rabea. Your master's been missing for two days. Where is he?'

Rabea's confused state and his longwinded response surprised me. 'I really think he's gone and done it this time, Ilyas. Come with me, and bring some of your friends. Let's go to the inn and maybe we'll find him there. Hamud was with him, and Ashraf too. Both of them are yet to come back. Let's go now.'

Suleiman, Juma', and Eid the wheelman went with them. I stayed back, watching them till they disappeared from view. A strange, sarcastic smile slipped across my face. If I had been more naïve, or maybe younger, I would have said that the man killed himself because he loved me. It was near impossible for a woman to make Sultan lose his head. *The man's probably in some prison somewhere, beaten black and blue after they discovered he was arming traitors with weapons. Let them kill him, for such a man needs to be stamped out.*

As time passed, I grew worried. Then slowly, slowly, I was seized by fear and I started to sweat. What if they really had killed him?

Oh, poor Sultan. No matter how vile he is, I don't want him to die. Let them break his nose, but not more than that, not more.

'Worried? Wondering where the great thief is? He deserves all that he gets and more.'

'Saleh, by God, I can't handle you at this moment in time. Leave me alone.'

'But he sneaked out of your room two nights ago into the dead of night. I thought you were honourable, but then you're like all other women, a slave to the rupee.'

'You're forcing me to raise my slipper.'

'So then, he didn't touch you?'

'What ugly words you're saying. No one dares touch me. Why aren't you with them searching for him?'

'Because I want him to die.'

The venom in his words took me aback.

'Look at yourself, you're shaking with fear. You love him, don't you? You fallen woman.' While he spoke, his eyes drank me in. My hands, my face, my feet. Only a crazy man would say what he was.

'You don't know what you're saying.' *How did we get here? It's like we're in one of my grandmother's tales, time making me into a princess once more. The battle raging around me is for the sake of winning my heart.*

But this time, the image of the fighter was a shabby one: a despicable sailor. Saleh glanced around, and then his facial expression turned to pleading. 'I'm the one who will make you happy. Even if you made a mistake with him, I forgive you and will marry you. Just don't believe him, he's seduced many before you, and they all despise him now. They weren't able to keep him.'

I trembled at the change in his voice and expression. Saleh had done whatever he had to do to get what he wanted: me. He wasn't good at ordering his thoughts or choosing his words, but he always did make me feel special.

'So, you planned it all? You've betrayed him.'

'No ... no.'

'You hate him so much. He hasn't left anything behind for you. You want him dead.'

For so long, I'd imagined Salim as the perfect man, like one of the heroes from my grandmother's stories. But I was delusional, because all that time the princess he wanted was hidden in a far-off jungle. I was cast aside, left to dream of him.

'Marry me. He has others. He'll never be loyal to you. Every beautiful woman delights him. He's only good at deceit and betrayal. I've known him since we were boys. He was a sweet talker. A liar. Always getting what he wants. Despite all he's done, he always gets the girl, the money, the connections.'

'And who told you that I want him? I hate him.'

'No, you love him. You're saying that just to find out what I did to him, to know how to save him.'

'Where is Sultan, Saleh?'

'I won't tell you unless you promise to marry me.'

'Have you gone mad? Me, marry you? Should I starve and debase myself?'

'What's wrong with me? What do you want?'

He spun in a circle and then knelt before me, somewhat awkwardly. 'Every day I bathe and perfume myself with oud that I bought from one of the most expensive perfumers. I even put it on at night now. Whenever I see you walk by in front of me, from your room, I imagine you'll take notice of me. I went to the barber, got my head shaved, and washed my teeth a hundred times. Every day I walk by you, intentionally working nearby, but you don't see me at all. Even vermin passing by get more attention from you. The one your eyes are stuck on is lower than every creature. But he's still a saint to you. Is it because he's good-looking and I'm not? Is it because he's a great charmer? Why are you worried about where he's gone? I've been watching you, and I nearly exploded. You were moving round your room like a madwoman. I'm the beast doing everything to get your attention, but you don't even look at me, not ever, even though I'm not the one selling slaves or guns, or seducing women. I'm not the one with a wife on every coast.'

I found myself having to defend myself, to contradict all the ugly truths. 'I don't care about him at all. You're imagining things.'

What's the story with this Saleh? Wasn't he against me being here in the first place? Whenever he got the chance, he'd tear me down, and now he's turned into a lovelorn sap who could almost kiss my feet. I stifled a cackle at the sight of his pleading face. He looked like a hungry puppy. There was no way this puppy could be the fighter that I needed; the time had passed for me to impose conditions.

The men came back after sunset without Sultan. Rabea's head hung low, resigned.

'Where's Sultan?'

'We didn't find him,' Rabea informed me. 'The inn's guests and its workers all said they hadn't seen him for three days. I asked the villagers, the children. None of them have a clue where he is. He's disappeared from Malindi completely.'

*   *   *

What's the point of all this searching? Another day and the poor fellow's elsewhere, being humiliated on all levels. I saw Rabea, his head between his knees. How could he be upset after having experienced such humiliation at the hands of such a man? *Doesn't he know how to hate?* I thought of comforting him, but I hesitated and then walked away. Suleiman was sitting with his friends. They spoke wearily of what they had done and how, despite it all, they hadn't been able to find a trace of the missing captain.

Suleiman raised his head and smiled faintly in my direction, then went back to talking with his friends. I guessed his interest in me had run its course. No doubt he'd heard my yell that night and saw Sultan leaving my room. *Saleh, that cunning devil. He's the only one who knows where the captain of this boat is. He's playing the fool, his eyebrows arched, while time stretches out before me with no end in sight. What if I tell the crew that Saleh knows where Sultan is? Would they make him talk? Would they believe me? Could I find one thing to prove how unique my circumstances were, my precarious position notwithstanding?*

My mind came up with fragile fantasies that quickly fell apart. The real solution was to accept my scrawny knight. But he should at least guarantee me a kingdom and a throne. The rest were dung—they were arrogant, and this scrawny one was my winning ticket.

Time passed, and I delighted in knowing how to get to Sultan. The man had probably had his fill of beatings by then. At least he'd gotten what he deserved for coming into my room late at night. *I wonder if now was the time to act.*

I had gotten used to my intuition. *The man has been tortured, but he isn't dead. I can wait a few more hours before settling on marrying Saleh.*

And the mountain people, Salim, Sultan: What if they found out I had married a revolting simpleton without any status? But how would they know? The mountain folk were a part of my past, and Salim was dead.

Saleh repulsed me. I hated him. Could I marry someone I couldn't tolerate—me, a woman of distinguished lineage? But the calculus was simple: I needed a refuge.

I did what I did, and I hated it, but I needed protection and shelter.

Time passed, contrary to everyone's desires, and the boat slipped further into silence. What was left of life for me to lose? I was old, and there wouldn't be another Salim. All paths were closed.

With one word from me, Sultan could live or die. Simply, in the blink of an eye, I'd be the knight in shining armour and at the top of the world. What else could I want?

* * *

But saying that I accepted his proposal was difficult. Saleh couldn't believe what I was saying.

'Just like that, without informing anyone? You think you can pull a fast one on me? How can I believe what you're saying?'

'I need a stupid man.'

'You're just trying to provoke me. Prove to me that you're not trying to deceive me.'

'Repeating myself is not something I'm fond of. I told you that I don't know how to lie. What do you want as proof?'

'Sure, sure, no woman knows how to lie. Convince me you're telling the truth. I'm not a fool, Zahra.'

'What do you want from me?

'Come with me to the Imam at the mosque. Nasser, Ismail, and Khalifa will come along, too. Khalifa can be your guardian.'

'It's a sham marriage, then. That's not possible.'

'Then there's no point in talking if there's no marriage ceremony. You won't get what you want.'

I stood in front of him, bamboozled by his quick planning. 'Isn't my word good enough? Also, Nasser and Khalifa won't agree to be witnesses and lie in front of the Imam.'

'Enough, Zahra. If you agree, then why would they disagree? Don't you see, the sun's already setting and Sultan's in the worst position possible.'

'I don't care about Sultan.'

'So then say yes.'

You didn't need to be clever to see what had to be done. It was my only way out. 'You're a real scoundrel.'

'Because I want you for myself? You've got to be mine.'

He made my pride purr in delight.

(11)

Flutter, seagulls' wings
And do not stop
I traverse distances
Chasing a burning call carried by yearning

- Mohamed Al-Balushi

I don't want anyone to ask how I'm feeling, I don't want to hear a thing about folly. Yesterday, I was with seagulls flying free and nothing stopped me, and today, I've become the wife of a man who has nothing except for knowledge of the sea. What will I do next?

After having traversed all that distance and left everything behind me, why does regret well up within me at this man alone, asking for my hand in marriage, all without any obscenities? Because he wanted me, I will exploit this fact, like any desperate person who's given the chance of a lifetime.

I'm miserable and now I condole myself with Saleh's affections.

There they are, having gone to bring back their kidnapped king. I informed them of his whereabouts, feigning humility about the gold that I paid to elicit this information. It was a lie, but worth it. For the first time I see respect in their eyes.

* * *

Saleh informed me of Sultan's whereabouts as soon as the contract was signed in the presence of the imam at the mosque. His sheer delight was laughable. The scent of musk and oud wafted off his body. He wore a white dishdasha and an expensive turban tied carefully around his washed and combed hair. I bathed and wore my normal clothes and perfumed myself with some musk that Ismail slipped me just before heading off to the mosque.

I still remember Khalifa's frown when Ismail whispered Saleh's intention to marry me in his ear. Khalifa took me aside and spoke to me about the right of refusal and how one should think deeply about marriage.

But time was running out, it was already *isha* prayer, and poor Sultan couldn't stomach another day of torture. He had been pursuing a slave deal with a regular client in Malindi, and Saleh's snitching had landed him in the hands of a chieftain, one who had lost his son the previous season. The chieftain learnt that Sultan had kidnapped his son and sold him into slavery in one of the Arab countries. Saleh's tale about Sultan had made me sympathise with Sultan just a bit. But this Sultan, with brute force in hand and at the ready, I couldn't stomach for even one day, so I married Saleh, saving him and my reputation. Saleh, my husband, was easy enough to steer. I didn't have to deal with him tiring me out with refusals, and there wasn't anyone else who came along with him to make my life encumbered, say a sister or a mother-in-law. Getting rid of Sultan himself was a great deliverance. He was a miserable man that would make my existence a hell, or a prison. And there was no time to think about why I married Saleh.

* * *

'How did you know where he was, Zahra? Are you mixed up with witchcraft?'

'I paid all my gold and ...'

'Your bundle is still where you left it. So basically, Saleh told you where he is.'

'How dare you say I'm lying, slave! Know your place. You're much better when you're quiet.'

'Sultan isn't stupid enough to be convinced by what you're saying. You're marrying Saleh because the bastard bargained with you and won.'

'May God have mercy on him.'

'You're fucking acting. You just did it to save him.'

'No, I did it all for myself. Whatever the case, you should kiss my feet because your boss has finally been saved.'

'That's *if* he's still alive,' he said bitterly. 'If he's dead by now, then you're the loser.'

His words froze my blood, and my body stiffened.

* * *

What if they've killed him? Will everything I have done be for nothing? I started to gaze in the direction of the port. What if they had killed him? No, it couldn't be. He was like the proverbial cat with nine lives. *But what are these crazy tears, then?* They brought him, and my heart stopped when I saw them carrying him in like a corpse. Rushing to them, I took a closer look. His face was torn up and bloody, his wrists inflamed from where his shackles had been. His legs were static, and he was barely breathing.

'We'll put him in your room, Zahra.' The colour drained from Saleh's face, but I nodded.

'They quartered him with horses every day. Another day and he'd be dead. He hasn't eaten anything. He's suffered terribly. The other two were killed.'

I stood looking on, my eyes riveted on Sultan's face. 'Why didn't they just kill him too?'

'They enjoyed torturing him too much. We found him in a hut, chained up in the shape of a cross.' I glowered at Saleh, but he feigned innocence and said in a broken voice, 'Take care of him, Zahra. He needs intensive care.'

I nearly threw up there and then, but I stopped myself in front of the utterly broken Sultan. *You eternally arrogant being, who would believe you'd now be at my feet asking for mercy and charity? There's nothing better than seeing you so weak, barely breathing.* I touched his brow. It was burning. 'He's got a fever. Leave him here. I'll look after him.'

Everyone left the room, except Saleh and Rabea. Saleh took me to one side and whispered furiously, 'Leave the door open at all times. Don't get too close because he bites!'

'Damn you, now you have something to say about him! Have you seen what they've done to him?'

'He deserves it.' He left while Rabea remained kneeling by his master, checking on him. He looked at me pleadingly. 'They've completely destroyed him. Nurse him back to health, Zahra.'

Sultan stayed where he was for two whole days. I asked Ilyas and Rabea to wash him with sea water, as maybe that would help heal his wounds. When I went back in, he was exhausted. *Oh, you who are near to my heart, yet far from my grasp, how long will you last like this, helpless?* I wished he would flirt with me again like he had that night. I asked for forgiveness every time the thought came to me because I had come under the aegis of another man. Saleh would pop in from time to time, envy glowing in his eyes. But he didn't dare say anything, always going back to where he came from, distressed.

When Sultan opened his eyes for the first time, my feelings were a mix of joy and trepidation. But he slipped back into unconsciousness. I fed him against his will. I'd crush the food with a mortar and slip it between his lips, forcing him to swallow, but most of the time he threw up the food. Despair hovered over me. Every night, I barely slept, and Sultan's condition didn't improve. The boat set off again, the sailors quiet and fearful. They kept stealing looks at the open door and, when they saw his body laid out, alarm and gloom would be etched on their faces. Three more nights passed, then I heard his voice in the dark of night.

'Water, Zahra.'

I was taken aback that he knew I was beside him. As soon as he started drinking, he began to cough. I raised his head and propped him carefully against the pillow. 'Are we married? Of course! You're here next to me every night. Married at last. I'll bring my children. Be a good wife, Zahra, and don't you dare try running away.'

'Don't speak, you're exhausted.'

'I wish I could hug you, but I'm broken. The sons of bitches destroyed me. There wasn't a single moment without torture. They put their cigarettes out on my body. And the horses... Oh, the horses.'

'Quiet, Sultan.'

'I'll kill all the horses I own.' He slipped back into sleep.

'He's fine now,' Saleh said. He'd come in without me realising it. 'Leave him and come with me. I'm your husband.'

'He still needs me. Don't you see?'

'You're stalling.'

'You're the one who asked me to look after him. Watch yourself, Saleh.'

'For ten days, you've been sleeping in the same room. We're in Mombasa now. Didn't we agree to stay here, buy a house, and make a home?'

'I'm still in agreement. I'll come with you after the afternoon prayers.'

'And why not now?'

'Because he needs me. He's started to move and talk. Two more days and he'll recover.'

'But he won't walk. His legs are too weak.'

'Don't say that. You're the reason for what happened to him. I said after *asr* prayers. End of discussion.'

'Come here at least. Let me kiss you. Aren't I your man?'

'Shame on you. When we're in our home, you can do as you please, but hush now, he's started moving. Go on.' Saleh fought the raging urge to plunge his dagger into Sultan's stomach, furious as he was. But he finally shrugged his shoulders and walked away.

'Have you married someone else?'

I trembled, alarmed. How much had he heard of my conversation with Saleh?

'Why, Zahra? Did you think that I'd lost my virility? I'm still strong, able to satisfy a hundred women. Don't you love me? Don't you love talking to me? If you weren't so modest, you'd kiss me.'

'You're hallucinating.'

'Don't go. Stay here with me. Say what I heard about your marriage was a lie.'

'I've married Saleh. We'll live here in Mombasa.'

He closed his eyes.

'I told you, we're not good for each other, Sultan. You're a slaver and I'm searching for what you don't have. Saleh suits me well enough. He's honourable and wants me, and I'm not just another wife to him.'

Sultan didn't say anything.

'Your wife is waiting for you. But I'll find a place to live here. I'll give you the rest of the gold, and then we're even. You'll go your way and I'll go mine. Isn't that what we agreed? With you, I'd just be thinking about your wife, and I'd hate being in that position, I'd absolutely hate it. I saved you because now I'll be seen as a woman worthy of respect. You've been the curtain I've been hiding behind for too long. But now I'm as radiant as the sun, a heroine. No other woman would do what I did.'

'You're a cheap bitch.'

'You're swearing like you used to, so you must be well. Allow me to leave with my husband now.' He suddenly spit in my face, scowling at me as I calmly wiped away his spittle. Then he closed his eyes without further comment.

*   *   *

'I'll buy a clove farm and put it in your name. And the house, too. I'll leave the boat behind. I won't work at sea anymore. I'm tired of travelling and its hardships. I want children and a loving wife. My mother died and, when I was a baby, my father threw me to my aunts. I was a hated burden who never knew love. Not a single woman has loved me. And the day you love me, Zahra, I'll give you my life.'

'But didn't you call me a slut?'

'Sultan stole my first love and any power I had. He left me with nothing. I've always lived my life as an unknown, in everything. I don't know what ugly power made me snitch on Sultan. Me and the other sailors stayed silent for so long about his shady business. I didn't do this to get rid of Sultan. I did it to get you. You're the dream of my life, the dream of my whole life.' Saleh said all this while perfumed and smiling. I avoided touching his hands. How they repulsed me! Despite all that I wanted to say, I'd never thought marrying him was the right thing to do. I hated his breath next to me. The coughing fit I'd had two nights ago came back. The coughs were dry and painful, but they didn't last long.

I spent the whole day searching for a small farm for a reasonable price as the land brokers pounced on us at every turn. They promised us we wouldn't have to wait long, but all the farms we inspected were extremely expensive, especially since the owners didn't really want to sell, but were only doing so under pressure from agents and Saleh's friends.

'They don't seem willing to sell, so why are your friends pressuring them?'

'We come first; we have money. They're poor and can barely pay their debts.'

'But they own that land. They're free.'

'They're not free, they're just lazy.'

'Don't say that.'

'You're such a sweet hypocrite, Zahra.' He was standing by a stall buying clothes, perfume, and expensive English soap for me. Then he stopped at the gold stall and bought me a pure gold necklace, a silver clip for my hair, some rings for my toes, and another heavy, brilliant necklace.

'That's enough, Saleh.'

'You deserve the treasures of the world. Don't ever regret marrying me, because I'll give you everything you deserve and more.' He was as cheerful as a kid who had been given back a toy after a period of painful separation. To him, I was a piece of candy that one leaves until the last possible moment to savour, because the longer you waited, the sweeter it would taste. *Temptation increases for a man who has never tasted such candy.*

Like me, he hated overachievers, or, to be more precise, he hated their success. Like with Sultan, for instance. Hating someone like that was the only way to be at ease, especially for someone filled unrequited love, whose dreams were a suffocating cloud of smoke, and holding on was illusory, a mirage.

Maybe if we join forces, we'll be able to do what we want. What we truly want with all our heart and soul can't be achieved by our hands. We second class citizens can only look on.

*   *   *

And Salim, your handsome, quiet cousin? And his secret marriage to the black woman? Where are you in all that, Zahra? Are you going to have a house with a man whose touch you flee? Are you going to live on a foreign coast, leaving behind the mountain and the people you're used to, the morning stream you passed by to reach your afternoon coffee?

In any case, Saleh is much better than my uncle's son Abdallah. At least this time I won't be a slave.

You're kidding yourself, Zahra. You know that a house or a small farm won't tame you. A day will come when the straw house that you've woven will come tumbling down around you. Then you'll be on the run once again, and you'll stay homeless until the day you die.

When I've had a child or ten, they'll carry my blood and my name. They'll make a statue for me, and they'll talk about me all the time.

But you'll destroy everything and run away, Zahra. No doubt you'll run away. They'll tear down your statue and hurl rubbish at it.

*   *   *

We returned to the boat a little after sunset. Saleh had settled on one of the beautiful farms in the middle of town and agreed on a price that he would pay the next morning. Some sailors met us with knowing, exaggerated smiles, and others were positively beaming. But Saleh ignored them and their mocking comments and said to me politely, 'Go and check on Sultan. If he's better, then he should leave your room tonight.'

'And you?'

'I'll wait here for you. You made me forget all about Ismail, and he'll want to catch up.'

I found Sultan sitting up, deep in conversation with Rabea. They fell silent when I entered. Then Sultan commented caustically, 'You both had your fill? At least you've got to pretend to be tired, Zahra, like all the other virgin brides. Then you could at least appear to be somewhat decent.'

'Shut your mouth! I don't have to prove my honour to anyone. I see you can sit now. What about standing up?'

'Aha ... so you want to get rid of me so that Saleh can come sleep here beside you. In that case, you'll have to lock the door the whole night, because you've married a man who doesn't lack manliness.'

'I won't wait to find out why you're so angry—you're probably just jealous of my husband.'

'I won't leave this room, at least not until my legs heal. And that will take some time. Why don't you both stay in one of the inns nearby? There, you can spend a refreshing sweet night far from any prying eyes. I have a friend who won't take much from you two. I'll write a letter you can show him. May it be a blessed marriage, inshallah.'

'You're just jealous. I'm sure after reading the letter your friend will decide to slaughter us. '

'He'd never hurt a hair on your head, not before I get what I want from you.'

'Soon, you'll be with your Zanzibari wife. Try to control yourself till then.'

'But Saleh will just throw you away after he's had his fill of you. And on that day, the promise of marriage won't do you any good. You'll come crawling back and I'll just kick you away.'

'You're unbearable, and your envy is eating you alive. I don't want to keep my husband waiting any longer.'

'Spend your night together on the sand—it's soft and cool. We'll find you both in the morning, all bitten up by the snakes and crabs.'

'We'll spend it on the raised beach hut next to the sea. That way, we'll be safe from the snakes.'

'You're such a vulgar woman. No self-respecting woman would talk about what they do at night. The bastard will regret marrying you. You'll teach his boys how to be savage and his girls no shame. You're only made for the bed, not for giving birth.'

I was beyond furious at how cruel he could be. I stood, trying to fight off the coughing fit that had come over me. I said, mid-choke, 'It's my fault for having stood by you. You should have been left there to die like a dog.'

'I didn't tell you to come after me. You're here because your husband is a chicken. If I were in his place, I'd have made you stay in the house and wear the burqa again.'

'I'm not staying here forever. And if you die, I'm not attending your funeral.'

I never went back to the room after that.

Saleh rented a European-style room for us in a clean inn. I was tense the whole time, until he came to take me out to eat some new, strange food in a hidden corner of the inn's restaurant.

'Eat the food however you'd like, Zahra. Forget about the knife and other utensils.'

'People are looking at us. My clothes are making them laugh.'

'God forbid! You're one of the most beautiful women, and that's why they're staring. They're probably laughing because an ugly guy like me is with you.'

* * *

He was kind in a way I hadn't imagined. Even when we went back to the room, he asked me to sleep on the strange raised mattress and said he'd sleep on the floor. When my eyes bulged in surprise, he said quietly, 'I won't ever get angry with you. It's enough for me to smell your pure breath. Sleep, and I'll pray for God to forgive our past sins.'

At that moment, I was no longer afraid of the future, nor did I have any regrets. God be praised! An enemy could become as kind a lover as Saleh—a man who gave me silk and his deference. I could sleep peacefully and forget the many insults I'd received earlier on the boat. I woke up once or twice because of a bad dream and found him looking up at me lovingly from the floor. He held my hand and patted it. 'You have skin silkier than water. What colour is your hair? Light? How lucky I am.'

I went back to sleep smiling. The man really was in thrall to me.

* * *

'I bought some land, and on it there's a small modest house. And here's the contract with your name on it. All that I own is yours. I promise you I'll be a good husband. Promise me your loyalty, Zahra.'

'How did you get that done so quickly? This bed is magical, I slept, and I didn't wake up till now. Did the call for morning prayer go and I didn't hear it?'

He smiled at me as he stood up. 'The call for afternoon prayer went a little while ago.'

I trembled. 'If I'd been with my mother, she would have whipped me within an inch of my life.'

'Take it easy. You're the bride here. Brides live well. One of the women slaves will bring your meals here, since I saw yesterday that you didn't eat well. If you're worried about what others think, we'll eat here for now. That is, until our house is ready, and you have two slaves of your own to help you with housework.'

'I want to grow cloves, Saleh, not just do housework.'

He laughed loudly. 'And grow cloves, too. I've got nothing to lose. We're in Africa, where it isn't strange for a woman to manage a home and do business. If we were somewhere else, I would have said no.'

'Really? You would have refused me?'

'No, I would've given my eye for you, but you know what they say: If your beloved is honey, don't eat them all up.'

Another coughing fit seized me.

'Zahra, that's a drop of blood. Are you sick?'

'No, it's just a nosebleed.'

'A nosebleed from your mouth? What's wrong?'

'It's just a simple cough, Saleh. Stop worrying, I'm fine. The slave is knocking on the door. I feel so alone now, I don't know why.'

'But I'm here with you. I'm always with you, Zahra. Always, I swear.'

He walked to the door while I wiped my mouth and went to the bathroom to wash my face. I looked in the mirror and found my face inflamed. *Why am I fooling him and myself? I don't have any feelings for him ... Saleh isn't my dream.*

But dreams are always just that. They seem beautiful and fascinating, and then gradually they evaporate. They leave us laughing bitterly as we stand at a dead end. Saleh is being chivalrous, unlike anyone I've met before. Despite our rough start, he respects me now and didn't turn his face away from me like the others. But I'm a cold woman. I know that enthusiasm and courage aren't the only sources of power. There is a much stronger source, and that is hope, which demands many sacrifices from us and more effort. And me? The problem is I'm very feeble. During Saleh's break time, I asked if we could go look for Salim's wife and son. I don't know why I had this obsession, but I found it pressing. The man didn't refuse my request despite his evident exhaustion. He fastened his turban hastily and started walking. He was happy just to be with me and didn't complain. *At least he hasn't yet.*

But we came back emptyhanded. The woman, her child, and her parents had just up and left. As for where they went, people gave different answers.

Some said she'd gone south, and others said they were on their way to the mountain. Many of their answers suggested the field she used to till no longer satisfied the needs of her family, which was why she sold her house and moved elsewhere, to hire labourers using the inheritance she got from Salim. All the talk was about Salim's wife having simply disappeared, and how her son, my beloved's son, would live far from his family, getting lost in the vast jungle. There would be no memory of Salim on the mountain. He would go up in smoke, as I had.

Maybe on nights when grandmothers regale their audiences with tales, our tale will be a bedtime story, or one of those legends told with a string of emotions. Salim will be turned into a hero, and I will be a villain or devil. And day after day, our tale will be twisted a bit more, until it's completely removed from the truth.

It was no use. She was the only one who tied me to my people. That day, I felt an all-consuming desire. But the woman had disappeared, along with her son.

'They've up and left. I had wanted to see Salim's eyes on his son ...'

Saleh didn't hear the last of what I said. He grasped my hand in a contrived movement and said with laughable sincerity, 'Don't worry, I'll comb every corner of the land. I'll do it all so you don't regret marrying me.'

That night, Saleh was less chivalrous, but he was still sensitive. He kissed my feet like a madman, his cold saliva like the sea on that hot salty night. Seeing him at my feet delighted me. He was completely preoccupied, his eyes polluted with desire.

But my heart was cold, and I nearly threw up.

* * *

It wasn't how I said it was. It was odious, and Sultan's image became my refuge.

(12)

O how quickly passes away
the glory of the earth

– Thomas à Kempis

Saleh told me that they would be leaving in three days. *And just like that, my journey with them—with their ballads and their ridicule—comes to an end. They go, only to return as guests. I see them in a way I never have before, and we go back to how we started: as strangers.*

But the clove farm was beyond wonderful, dispelling that feeling of being unmoored that one gets on arriving in a strange land, making me enthusiastic to work. Saleh, my dear husband, who had been a mystery till now, was happy with my happiness, providing me all means of joy and comfort.

I poked him and whispered, 'I thought you were evil and a coward for such a long time. You remember how you cursed me so horribly?'

'I was a fool. After our marriage, I learnt what a pure gem you are.' He tried to kiss me, and I yelled coquettishly, 'The workers are watching us!'

'I love you, my wife. Nothing in this world makes me feel as happy as I am with you right now. God protect you. I'll go today to bring labourers for the house. I'll buy two male slaves for you and two female slaves, or maybe five.'

'No, no, it's enough. I don't want a crowd. Don't forget that we have to pay for irrigation, transport, and harvest. Do you think you're sitting on a treasure chest?'

'Seems like you're thinking seriously about the future. Do you want to have ten children for me?'

'I said five is enough. I want to raise them equally, the girls just like the boys, no difference between them.'

'I'll marry the girls off when they're ten years old. That way we'll make sure they are still pure.'

I grabbed his neck and said jokingly, 'I'll have to kill you if you do that.'

I wish I could love him. I'm as dried up as they come, barely able to smile and keep up with what he's saying. I know he deserves love and appreciation, but I haven't known how to love for such a long time.

There was a sweet breeze, and our place was magical, perfumed. The farm stretched out in front me, a vista of splendid greenery. I didn't pay any mind to the furious, envious looks of the neighbours and my slaves. I was floating atop a cloud. In the flash of an eye, I had become a grand lady, waited on hand and foot, far from the blistered hands and dawn wake-ups of the mountain. My word was law, and with the mere gesture of my finger, the man got up or sat down.

I really tried to show him my gratitude in one way or the other. He would wake up from beside me at dawn, bathe, and go for prayers. Then he would wake me up to pray, all kindness and love. Who would have thought that Saleh was such a tender soul? Who would have thought that the love in his heart was a small river that never ran dry, forever seeking a suitable estuary? *And today is the day it drowns people, especially me.*

In all honestly, what a good man he is and how close we have become.

*   *   *

But ... destinies don't change. The crow of bad omens that appeared on the mountain on the eve of my birth still trailed me wherever I went, even after I'd crossed oceans. Even after it was driven away.

What is written for me, what is recorded for me on the eternal parchment, will become clear.

On the very day that I'd decided to say a sweet word to bring him some joy that humid summer, on the very day I found a golden anklet next to the bed after I had told him that I liked it on an Arab neighbour, on that orphan of a day, they killed him.

They took him.

I had started to use perfume at night to please him, because he had transformed me into a lady.

They stole him.

The poor man, who like me had been living at the centre of his own life for the first time. He fell from his throne and was lost. We had just gotten married, I had just begun to know joy, and now I was alone.

They killed him.

I stood looking at him. *Why have they brought you to me, oh Saleh? You suffered and cried like me.*

'They stabbed him and ran away. Forgive me, madam. We were busy buying the almonds you had ordered and, just like that, in the darkness of the souk, they killed him.'

I bowed my head, baffled. The anklet tinkled when I moved toward him. His ugly face was bloody and frozen. His eyes were open, looking at me. I shuddered and went outside the house, blubbering.

* * *

The old nightmare comes back to me. The question about the near future and the dagger that ended Saleh's life. How I hate the night in this strange land. I hear the rustle of corpses buried under the house. Each of them buried, their work unfinished.

* * *

'God make you strong, Zahra. Better luck next time.'

I recognised the revolting voice. *He's come to gloat. He killed my husband, and now he's come to see my humiliation, rub it in.* He spoke to me from behind the purdah with all politeness. 'Get out of here, you criminal. Is this how you pay me back for taking care of you?'

'Poor Zahra, are you hallucinating?'

I flew into a rage at his coldness and yelled, 'If you don't get out of here, I'll order my slave to throw you out!'

'Let's come to an understanding. We haven't yet settled our account. I have some other news.'

'I said, get out!'

'Show me your face. Don't tell me that you're in the *iddah* mourning period. Are you going to spend another four months away from people? Come on now, Zahra, it was a sham marriage, you know that.'

My nerves started to fray. After a hiatus, my cough came back. I called out to one of the slaves and yelled hoarsely, 'Get him away from the house! This man must never come here again!'

I heard him resist the slave with an ugly laugh, then he yelled from the threshold into the house, 'Your brothers are here. They came for you. Mabrouk!'

His words were a thunderbolt that only preceded death. Death came for me in a flash that seemed long and hard. I couldn't breathe. I felt my brain burst and ooze onto the floor. I didn't know whether it was death or just my desire to die.

But I didn't die. God wanted me in one way or the other to see the gleaming dagger in my brother's belt. Revenge for mountainfolk meant shaming. Today, my shame was branded on my skin, and my destiny would be exactly like Fadhila's, whose father had killed her on a dark night because she was carrying an illegitimate child. The slimy mud that swallowed Fadhila's body on that day made for a despicable grave. I could almost feel the mud flooding my eyes.

Worries. When they come, they come in waves. Today I feel hollow everywhere.

Fadhila preferred to die rather than reveal her baby's father. She knew that saying the name would almost definitely lead to even more shame, to thunderous scandal. She knew that she'd be killed, and that's why she kneeled before her father's dagger and didn't make a sound. She surrendered, and they buried her with her shame. She got rid of her fear and any feelings of emptiness.

As for me, well, I'm still breathing. Time drags its heavy form over my exhausted body. Destiny won't kill me as easily as it did her. I die every day, in fear, from the moment I was born until feeble old age.

It was laughable that my brother would come with his dagger to get rid of me, a shameful stain. This defender of honour used to sneak out every night to Fadhila's house and, after an hour or two, would return for another brother to take his place. My father would look on wearily, worried. It was beyond comprehension how much they railed against her, how they set her on fire. And there was no escape from a dark night and a sharpened dagger. When Fadhila was disappeared, no one reprimanded those men. They were simply deemed reckless and crazy, and she, a whore.

Fadhila didn't wait to see how the end of her story would shame her family further, pushing them off the mountain, forcing them to set up their tent in sands where the Wahiba tribe stays. She was at rest. *As for me, it's out of the question. Behind and before me are hundreds of endings, and I don't know exactly when I'll surrender my neck to the dagger of shame. I'm not carrying an illegitimate child, and I won't naively gift myself to countless men. But shame is shame, no matter what form it takes, or what its reasons. That is what my uncle would say anyway, and what my father would parrot back.*

But why should I have to surrender to the dagger? I haven't been waiting for it, with my neck ripe for the slicing. I won't give in to the fear rooted within—it's become an inescapable reality. Fadhila made a mistake. That was a real reason for shame, while for me, I won't ever bring shame on myself like that.

Forgive me, dear husband. I'd wanted to offer you complete devotion, but I survived. And you, Saleh—you lived an orphan, and you died an orphan. I've got to live in any way possible. I haven't come to die.

I secretly sent my male slave to summon Sultan. I waited in our sitting room, watching the female slave in front of me cleaning up and organising the place. A long time passed before her counterpart came back breathless, the smell of sweat a harbinger of his arrival. 'Sir is coming. Will you allow him to enter?'

At this, the female slave jolted and looked at me, astonished that I was going to meet a man face-to-face during my mourning period. I chased her away and told the male slave to bring Sultan in. The moments of tension that preceded his entry were enough to make my expression dark, leaving me agitated by the time he finally entered. 'What happened? Lady of the house, you're meant to stay in mourning for four months and ten days. Did the news of your brother looking for you shake you up?'

'I'm forced to speak to you, and religion allows it in exceptional circumstances.'

'You're always so hypocritical. Have you wet your pants in fear?'

'You're a scumbag, Sultan. You're rotten to the core.'

'Ilyas told me that a man called Saeed is looking for you. He says he's searching for Zahra, daughter of Nasser bin Zahir. Ilyas didn't hold back, he said that you've married and that you live on a farm in the middle of town. Thankfully, Ilyas didn't come with us when we came to congratulate the newly married man, now *deceased*.' He emphasized his last word.

I cut him off nonchalantly. 'What should I do?'

He laughed, dripping pure sarcasm. 'What happened to the strong Zahra? Why are you trembling? Do you think he's come to kill you? He's just come to make sure you're okay.'

'When does the boat leave?

'The man's just come to make sure you haven't been kidnapped. No need to get so worked up.'

'Ha, you don't know my brothers! You don't know my family. We don't know anything like abduction or running way. All we know is shame. I'll sell all my possessions and come with you to Bemba. Are you okay with me coming along? I have a lot of money, and gold I didn't give you the first time round.'

'That's it?'

'What do you mean? What else do you want?'

'I want everything you have, since I'll also be a walking target.'

'What is it that you want?'

'The farm, the gold, you.'

I stood where I was, overcome by a coughing fit. 'You bastard! I'll get on the boat for a cheaper price.'

'I'll tell him where you are, like you and your husband did to me with that sheikh.'

'I didn't inform on you to anyone. You killed my husband. You're a born criminal, a real despicable bastard. Here you are, taking advantage of me in my time of need in the worst possible ways.'

'If you don't want a favour from me, should I go then?'

He stood and picked up his thin bamboo cane, about to leave.

'Hold on. Where are you going?'

'To get your brother. He really misses you.'

'I'll just give you the gold.'

'And the farm?'

'Not happening. I'll be penniless. I can't do it.'

'Then I'll bring him here.'

'Damn the day you were... Take the farm and take me to safety.'

'Now, give me everything, Zahra.'

My God, how did things get to this point so quickly? Getting married to Saleh and now a widow, in what seems like days. Happiness, money, and power all up in smoke in a matter of moments. The past alone is heavy. The past, when it comes back, comes slowly. It comes to humiliate, strangling me, squeezing out every last breath.

*   *   *

After I thought that I'd achieved my ultimate dream, the past came to remind me that I was a wretched, homeless person, that my transformation wouldn't be forever.

How ugly this damned boat is, how ugly these mocking sails are, protruding like ribs, and these familiar facial expressions hiding all their mockery at how far I have fallen. Just yesterday, my husband was sitting in that corner looking at me, and today that corner is only a reminder of how he was betrayed by one of the men on this boat. Here I am again, penniless, homeless, with no tomorrow.

If only I hadn't left you, my dear mountain. If only I'd closed my eyes, clung to your pure soil, and kept my mouth shut. Don't make me feel guilty now, mountain, for I'm not in the wrong; wallah, I haven't made any mistake. By the Abrahamic faiths, I haven't done anything wrong, and by the prophets and by existence itself, I've lost my success again, lacking peace of mind and security.

Oh, harsh times.

Oh, harsh times, forgive me.

Tears pour from my eyes, and nothing can stop them.

Swallow me up, oh sea. Take me to your depths, take me to where Salim is, he with his high morals, tenderness and great understanding. Take me to my cousin and take my life while I'm in his embrace.

'You're crying. No, no ... why, Zahra? Do you taste a strange bitterness on your tongue? It's really bitter, isn't it?'

I stayed quiet.

'I'll never forget the pain that I went through. Don't you remember?'

'You brought that on yourself. You went chasing death by stealing a sheikh's son.'

'No, no, let me tell you how it was. Your dead husband snitched, and you covered it up. You rewarded him by marrying him. You both conspired against me, like a cripple at the end of his tether. You felt guilty, so you stood by me for a bit, but as soon as the slightest bit of life came back into me, you got rid of me and went off with him to live happily ever after. And me? I couldn't walk. You thought I'd be useless in bed because of the torture? No, no, I'm still a man. The girls at the inn told me I'm stronger than ever before.'

'Shut up, Sultan! You killed him. Anyway, pain doesn't change a person.'

'Killed him? I didn't touch him. He killed himself.'

'I hate you with my whole heart. You're a slave to money. I wish I'd let them split you in two, one half for the wolves and the other for the sharks. One day, Sultan, you'll feel how I feel now, and you'll regret all you've done.'

'Did you even love Saleh? What did he even have for you to love? He was deformed, no good at flirting. You left me for a nobody like him.'

'At least he didn't exploit a helpless widow. What he did was preserve my honour. What exactly do you think you have? You forced me out of my rightful mourning period, and now people will think I'm unfaithful, a fallen woman.'

'You haven't even scratched the surface of who I am, dearest.'

'Shush. I don't want to talk to you anymore. I've been trampled on enough. I'm still mourning my husband. I want to be alone. After we reach Bemba, leave me there and keep going. I want a small hut where I can spend my mourning period, and then I'll take care of myself.'

His face darkened as he yelled in my face. 'Why are you so loyal to him? Why didn't you ever love me?'

'You're like a thorn in my foot, like a louse in the hair of one of your sailors, like a rotten tooth, you devil. I care for you as much as the foam on the waves that disappears–*not one bit.*'

He stood speechless and indignant, staring at my flushed, hard face.

'You really hate me that much? I still won't let anyone else have you, Zahra.'

I spit in his face, bitter hatred exploding inside me. 'I'll say it again, Sultan. I want a small hut where I can ask for God for forgiveness. And you? Without you, my life will be much fuller.

* * *

If I had been in a different state of mind, I would have said that the view before me was an earthly paradise that could not be matched anywhere else. The small, scattered coral islands were covered with lazy, green moss in an azure sea. The island was the definition of green, surrounded by large coconut trees, ships, and fishing boats. But I turned away from it all and sat still in my cabin.

Will I keep running away from death? How long will I keep looking to survive without having to face violence? Will I keep looking for security, with a fear that drains the blood in my pocket, a fear my family has injected into me. What I'm doing now is surrendering to shame, and, in the end, I'll meet the dagger. I'll meet Death.

I sat in the cabin all day. I didn't have the desire to go out, to go anywhere. I was weary and fed up. I wasn't even hungry, and I just swallowed some crumbs to stay alive, pouring the rest out into the sea for the fish. I was surprised to find a small turtle on the last mossy step of the bathroom, looking up at me with sad eyes. I couldn't fathom why it started to tremble. 'Why are you so sad?'

'Who are you speaking to, Zahra? Ohhh, the turtle. Give it here, we'll roast it for a tasty meal.'

'Leave it alone, you beast. It looks terrified. How have you come in without asking?'

'I came to speak to you. You didn't come out once. Truly, you respect your husband.'

'I revere God.'

'We all revere Him, maybe just in different ways.'

'Sultan, enough with your lies. You make me sick. What do you want?'

'May God forgive you for saying such things. I've come to make you an offer you can't refuse.'

'Spit it out.'

'I don't have any tricks up my sleeve. I want you, with all your faults. I've got to have you.'

'What else—'

'I'll give you back all your money and the deed to the farm in Mombasa.'

'In return for?'

'For you.'

When he saw my face harden and my body grow stiff, he added in a soft voice, 'In a halal way. Marry me. I'll be honest, my wife and I are on the rocks. We've been separated for the past year. She's jealous, you know. I'm going to end everything and come back to you with my two kids.'

Coldly, I cut him off. 'Just like that, singing the same old tune. And my husband's blood, do you want me to forget that? It won't be long before you'll fight with me, too, and leave me alone all over again.'

'Don't drag me into your husband's murder. I heard there was a dispute between him and the original owner of the farm, who hadn't wanted to sell, but your husband put pressure on the agent, who then took advantage of the owner, getting it for a cheap price. Maybe they killed him because of that.'

'And if I tell you that I hate you, and I won't accept even on the pain of death?'

'I'll tell your brother where you are.'

'Go on. Go get him, then.'

'How brave you are! *Wallah*, I didn't expect that.'

'I'd rather die than have you touch me.'

'Zahra, why are you always picking a fight? You'll sleep in the street and the Africans will cut you open.'

'I'll accept on one condition.'

He circled me, taking me in from head to toe.

'I want a small house and farm in Bemba in my name, servants and labourers, and I have complete freedom till you come back from your travels.'

'I have a farm here, but I already have a steward looking after it, and he's good at administering it.'

'I'll manage it myself, and no agent.'

'I wouldn't want my wife to mix with men. Her place should be in the house.'

'I said just until you return. Then we'll settle the matter peacefully.'

'I don't like it.'

'Fine, then I'll seek refuge with one of the Omanis in the country. Maybe he'll marry me and give me what you're not able to.'

'You won't go anywhere else. No one will have you.'

'You want to bet?'

'Bitch, I already said it.'

'So then?'

He murmured to himself for a bit, like someone pleased with himself.

'So be it, but I'll marry you now.'

'You're insane. I'm still in my mourning period.'

'The imam won't know you were married before.'

A bolt of disgust shot through me. 'Do you think you're marrying a girl off the street?'

'Religion allows it, you said it yourself.'

I smiled for the first time since he'd come in. 'You always come back with what suits you, but this time, I'll do what my religion wants.'

* * *

Here I am, surrendering to my destiny, which is to die, while Sultan still doesn't know who he's trifling with.

(13)

Loneliness fills my heart
Oh, dread of the place
I see myself as someone time has left behind
On whom the lights have gone down
Whose flowers are a wasteland
Alone,
Surrounded by ghosts

- Dr Hussain Debbagh

Today, I feel like bidding the world farewell, and if the distances don't swallow me up, then the dagger of shame lurking in wait for my body will be the end of me. What a miserable feeling of emptiness! I wrestle with all the men in my life trying to pin me down. I just want to inhabit the whiteness of the wave. I find myself traversing dark alleys under the perpetual gaze of someone or other perched in every corner and doorway.

* * *

I know all the faces and they know me. All the faces that I know chase me like rabid wolves, drawing closer, baring their venomous fangs like knives, always demanding, always taking. Familiar faces: my deceased husband, Ilyas, Ismail ... all of them lying in wait for me, as if I'm a naïf, terrified prey for whom an interminable long march forward is the only way to survive. I see my uncle with his bulging arteries, his reddened, envious eyes, his bloodstained, bright-red hands. At the back is Sultan, that shrewd devil, with his seductive smile, and there I am crying, drenched by all my tears, my throat parched, butchered by coughing, but they are getting closer, their hands outstretched....

Oh sun, come out, kill all these germs rubbing against my body, making me ill. But the sun refuses to come out, its indignant light spitting in my face. The whole universe wants to stain me with shame, and within me boils a strong rebellion that defies regret. Now and again, a small pocket of light beckons to me to come out of the darkness that comes from the face of the lost beloved.

He stretches out his luminous hand to me, trying to rescue me from all these hallucinations, but they weigh me down, and I sink under the weight of contradictions that I can't shake. If it were up to me, my young love, I would live as I wished, but the truth, my bullet-riddled sir, is that my hands and neck are shackled. How can I find a place where I feel peace, when all I have today are cunning thoughts? I'm not a slave to the devil but I'll fight him with the same weapons and, perhaps at that point, I'll find light.

* * *

The sun was breathing in the morning. The evening had been banished, the darkness still collecting itself on the beautiful dirt hills of this the new land. There was a sweet aroma wafting through the air, the smell of cloves everywhere.

How breathtaking this island is, more beautiful than anything I've ever seen. There are small and large sailboats spread out on the still, cold sea and the hilltops are shrouded by thick, reddish-orange clouds that look like the wool of mountain sheep. The smaller islands have a bright-red hue, their sweet redness mixed with the green of lazy dark seaweed. This smooth, quiet island delights me. I raised my hand unintentionally to greet a small boat, its black sailors readily waving back, seemingly ecstatic about the splendour of the morning.

'So you're really leaving us this time, and not coming along to Zanzibar?'

'Yes.'

'And your relative over there?'

'All lies.'

I didn't turn to see what impact my words had on the solemn old man, but he said, 'Ismail told me you ran away from the mountains. He still has it in for you, since you stole Saleh, one of his dearest friends.'

'What I do is none of your or Ismail's business, so stop talking about me in secret.'

A long silence fell between us. I breathed in as deeply as I could, taking in the refreshing air.

'Okay, fine,' he continued, 'but I just wanted to warn you of the danger that you're heading toward. It's hard for me to see someone like you lost like this. My girl, Sultan is reckless, and he doesn't ...'

'I'm not going to marry him.'

'He said he's going to come back after the end of the divorce waiting period to marry you, and he asked me to be a witness.'

'Sultan is mad.'

He smiled calmly. 'Is it okay if I tell him that you intend to trick him?'

'I don't care what you tell him.'

'You're playing with fire, my girl. A woman like you can't live without a man protecting and respecting her.'

'Tell me, did he send you as a go-between? Or do you also want to propose to me?'

'Oh daughter, be guided by God, and don't be so headstrong. Go to Sultan's wife. She's got a lot of property, she's very rich, and her father was a religious man. She'll protect you from the world and Sultan.'

'Sultan's wife? Even if I were starving to death, I wouldn't go anywhere that wretched man has contaminated.'

He thought deeply for a moment, then said, 'I will recommend you to dear friends in Shek Shek and Waita. Don't go easy on the slaves—they'll turn on you and take everything you have.'

'Argh, don't make me listen to your dull warning again. I don't need help from anyone. I know how to take care of myself.'

* * *

Oh, hot sorrows,

Oh, masts that I stare at every day,

Oh, hallways of boats, oh beautiful smell of my country,

Oh, fragrance of the keedha tree and bitter orange,

Oh, evenings of conversation by the stream,

Oh, my distant country, what sadness is tangled in my heart now, leaking misery.

What's wrong with me? I feel so alone, I feel out of place, right from my depths.

Oh, Zahra of long journeys, oh Zahra of strange sorrows.

Oh me, oh migrant, oh my resurrected longings, how painful is my misery!

* * *

They came all at once when Sultan announced my final journey with them, their eyes full of pity and their hands pinned behind their backs. Some of them greeted me and got back to work, but Ilyas was visibly affected and vainly tried to force a smile. Old Khalifa started to give advice steeped in tradition. His son Ismail was the only one who seemed relaxed and happy, staying in front of me when they all hurriedly went on their way.

'So, you're going to get married again?' Ismail asked. 'You killed him and now you're looking for another husband. I told him you had no morals, but he was foolish, happy with you, and then you killed him to get everything he'd worked so hard for. And now you're back. At least have some sort of respect for him. He cherished you and gave you everything you wanted.'

'I didn't kill Saleh.'

'You planned it with your lover.'

'Watch it, you bas-'

I saw Sultan coming toward us while I was exploding at Ismail, who then breathed his final malevolent words at me, 'He betrayed our long friendship for a whore like you, one stalked by shame.'

Rabea and another slave called Hamud came along with us. Hamud was tiny, a chatterbox, unlike Rabea. Sultan was sluggish, leaning on a thick cane.

'You're done, Sultan. Why are you even trying to convince me to marry you?'

He turned pale at my mordant quip. 'But you still haven't even had a go ...'

'It won't make a difference. You've become like a pet cat.'

He ranted and snarled at me in Swahili, making the two stiff slaves laugh.

After that out-of-place outburst, I preferred to sit in silence, staring at those passing by. A lot of people from my country were plying the roads. There was also a very old man selling coffee with the same marvellous, unforgettable smell, and women wearing black hijabs whose shiny, fleshy brown legs rather incongruously poked out from under their short clothes.

A simple comparison between these women and me was laughable: next to them, I was a faded stalk of wheat, while they were plump, soft, and desirable.

'Stop staring. Shame on you! Don't you have women already?'

Hamud the chatterbox sighed and whispered, 'Madam, my woman is very thin. I wish she had even just a little of that flesh.'

'Have you no shame? Your eyes are popping out of their sockets. It must be their short dresses.'

'No, that's normal to us now.'

'So, you'd let your wife wear such things?'

'That's the way of life here.' He squirmed. 'Men are used to it, so they don't see it as anything special.'

'That's for sure. Your eyes betray you.'

'You're just jealous, Zahra. I know you want to see yourself in such clothes.'

'I wasn't speaking to you, Sultan.'

'When we get married, I want you to wear such things, maybe even shorter.'

I spit in his direction. 'In your dreams!'

'*Wallah*, I saw you in my dreams in the most beautiful clothes!'

I didn't know why I liked what he said, or why a surge of youth blossomed within me.

* * *

The ground was muddy from the night rain, and the trees a deep green.

The soil sparkled, its colour almost that of ruby coral, and the birds warbled joyfully. Some of the passers-by had on tall *tarabeesh,* red hats with black tails like those of horses. As for the women, some walked with their plump cleavage showing, decked out in short-sleeved dresses, their heads covered by loosely tied handkerchiefs.

Two women carrying huge sacks of hay on their heads caught my eye. On their backs, their babies were tied up with old cloth. *Would I be able to carry so much weight?*

Sultan stood at the mouth of the souk, where the livestock sellers were. He made his way to a donkey merchant and haggled with him over the price of a donkey. He then ordered me to ride it.

'The farm's a bit far from here. They'll take you there. Like we agreed in front of Rabea, you'll get to run the farm. This will surely bother my foreman, so just leave him alone. Do whatever he tells you, because he's an experienced man. Do not, and I repeat do not, get mixed up in what he does otherwise. As for going out, you won't go anywhere without these two. No going out alone.'

He stopped barking his tall list of orders, seemingly unsettled, his hands shaking. He avoided my gaze. 'No one will insult you. Take heart, I'll come back before going to Zanzibar. I have to tell you something important. Wait for me and ....' He swallowed his saliva like a guilty boy. 'Don't run away. Everything will be fine. Now, I have a hundred things to do. I missed out on a great opportunity in Malindi, and I mean to make up for it.'

This stupid donkey is so sleepy that we would move faster if I carried it. I wasn't wrong in my assessment of it the first time I laid eyes on it; it was a lazy brute. I kicked it once, twice, thrice, and all it did was bray loudly, and then it became quiet. It was looking at me now and again, its eyes reflecting its stupid smile. In that moment, it reminded me of my recently deceased husband, Saleh, when he was next to me on the mattress and I felt the sudden urge to vomit. I got off the donkey, annoyed. 'Rabea, take me to the closest souk. I'm going to sell this donkey.'

*   *   *

I didn't like Sultan's foreman one bit. He was arrogant beyond belief. He towered over me as if I were a mere ant, and when Rabea showed him Sultan's instructions, he exhaled like a bull ready for a fight, his eyebrows raised in disapproval. I reacted to his behaviour with a commensurate chill and didn't pay him any mind. *This place is now under my rule, and he's nothing more than a labourer. Having this European-wannabe next to me is no problem at all, because from today I'm his master, and I'll treat him however I wish.*

No one could deny that the other African workers obeyed him, while they reserved hostile looks for me. He was their prophet.

I didn't want to get into a battle of wills with him as I was completely spent, not wanting to admit, even to myself, how my slave "bodyguards" were right to oppose my sale of the donkey. However, I felt better when I thought about how much I'd gotten for the beast.

The house was charming, but somewhat cramped: four furnished rooms, a kitchen, and a clean bathroom.

Dust had settled on the chairs, the tables, and in the hallways. The whole place needed a good dusting. I liked the room that looked out onto the clove garden and storehouse. It had a large window with wooden bars, and the view was captivating. I didn't hesitate to call it mine. Pure bliss is what I felt looking out at the land. Who would have believed that I, with nothing to my name, kept down by my family, would be in sole charge of this whole place?

Rabea finally spoke. 'No one will bother you here. But the place is a bit out of order.'

'You mean the dust? We'll have it cleaned.'

He exchanged looks with Hamud and calmly said, 'I mean the people, madam.'

'Oh, you mean Khamis? He's cocky. Don't you worry, I'm going to sell him.'

'Don't ever say that in front of him,' Hamud interjected, his brow furrowed. 'He was educated in Europe and considers himself a national hero.'

'What do you mean by that?'

'The people take part in a lot of small revolts. They want their land.'

'Which land? Didn't they sell it to us?'

'They say they've been humiliated and robbed in their own country.'

'Well, I guess they're right in a way. You kidnap them and sell them like ewes ... isn't that what your master does?'

'They're not only disagreeing with us using them as slaves.'

'They've become civilized working for us. This makes me want to sell Khamis even more. Did you see how he was looking at me?'

Rabea cut me off abruptly. 'I am dead serious. Sultan warned you about that man in particular. All the workers are in the palm of his hand—he's in a different league. But wait, aren't you the one who said everyone is equal? Why are you changing your tune now?'

'No, no, I'm not changing my tune. They're all equal, but it's just this Khamis I need to deal with, and then I'll repent.'

'Don't pick a fight with him, madam. The slaves listen to him, so try to win him over instead.'

'Let him and his helpers go to hell. All he's got to do is listen to me. I'm so tired. Get a move on and clean the place, you two. And from tomorrow, look for a slave girl who knows Arabic, can serve me and cook for us. As for Khamis, he can cook for himself.'

I tried to observe the widow's mourning period again, but it was out of my hands. Things grew tense in the country, and I didn't understand why, and things at the farm weren't easy at all. Khamis found a new way to annoy me every day, and one word from him was enough to stop the clove harvest. The timing of the harvest made me anxious. The farm was bursting with cloves, coconuts, and corn. Without workers, the harvest would be impossible.

* * *

The morning started with a quarrel with Khamis. He insisted he should be able to sell the harvest without my permission. When I came out of the house and he saw my eyes heavy with sleep, he said, 'The farm needs someone who can manage it, not a lazy woman basking in silk.'

'Why are you always fighting with me? Can't I have one day where I enjoy myself? What do you want?'

'I wanted to sell this sack, but apparently I'm not allowed to. I don't appreciate anyone doubting my loyalty.'

'Sell it without my say-so? How many times have I told you to not do anything without running it by me?'

'I came to see you, but you weren't available. It seems sleeping takes up all your time.'

I held back from cursing. *This coastal man with his deliberate Arabic will give me more white hair. He'll lead me to the grave.* 'Enough. Have some respect for yourself when you're talking to your boss.'

'I have no boss. I agreed to work with Sultan, and to make my own rules.'

Before I could respond, Rabea interjected, 'I think this needs some more discussion. How about we go inside and speak after we've taken a few breaths.'

'Shut up, you!' I snapped. 'Listen here, Khamis, if you want to work here, you're welcome. If you don't, take your ignorant followers with you, and I'll find a hundred other labourers.'

'Are you throwing me out?'

At this Rabea yelled, 'That's enough! Let's go inside!'

I gave in. It was clear to me how this man could make the farm die of thirst.

'This is the first and last time you can sell this amount of goods.'

At this, he tilted his nose up and said quietly, 'There won't be many times when you say such things.'

I turned away from him and, without having any breakfast, I went to supervise the labourers in the field. They were full of the same hatred that

Khamis had for me, but they were too weak to show it so openly. Instead, they were outright hypocritical, smiling before me and whispering insults behind my back. I didn't pay them much attention though, or let's say I didn't want to pay them much attention.

* * *

Time is charged, and the weather is, too.

What happened in this supposed land of dreams, my cousin? I just came for some peace and quiet ... If only ....

'Mutaka, enough with your empty talk. Have you given the cows something to drink? We won't get meat from the market, since these days the Swahili folk will starve us to death. They hide their cows and ewes so we won't eat them. And because of the Hindus, the cow has become sacred. They'll also die from hunger. Where is Kaghudi? Why is that idiot always late?'

The simple man before me trembled, and said in broken Arabic, 'Kaghudi, wife ...'

I spared him from having to talk anymore. There had to be some way to get them onside. So, I invited them to eat a meal under the giant mango tree in front of the house.

'From now on, all food will come from me in exchange for some more effort and loyalty.'

They whispered feverishly amongst themselves and then darted toward the courtyard, where the mat that had been laid on the ground was overrun by food.

It was fine for a start, and Khamis' amused looks didn't bother me. They started to wish me good health–without any sincerity, of course–but I smiled and went inside to eat my own food.

*   *   *

After having known such a thrill, I wouldn't give it up for anything. I really loved that life, and on that day, I truly felt I was where I should be, a place where I was a queen ruling with my sceptre in hand, where no one dared–except for Khamis–to go against me or be unfaithful. *Finally, a dream come true.*

Oh, how I longed to see myself as a real princess!

(14)

*'You can bite into an apple
with gold teeth ... but
you can't bite it in the same way
that you would with your own teeth.
The taste, the juice
won't be the same.'*

- Rasul Gamzatov

'I told you I won't sell the clove to the locals. I'll sell it for a higher price to the merchants on the foreign boats that have docked here, without needing your friends' help.'

'But Madam Zahra, we can't reach the port easily. It will be such an exhausting trek. The transport will be expensive.'

'Think about it, you know-it-all. The price of transport that you're gnashing your teeth over won't be anything compared to the price that the foreign merchants will pay. You just want your friends to benefit at my expense.'

'But Sultan ...'

'Sultan should have kept a tighter grip on you. What you brought in last season isn't even enough to pay the workers' salaries or for the animal feed or upkeep of the farm. You've been too generous with your friends, as if it's your father's money.'

'Madam Zahra—'

'Listen, Khamis. Sure, you're educated and experienced, but I won't sell to your friends at dirt-cheap prices in the name of friendship. It just won't happen. The cloves from this farm are some of the best in Waita. If you were in my shoes, you wouldn't do it either. How hard can it be to buy a few donkeys to transport the cloves to the port? I'll take care of selling to the merchants there.'

He gritted his teeth and shot a livid glare my way, all the while towering over me. 'The local merchants need our help. If we decide not to sell to them at all, there won't be any work for the struggling merchants.'

'Goodness me! So it seems I should be giving charity to your friends and losing money to make them happy? Then let them buy land and farm cloves instead of depending on us. I didn't come here to run a charity.'

'This is their land. The way you're eating from their produce is why they're still poor.'

'Or because they're lazy. I won't sell to lazy people.'

'It's their right to get some. You've got to leave them some.'

'All I know is that the farm is under my control.' I saw him about to object even more. 'No, no, no. This is the last time I'm saying this, Khamis: I will never sell to your friends.'

He yielded to my angry tone, but his eyes betrayed just how much he resented me. Ever since our first meeting, he'd been waiting to erupt. After a moment he said calmly, 'However good you think things are now, it won't last forever.'

'You fool.'

He walked away.

Damn the day this crazy tall man was born! Just from seeing his arrogant face, I felt my blood clot, poisoned. *What I really hate is this perpetual fear that I drag behind me. Despite all my stubbornness, my body trembles in fear. No matter how beautiful this place is, cruelty reigns.* I leaned against the mango tree and took a deep breath. *There is no refuge in any world, no matter how hard we look.*

And here they are, coming to lunch with eyes full of hate. Some of them turned away from the food and left without asking permission. The weather foretold a coming storm, ominous rain like yesterday's. It all felt contaminated, asphyxiating. I started coughing once more.

*   *   *

Munira was a young woman of pleasing proportions, her curly hair braided tightly, accentuating her attractiveness. Every day, she plaited my hair the way she did her own. I liked how fast she did it and how she flattered me as she went along, and so I let her serve me. She would chat with me when I felt lonely. I knew all the farmworkers flirted with her, and that she liked it. She received many compliments. I saw her once joking around with Kuzi, a tall young man, very dark. It didn't escape me how Khamis was nearby, watching her, a peculiar expression on his face. He didn't like Munira being around ever since Hamud had brought her, saying she was an active girl, a good girl.

The truth was that I accepted her immediately because I wasn't strong enough to do the housework. That was why I didn't hesitate to part with some rupees to buy her a new wardrobe, more modest clothes than the short ones she habitually wore. How beautiful her slender build was, and she knew just how to move, the secret ways into men's hearts. Even Kaghudi, who had a child on the way, would look at her in admiration, soaking up her features.

'Hey, you sorceress, let them work.'

'*Wallah*, I swear, I didn't do anything.' How sweet she sounded when she spoke Arabic, melting even rock.

*   *   *

'Madam, there are five chickens missing,' Hamud informed me.

I looked at him coldly as he panted away.

'Yesterday, it was a female sheep, and before that it was two chickens. Today is Thursday and you've been asleep like a fool. I need a guard, a strong guard. If anything else is stolen, I'll sell you to my neighbour, and you know how he treats his slaves.'

I looked at Munira, who was flustered, and said jokingly, 'I haven't even accused you, and you're already shaking like a leaf. Do you know who did it?'

'Never madam, *wallah*.'

No sooner had she left than I said to Hamud, 'Just act normal. This thief has got to be caught tonight. At least, we'll get a new slave on the farm.'

'Madam, you're treading on toes here. If Khamis heard you, he would be up in arms. You know how much he looks after the sons of the soil here.'

'Ha. And what if I told you that Khamis had something to gain from all these robberies?'

'You're exaggerating. The man has been educated abroad. Can't you see how polite and put-together he is?'

'The best thieves are always most polite and well put-together. This man wishes me nothing but ill.'

'He's a good man. Don't try to see an enemy everywhere you turn.'

'He's scary, he's angry. Hang on, why are you speaking to me like this? Go back to guarding the chickens. You're getting on my nerves.' My body trembled spasmodically from a spell of dry coughs. I needed a long nap, and after that I'd think about some possibilities and long-term plans.

* * *

'No, no, no. I won't sell to your friends. We already discussed this.'

He interjected sharply, 'It's different this time.'

'Don't you get tired of making trouble? I just got up from my nap and I'm meant to go survey the field. I doubt they're stealing behind my back. I can't take any more problems, Khamis. You're just trying to kill me with tension.'

A faint smile danced on his lips and was gone as quickly as it had come. 'It's simple. You're a smart woman, which is why you won't hesitate to listen to my advice.'

'Advice from an educated man like you? Teach me.'

'Please leave us, it's an important matter,' he instructed Munira, and she left without asking my permission. In spite of my nap, I didn't have the energy to fight. He hesitated for a bit and bowed his huge head while appearing to carefully choose his words. Maybe he had finally come to ask to be let go, I thought. *I swear, if that's what he's going to say, I'll pay him handsomely and gift him a cow, too.*

'It's about your woman helper.'

'You mean my slave?'

'God didn't make her a slave. She's a helper.'

'She's my slave. What about Munira?'

Damn the disappointment I'm feeling!

'You know that the farm needs continuous, vigorous work to survive?'

'Yes, I've known that since I came here, Khamis.'

'And that the workers need to be able to work without any distractions? These are poor bachelors who can't marry, and they're barely able to keep up with what you have them doing.'

Like a fool, I whispered, 'What does she have to do with that?'

'She's a young thing, good-looking, and flirts a lot. They leave their work to watch her coming and going, which slows everything down. What do you think about letting her go, and I bring an older woman to help you?'

'An older woman? That's what you wanted to tell me? I'll end up working instead of this old woman, who probably won't show up half the time. Munira is young, strong, and I'll keep her.'

'Could you then perhaps get her to come and go a different way?'

'It's not a sin for men's shameless eyes to take her in. Should she sit at home to please you? These uncouth labourers are like all men, gawping at women, even old hags. Men are perennially shameless wherever you go.'

'Listen to me, madam. Let me bring you someone else.'

'No.'

'I have a strong woman, but she's married.'

'No.'

'Madam Zahra—'

'No.' When he fell silent, I added for good measure, 'And I'm sure you think I shouldn't work either.'

'I—'

'Am I not beautiful as well, so that the workers look at me when I pass by?'

'I—'

'You want both Munira and me out of work, it seems, so you can take care of the farm as you please. You think the whole world ought to answer to you.'

His eyes became slits.

'Get out of my face!'

As soon as my breathing seemed to be returning to normal, Rabea entered, his face clouded over. 'What's got into you? What you're doing isn't good for us. You know that rebellion is popular in this country, that there are thefts happening left and right, murders in secret. That man can turn everyone against us, and you're here treating him so rudely, it's as if he's one of your slaves. I told you a hundred times that the man has dark thoughts. He has a great following among the locals. Are you trying to get us killed?'

'We won't die, not by the hand of some Europeanised man who likes to be in control. We'll be fine. Now, stop being so agitated. As for the thefts, we're able to guard our goods. I'm going to guard the pen myself and kill the thief with my own two hands. I'll do it all on my own, you'll see.'

'How crazy can you get? You don't see what's going on, and you'll get us all killed. They're all just waiting for us to make one wrong move. Didn't Sultan warn you? If he comes back, I'll tell him that you're humiliating Khamis and provoking him. You'll see what he does then. He'll take back the authority document he gave you.'

'Let him take it back. It's not like he'll get anything out of it.'

'What do you mean?'

'When Sultan comes, you'll see what surprise I have in store for him.'

'Zahra, I'm tired of your games. You're beyond stubborn.'

'What happened to you? You used to be so calm. What are you scared of?'

'You'll only be happy once the roof of the house comes crashing down on us.'

'I don't think so. The roof will fall on Khamis's head first. I mean, after all, he's so tall.'

He shook his head in despair and quietly sat at a distance.

That night, I grabbed the rifle hanging on the wall of the house. It was fully loaded. I'd often thought of using it. I remember the first day I'd touched a rifle, back when my fingers had been soft as silk. My father had taught me that honour was more valuable than life, and that in wartime people go crazy, doing anything just to survive. He also took me aside and told me, 'If you're not strong enough to kill your attacker, then aim for your own head.'

My father was right–in general, I mean. He didn't know I wouldn't be strong enough to kill myself, even if it was to defend my honour. It was better that I be confident enough to kill someone else, to stay safe.

I chose a bush opposite the pen, right next to the chicken coop. It was pitch dark all around, with no sign of Hamud. Maybe, like me, he was hiding. A long time went by, and I lost feeling in my legs. Everything was quiet and peaceful. I wondered if the thief was a fox or a wolf. I was afraid that the ghost that has been with me since childhood would show up, a giant of a poltergeist, a ring in his nose like a bull.

God damn this stupid thief! My legs were completely numb now, and the weather so cold it made me shudder. I swallowed my cough and focused on the darkness all around. Maybe I'd be able to spot some kind of movement, but the place was quiet, with no movement to speak of, and with sleep pulling persistently at my eyelids. I started drifting in and out of sleep, and I seemed to have fallen into a deep sleep when the chickens made a noise and I started. I saw ghosts–no, black children–swirling round me, who then took off running. They were so young, so underfed that their bones were almost sticking out. They were as thin as the almond tree trunks that we used to plant back on the mountain.

'Stop! Stop there, otherwise I'll shoot!'

It seems I surprised them, for they scattered, running like the wind. I closed my eyes and pulled the trigger. I heard a yell far off. I grew frightened and held the gun in a defensive position. Before I could pull the trigger again, a strong hand gripped my arm. I yelled out and saw whose face it was. 'God damn you, Khamis! What are you doing here?'

'Give me the rifle.'

'Let me go. Look, I've injured one of the thieves, but he's still running. Let me go, you idiot!'

'They're hungry, they'll only take what they need. Give me the gun.'

'You're hurting my arm. Let go of me!'

As I tried to wriggle out of his grasp, my eyes locked with his fiery eyes in the dark. I felt so small next this giant of a man. What an animal he was.

'God damn it, let me go.' As soon as the footfalls had died down, he let me go. His body smelled of fresh soap and a strange cologne, and his brute strength was off-putting.

'I get it, you planned all this. Let's come to an understanding in the morning. I bet you've been protecting them every night.'

'The children of my nation don't steal. We are honourable, and all this is ours. We don't steal our own things, we...' He halted his speech abruptly when I wrenched the gun from his hands and started running in the direction the yell had come from. I searched all over, but the place was completely empty. My blood boiled at all this idiocy. Again, he roughed me up, this time grabbing my waist and pulling me toward him. I started kicking him. 'How dare you!' He forced me to look into his eyes as he ranted. 'Listen

The three in the pen are male.'

'We're in agreement, then. Tomorrow, I'll bring you six to choose from.'

'Leave them with me for two days so I can test them out and choose the strongest.'

'That's too much to ask, madam.'

'Not to me. As for the price, we'll agree on it without any bargaining.'

He muttered in confusion, then agreed.

Hamud was ridding the clove harvest of dirt and leaves, the only one carrying out the orders I had given at dawn. I sent Munira and Rabea to go ask about the injured child, and I waited the whole day to hear their response. Khamis didn't come to me that morning, and for some reason I decided to postpone wreaking my vengeance on him, maybe because I wanted to ask him about his cologne.

I asked the workers to carry the cloves and sugar cane on the backs of the donkeys. But Hamud sat rubbing his hands clean of the clove peels, stealing glances at me.

'We'll take these goods to the port.' At first, I muttered among the workers, but then announced in a loud voice, 'Whoever is late will lose a day's wages.'

Kaghudi protested in broken Arabic, 'No, no, too much.'

'Leave if you want, Kaghudi.'

I was pleased with myself when I saw them obey me. I kicked the pregnant horse and rode behind them. 'I'll go with you and Rabea will come, too. Hamud, you stay with the chickens.'

here, I don't want to be angrier than I already am!' I heard his heartbeat speeding up and was convinced in that moment of his intense patriotism.

'Leave me. Where is Hamud?'

'He's sleeping at my place. He got tired of guarding, so I took him to sleep.'

'Khamis, are you challenging me? Do you think I'm a weak woman who's easy to trick?' A violent wave of coughing cut me off. Hesitantly, he approached. 'Are you okay? Let's take you to the house.'

'Get away from me! I can't stand you, traitor.'

'Don't speak. You've got a serious disease. I'll call a doctor for you in the morning.'

'To poison me? I'm fine.' Again, I got lost in my coughing, wondering why my feet were trembling when I heard him speak. Why was he still so sinister even when he was trying to do good?

* * *

The donkey merchant came the next morning. He was from Bahrain, an Arab. He talked at length about the quality of his donkeys, their fatty feed, and everything else he could think to say about them. He didn't seem surprised to see me there, as if it didn't faze him at all. Or maybe he was used to dealing with women. 'I won't buy your donkeys without seeing them first. Did you see an injured boy on the way here?'

He smiled at my sudden change of subject. 'No. Is he a runaway slave?'

'No matter. Bring me two females and one male. I want them to breed.

The tense atmosphere exploded into rumbling laughter, and Hamud hid himself to avoid hearing their snide comments. I gave Rabea the rifle and made my way to the small caravan. The mare seemed happy that morning. The breeze refreshed my body and also made me feel lighter.

* * *

I have a secret. The veiled flattery of the merchants delights me, as do their looks, which are full of admiration. I like how they move hurriedly before me and accept my high prices, only because of the green heaven in my eyes.

* * *

'You know, Rabea, only now have I realized where the thieving child is.'

'Can't you just let it go? It's been a week.'

'Take me to where Khamis lives.'

'The man hasn't come here, trying to avoid your bitter tongue. Now you're looking for trouble.'

'He's the one who comes every day to ruin my plans. And now he's in hiding.'

Rabea grumbled and let out a long exhalation. When he was about to leave, I stopped him. 'Believe me, he's hiding the thief in his house, nursing the gunshot wound.'

'You always think the worst. Even if you're right, you should still leave it alone, because he's a difficult man. He loves everyone from this soil, so don't even think of making him angry. It's been more than a week, and Hamud hasn't shut his eyes while guarding the chickens, who are all still there. And the sheep, they've increased in number. You should just drop it.'

That day, it kept coming to mind that I had to find the thief and, if Rabea wasn't going to come with me, I'd go on my own.

'Go on your own,' he said. 'I'm tired of your crazy schemes.'

'Okay, let's see what I do with you.'

He grumbled once more and slammed the door in my face. Good thing I had my shawl on to keep me warm. With ease, I made my way toward the workers under the mango tree.

'Kuzi, come here.' As he came closer, I smiled. 'Do you know where Khamis lives?'

He looked flustered.

I quietly probed him. 'The man has been missing for a week. I just want to make sure he's okay.'

'He's fine, I am sure of that.'

'I want to see him, I've missed him.'

'He's busy.'

I clenched my teeth. 'Munira told me you have nine younger sisters and a crippled mother. Take me to him now or I'll throw you out.'

*   *   *

Khamis' house, or more like his hut, was old, rundown, made of clay and straw. The light inside was so faint that any passer-by would think it was abandoned, teeming with djinns. I motioned silently to Kuzi and then quietly knocked on the door. I heard a noise from inside, then Khamis' voice asking in Swahili who was at the door. 'Tell him it's you. I don't want him to know I'm here.'

Kuzi said his name quickly, his eyes guilty, his teeth pulling at the dry flakes on his lips. He put his hand on his heart, then said a word in Swahili I didn't know. 'What did you just tell him, you fool? If you warned him, you're done.'

'I didn't tell him anything.'

After a minute or two, the door opened to Khamis's smiling face, which looked exhausted. When he saw my face, he gasped and glared at Kuzi. He berated him in Swahili, but I didn't wait to hear their argument and slipped under Khamis' arm gripping the doorframe as I asked, 'Won't you invite us in? It's impolite.'

I looked around the house, which was pretty much empty.

'Wait,' he said. 'I have a guest. It's shameful if you see him.'

'Oh, you know I'm not concerned about things like that.'

I shook his cold hand and went around, looking for this supposed guest. But the room was completely empty except for a rag, cotton, and some gauze.

'Looks like your guest was injured.'

Khamis started swearing in Swahili at Kuzi, who tried unsuccessfully to defend himself. I picked up the blood-stained cotton on the ground. 'Don't tire yourself out. I threatened to take away his salary. He has a large family, as you know, and had no choice. Did your guest just leave? You must be tired from stealing all those chickens, distracting guards, and inciting people to rebel.'

'What do you want, Zahra.'

This was the first time he had said my name without prefacing it with madam. His white teeth gleamed in the dim light.

'I just missed you, that's all. There was no one to yell at me or hatch plots. When will you come back?'

'I don't know. Just stop inspecting my house and get out.'

'Oh goodness, throwing out our guests, are we? Have a look at my finger here. I've got a long thorn stuck deep down in it, which I can't get out. You must have studied medicine, seeing as you have some medical supplies here.'

He said with the utmost chilliness, 'Human beings are peace-loving creatures. I didn't study medicine. Now, go home. It's dark out, and there must be people worrying about you.'

'Where's the young thief? Give him to me. I won't punish him. I just want to ask him to work for me. I have a good heart.'

'I don't know where he is.'

'I want the thief.'

'To make him a slave?'

'No, no, I believe in people's freedom.

'Such a hypocrite.'

'I said, *bring him here.*'

'Don't you dare raise your voice at me. You searched for him. Did you find him here?

'And your guest that you mentioned, where is he?'

'You mean she. I think she heard your voice and slipped out the back door.'

'A woman? You're lying. Then why the bloody cotton?'

'Maybe you'd know more about that, seeing as you're a woman.'

'Filthy liar.'

I threw the cotton in his face and called Kuzi to the door. 'I'll get the boy by whatever means necessary.'

'You're digging a hole for yourself, Zahra.'

I spat in his face. 'You're fired.'

'I'll come by tomorrow when you've thought more about this. We're like the clove tree, and you are a weed to be removed.'

Someone like Khamis won't keep me from my destiny of absolute freedom. I'll crush him under my foot like an impudent insect.

(15)

*'While chasing after hopes of a treasure,
I lost the profit I held in my hands!'*

- Jean de La Fontaine

Today I'll laugh wholeheartedly, and the legend of the rogue will be destroyed by my hand. Sultan will taste, for the first time, perhaps the most difficult of deals with someone he thought was beyond weak. He can ask me for everything, except for this beautiful farm. So let him take everything, but this magnificent clove heaven will be the final compensation for all he's put me through. Now, with the authorisation document in my possession, I'll throw Sultan out of Bemba. How his heart will burn when he finds out!

It's a fair division. Didn't he strip me of my life, my dreams, and make me cut my mourning period short? Now it's his turn, so let him squirm, and let me get him out of my life for good.

I bid the lawyer farewell with such warmth that Munira came and whispered, 'Do you like him? No one else does.'

'Yes, today I do. He works with such alacrity and doesn't object to anything. That's how he gets what he wants.'

'But he's a cheat. I swear, *wallah*, believe me.'

'I'm happy, Munira. I like this place. It's the one thing I want. Without it, I have nothing. You know my brother, who I told you about? He's the reason I ran away from Mombasa. I wish he could see me now, here, as a queen that he can't touch. If he did, I'd order the slaves to whip him, one thousand, no two thousand strokes. Maybe once I'm over my fear, I can look forward to meeting him.'

'Is he beautiful like you, madam?'

'You sly one! Even more so. If you can believe it, God gave him more, better of everything. I was born a nobody. Let's start our Swahili lesson now. Where's Kuzi?'

Her face grew red with embarrassment and she ran to call him. It was as if he had been waiting for her. He straightened up as he greeted her. *What fools they both are. Is there even room for love in this crazy world? Love can shackle freedoms, leaving you with regrets and old age.* But why would they listen? They were enchanted with the verdant land, taken in by the charm of youth. What else did they have? They both were poor, a hundred weights hung round their necks. They knew very well that love wouldn't provide them with a living, but they blocked their ears to any warnings, these young things in need of a dream to ease their worries. They needed something, even if it was an illusion, that gave them hope.

*   *   *

'Do you see all this money, Khamis? If I'd made a deal with your friends, then the farm would be uninhabitable. Look how green it is, full of water and workers going about their tasks.'

'You're good at making yourself seem important, but the land you're standing on is already so fertile that, if you breathe in, you'll smell clove and sandalwood.'

'I won't get angry at you today. You're all bark and no bite. As for the child that you hid from me, he'll be here today. You know who'll bring him? My slave, one of your dearest friends. You know why? Because I own everything and they're needy.'

He swallowed his saliva. 'It doesn't mean that they're traitors or that they love you. They're doing this because they have many mouths to feed. You've taken everything from us, even the feeling of freedom. They burn with fury inside, and all this won't last long. One day the scales will tip. I myself will buy you, and you will serve me, my slave forever.'

'I like how much effort you put into such dreams. But all of you–and I mean them, too–you're slaves, and a slave is always a slave, and a master, always a master.'

'What about religion?'

'So you also call upon religion when it suits you. We're all two-faced. During the day, you work with me but then, at night, you stir people up against me. I used to be the same, but I can't go on being so hypocritical.'

'I'm not two-faced, I'm nationalistic.'

'I, too, love this country.'

* * *

He was young, trembling, but tall like the rest of his kind. His arm was wrapped in gauze that had started to go black because of how dirty it was. He stood in front of me, his eyes, wide with fear, filling his entire face. A hungry child, his cheeks sunken. Before him I felt horrible, as if I must like tormenting others. *But I've got to be strong, I've got to make myself strong.*

'So you're the one who stole the chickens and the sheep.'

He didn't understand me. He looked at Munira, befuddled, so she translated for him, and he started speaking to her in Swahili. From what he was saying, I made out that he was responsible for five siblings and two elderly parents. Using gestures, I showed him that thieves usually got their hands cut off. Calmly, he brought his hands before me and said, 'Here you go, but make sure to pay my family.'

'What a smart boy you are! They've taught you well. Are you trying to make me feel bad? But I'm going to offer you some work.'

'I don't want it. You all treat us all like donkeys. My father worked like a donkey. And when he grew old, they threw him away.'

'Not all people are the same. Did Khamis tell you we're all the same?'

'No, no one told me. They just told me to refuse to work with you. They say you make the workers tired and ask them to work at night.'

'That's not true. They hate me because I'm not from here. Also, you won't work in the field, you'll work with Munira, helping her around the house, and you'll get good daily wages.'

'Why would you do that for me?'

'For God's sake, so that you don't steal again. You can even bring your friends to work for me too, but make sure they don't steal from me.'

'I don't believe you.'

'I just want to stop the stealing. And I want one of you to be my personal helper–you, for example. Does your arm hurt? I can get you a doctor.'

'You'd do all that to stop the stealing?'

'Yes.'

He thought for a moment, and then reached out his hand out to me. 'I'll do it. You're not like they say you are. You're kind.'

I felt a strong prick in my chest at his last words. He was so innocent, so naïve, and his eyes were so beautiful. I *really* was horrible.

I felt nauseous and dizzy. The weather was unbearably humid, and the cough was a reminder of how fatigued my body was. The boy ran behind me, panting. 'There's a guest for you, madam. Should I let him in?'

'Guest? Is it the merchant?'

'No, no, he's from your country. Really big.'

And then, just like that, Sultan stood in front of me, like a ghost from my past, clean-shaven and in fresh clothes. At that moment, I didn't know how to arrange my face. I just froze in my seat, a wan smile affixed to my face.

'What's this welcome, Zahra? I thought you'd jump up to welcome me and kiss my face, but you're so cold. I've missed you.'

He took my hand in his and shook it. It was a hard handshake, and his hands were hot.

'What's with you? Don't you know what desire is like? Don't you know how to act toward your future husband?'

'Aren't you going to your wife in Zanzibar? Why are you here?'

'My God!'

He sat next to me on the couch. 'I've only left you here for three weeks and you've gone and found someone else. Who is it this time? Will your slave kill him like your last husband? Or maybe I will.'

My entire being trembled, and I felt dizzy. 'There isn't anyone. I'm not marrying anyone.'

'Except for me, of course. Come here and tell me the plans you have for your land.'

'My ... my land?' How did he know already? I started to feel even more unwell than before. I flopped down in the seat.

'Aren't you going to be my wife? What's with you, why are you so yellow? Are you hiding something from me? Why are you trembling? Zahra, what have you done behind my back?'

Oh God, where did all my courage go? Why do I feel like running and hiding? Why do I feel like throwing up? Why I am feeling guilty? I only seized what I deserved, what's rightfully mine.

He looked around, surprised. 'Where are Rabea and Hamud?'

'I sent them both on an errand.'

'A secret mission, it seems. You've become quite a strong woman, I see. When are we getting married? Now?'

I swallowed my saliva, geared myself up, and replied, 'I won't marry.'

'You're starting to get on my nerves. What's this?'

'I won't marry. Take what you want.'

'Why are you saying that? Is there someone else better than me?'

'You aren't good for me. You've got a bad reputation, and a future with you would mean I'd move from one place to the next.'

'Look who's talking! Ms Noble Lineage.'

He circled me, shock all over his face. He was trying to suss out whether I was joking, but I bowed my head and kept talking. 'I took advantage of your power of attorney and put the farm in my name. I won't marry you, so just take whatever you want as your compensation. Except for the farm—that's mine.'

He grew pale as he stood in front of me, speechless, as if stung. So I kept going. 'You killed my husband and took advantage of my fear. Today, I'm not scared anymore. Bring my brother today if you want.'

He sat in the chair across from me, staring at my face, hoping to see a smile. But I looked at him stone-faced. 'You can sit there in that chair till it's time for you to leave the country, and I'll give you all your money. This is now my property. I won't share it with anyone or fight anyone for it.'

'My God, who taught you to betray me like this? Even Khamis never tried such a thing. I saved you from being humiliated, I helped you and protected you. And you're punishing me by acting like this.'

'You did it because I paid you good money. And today, I'll give you more. What else do you want?'

'You're really doing this, you bitch?'

'Calm down. If you don't, I'll call my slave and he'll take you and your luggage back to the boat.'

'You think you're done with me?'

I stood up in front of him, staring into his deep, gorgeous eyes. 'I don't want to get rid of you, but we're not made for each other.'

He smiled his cunning smile, and it scared me to guess what he might be thinking. 'I'd expected a surprise from you, but this is too much. No worries, you'll come back to me one day. Will you allow me to stay here for just a week? It will be embarrassing for me to go back to the boat early.'

'I warn you, don't play with me, Sultan.'

He forced out a chuckle, resentment clear on his face. 'The stab in the back hurts.'

'If I've got to protect myself, Sultan, I'll order them to take you to another sheikh whose son you've sold off.'

'The believer doesn't get stung twice. I came to tell you that this slaving season went well, and I think that, after today, I'm going to retire from that dangerous job. The boat's enough for me.'

'And the weapons?'

'Now that I won't give up. Especially because of the people of Bemba.'

'What do you mean?'

'I'm tired now. Tell that girl of yours to get a bed ready for me, and to bring me food to my room, alone.' Then he got up. 'I swear, God made your head too big, Zahra.'

*   *   *

'You two' I snapped at Rabea and Hamud, 'be quiet! Your master is tired and there's no need to wear him out any more with this silly talk.'

But Hamud ignored me and went on. 'But she didn't listen to Khamis. She treats him like a servant, stripping him of his dignity.'

Rabea added furiously, 'She always does the opposite of what he wants. She's such an idiot.'

I yelled, incensed, 'Shut up!'

Sultan didn't object or even look surprised. He just looked back and forth between his two gossipy slaves.

'No, no, Zahra. How can that be?' His words were scornful and gave the two slaves pause. They then started whispering and quarrelling with each other. 'Khamis is a very skilled man, very reliable. I know him well. He has great sway over the minds of the locals.'

'I'm going to throw him out, Sultan.'

'That's so rude. You should marry him. That way, you can stay on the farm,' Sultan replied.

'Tell her, master, tell her. That man will lead the rebellion against us. The country reeks of treason, and she's treating him like a child. Tell her how much you suffered to gain his favour, and for him to manage things here.

Tell her why you used to turn a blind eye to him favouring his people.'

'She knows all that, Hamud. Zahra always likes to make problems. Let her be.'

'Master, you're just encouraging her. Does that mean you're not going to marry her?'

'That's what I've always liked about you, Rabea. Always looking out for me.'

I looked at Sultan's cold features. He kept stealing glances at Munira, who was sitting by me on the ground.

'I'm going to sell these two slaves to the first slaver I chance on, to get rid of their salty tongues.'

'I don't think you have the right to do that, Zahra. I own them, and I'm going to set them free when I leave here,' Sultan countered. 'Would you believe that this woman tricked me and has put the farm in her own name?'

The two men exchanged looks and then turned to me. 'Really?'

'Yes,' I responded. 'All the papers are in order.'

'And us?'

'If you want, go from here and leave her on her own, they'll still come for her.' Sultan replied.

'I'm going,' Rabea said.

Hamud followed.

The evening slowly cloaked the branches of the massive mango tree, the small birds finding shelter in its branches. It was a silent evening, in which only the grasshoppers and the frogs' croaking could be heard. The workers were stretched out on the ground, chatting in low voices after realising that I understood a good amount of Swahili. Those days, all of us were working. I would toil alongside them, no longer sleeping away the day in my room. I got addicted to work and having the upper hand. I enjoyed bullying them. Whiffs of smoke, infused with the smell of fried chicken, drifted around me. People were laughing loudly. I could make out Abdallah, Sultan, and Khamis. In the clouds of smoke, I sometimes saw my father's rusty rifle, and at other times I saw a worn-out silver dagger. I myself was akin to an amorphous wisp of smoke. I couldn't fathom why I suddenly yearned for home. It seemed that, at the time, I was clinging to that place like a drowning person, like someone with nothing.

What are you thinking about? Looking into the sky. Are you missing your dead husband?

It was Salim himself, with all his ideals. He was also fleeting, a wisp of smoke on his own path. He too evaporated, swallowed up by the sea.

Are you thinking of tricking someone else?

Even though the sea is my friend and doesn't pester me for even a day, there is another wide space I welcome, a wider one than the sea that swallows me bit by bit. I don't know what I want anymore, really. What was the point of coming on this reckless journey to begin with?

I don't look at him, I feel myself walking in an endless spiral, sea spirals that I'd heard about and now suddenly feel. Something is scaring me. I'm cold even though the weather is warm. None of you know who I really am, what I really want. Would any of you be surprised if I told you that I don't know a thing about myself? I was born to break rules, to say no even to things that make sense.

* * *

He was blatantly flirting with her and she, as usual, was walking with exaggerated coquettishness, swaying with the breeze, carrying a platter of rice on her head, humming a lovely Swahili song. Her voice itself was seduction. Everything in this African woman was femininity personified. Outright flirting like this would have been scandalous in my country, but here such behaviour didn't turn any heads. Like someone who bought bread from a bakery, or someone who bathed in a pond, it was just a daily occurrence. Just as flirting was normal—bread in a time of hunger.

Sultan was a seasoned flirt. He practiced in silence, and he followed her exaggerated movements with wide eyes and a sly smile. *What a sight! A few hours ago, he was trying to change my mind about not marrying him, and now here he is shamelessly flirting with my slave right in front of me.* 'This is the height of rudeness. Are you flirting with her in front of me?'

'You're not being fair to me, Zahra.' His eyes followed the movements of her body, his face showing how pleased he was at the sight he beheld. He scratched his head in confusion. 'How beautiful she is, Zahra. Where did you get her from? I haven't seen her before. You've struck gold.'

'Leave her alone, Sultan.'

'You're jealous.' He cut his words short when he saw her chatting with one of the workers. She stole a look at him.

'God damn! She really is attractive.'

I got up from sitting next to him, hating the feeling of being sidelined. I entered the house quickly and sat on the couch beside the window, watching the workers and their continual laughing. It wasn't long before Munira brought me some dinner. She looked at me with great interest, but I didn't pay her any attention. Then, without any particular reason, she asked delicately, 'Will the guest be having dinner here with you?'

'No, give him his dinner far away from me. Why are you asking such stupid questions?'

She stared at me for a moment then quickly left. I saw her catch up with him and speak to him for a bit. I wasn't disappointed when I saw him follow her soon after and disappear into the night.

They were like stray cats in the field: the night call and the stalking male. Back home, I would follow the cats to see the end of the chase in the middle of the *qat* in bloom.

The workers' tales were entertaining, but my chest was tight, and I was scared. I had a coughing fit. The spots of blood were getting bigger and bigger each day. I wiped them away quickly, turning so that no one would see.

I then remembered the story of Suleiman and the needle. A tear dropped unexpectedly from my eye, because it reminded me of my husband, who I had forgotten, the one who had been betrayed and killed.

I felt the same tightness and congestion. The tap in the bathroom was being stubborn. While I was trying to fix it, I heard Munira's faint laugh through the wall. I tried to eavesdrop to figure out what was happening behind the clay wall, but I could only hear a faint rustling and grasshoppers singing a monotonous, depressing tune.

The night was bleak, truly godforsaken. I felt a burning sensation in my chest and an odd gnawing in my stomach.

Ahmed came to see me as usual after dinner and sat next to me, smiling.

'Where are your friends?'

'They're still eating dinner and wish you good health, madam.'

'But there are others who want me dead, Ahmed.'

'That's not true. You're a good woman and treat us well.'

'There are those who are planning to get rid of me.'

'Who are they? They must have a death wish.'

I smiled in spite of myself. 'You'll fight for me, Ahmed. Will you be loyal to me if there's a war?'

'What war? God forbid!'

'They say that Khamis wants to steal the land and kill me.'

'No, Khamis respects you, madam.'

'So many people have told me this. At first, I didn't believe them, but now it's gotten out of hand. And people are warning me about him, too. I'm scared, Ahmed. There's no one to protect me if he gets angry.'

He beat his chest with his palm. 'We're all here for you. Me and my friends and my brothers.'

'Khamis is planning something. If only I knew what he was planning, then I could protect myself before falling into their trap. I'm an honourable woman, a good woman. If I become a prisoner, then you'll all be out on the street again. How I worry for you all.'

Silence fell between us, and I started coughing. I didn't have to wait long to hear what I had been fishing for all along. 'I'll find out what they're planning.'

'No, they'll think you're spying for me.'

'Never, they won't know. You can trust me.'

'What if they find out that I'm the one who gave you the idea? No, boy, stay with me. Just promise me your loyalty.'

'I'll just follow them and tell you secretly what they're up to.'

'No, don't do that, Ahmed. You speak sometimes without thinking, and they might cut out your tongue.'

'I'll do it to show how grateful I am.'

'Oh, Ahmed, just forget it. I wish I hadn't said anything.'

But he stood before me and said, 'I am loyal to you, and so thankful.'

At that moment, I felt somewhat relieved. *I don't have any country today aside from this one, and I'll fight for it to console myself for all I've been through.*

Rabea entered, the look on his face telegraphing his knowledge of the ugly game I was playing with the young boy. But he didn't say anything, so I thanked God because I'd had my fill of barbs.

'You know, Rabea, Khamis warned me about Munira. He said she'd distract the workers with her beauty. Does she distract you, Rabea?' He smiled, then shook his head.

'Don't deny it. Even your master runs after her like a fool.'

'It's his hobby, he can't control himself.'

'Did you hear what he said? He hates me because I beat him.'

He laughed loudly. 'And did you really?'

'It's the biggest disappointment of his life, really.'

'But he's not done with you yet.'

'What do you mean?'

'When people like the two of you get together, no one ever gives in, and usually the man has the last word. He said I've become more loyal to you now than to him. Obviously, that's painful to hear.'

'He's only got two days left and then he leaves for good. He won't come back, right?'

'No, he won't.'

Munira came back into the room. Her face was flushed. She told me there had been a lot of dirty dishes and…. I kept listening until she ran out of excuses. When she finished, I smiled at her and ordered her to go to bed.

'You know, I wish I could see Salim's wife now. If she looks anything like Munira, I'll forgive him. I used to think African women were ugly.'

'Ah, yes, your dead cousin.'

Sultan had shamelessly been standing right behind Munira. *If only I knew what he'd being doing that whole time to make her dark cheeks so flushed and her eyes light up!* 'Hello Sultan. You're also glowing, too, but also seem to be tired. Sore maybe? Do you want some water? Or a duvet?'

'No, I need to speak to you privately.'

Rabea jumped up to leave. I stared at Sultan calmly. 'No, I can never allow you to sleep with her, Sultan. Have you lost it? Remember God.'

'Don't be so jealous. I want to talk about your coughing. Are you sick? Don't hide this from me, Zahra.'

'Are you trying to say that you've forgotten already what I did to you, and now you care about me? Leave it alone. I know all your tricks.'

'I haven't forgotten, and I won't. But not everything is about the farm and how you tricked me.'

'The contract is legal and as for—'

'I won't take anything from you. I'll come back after a year or two to find you penniless. Then I'll win you back, and the farm, too.'

'Actually, that's when I'll sell you off as a slave.'

He laughed loudly. 'I still want you, Zahra. You're my wife and, believe me, I'm still strong. Just marry me for one night and you'll see.'

'Stop talking about the impossible. In two days, you'll be gone, and if you don't leave, my men will drag you to the boat.'

'So you'll be fine with me being dragged like a donkey?'

'Why not? You're here to exact revenge. I'll have you for lunch before you have me for dinner.'

'You always think the worst. I'm a kind man and...'

He took my hand, and I wrenched it away. 'Go back to you bed. I don't think you can handle another round.'

'I haven't done anything yet.'

*   *   *

Sorrow upon sorrow, and what a bleak night! My pure country, my mountain, the streams, the passing phantoms. My heart is burdened with sorrow, my eyes fighting off sleep. The sea swallows me up, and my heart is full of plotting. What has possessed me? Why have I gone mad?

*   *   *

Sleep had barely touched my eyelids when I heard a knock on my door. I stiffened, but the knocks didn't stop. *Who could it be this late at night?*

'Zahra.'

Had he come to say something childish to me so late at night? I pretended not to hear him.

'I know you're not asleep. I've come to give you one last chance to stop all this. Things have got out of hand between us.' I didn't move. He whispered so as not to wake anyone else in the house. I wondered if he had just left Munira's room, drunk on her youth.

'Just show me your face, Zahra. Let's just finish it and come to an agreement. I cherish you, and I'm ready to forget all that you did to my property.

Don't let me go away resentful or you'll regret it, my darling. I don't want to hurt you.'

Then it went quiet. I heard him muttering angrily, but I didn't show him my face. It was all meaningless. No use. I was already at the bottom of the sea. No point to all this hot air.

'You'll regret this, Zahra.'

There's something stuck in my chest. It's heavy, weighing down on all my dreams and hopes. It must be regret or yearning, I don't know, I don't know. But it's so tiresome, paralysing me.

* * *

'So you send child spies, how clever you are! I'm so impressed with how you think.' Khamis surprised me that morning with these words, even as I was feeling unwell.

'You're imagining things, I didn't send anyone.' Then I added, 'Is there a reason I'd send a spy to you? You're loyal, doing whatever you can to make me happy.'

'You're so cunning, Zahra. But I warn you against turning our children against us.' Before he could add anything else, my coughing fit cut him off. He looked at my face and my trembling hands. He said in a low voice, 'You're very sick. Should I call a doctor?'

'I don't need help from you. You've come and accused me of this and then you dare ask if I'm sick.'

'So many people in my country fall sick, but aren't able to go to a doctor, and then that's the end of them.'

'That's their destiny.'

Suddenly, he yelled in my face: 'Destiny seems to work out well for you. You say that slaves will always be slaves.'

'Why are you acting like this?'

'How could you send one of our own children as a spy? Did you think you'd pay him in candy? What do you call this?'

'Who said I sent him? He made a bet that you wouldn't conspire against me, and I said that you want me to leave. That's it.'

I held my breath a bit to allow myself a cough. He believed me and said, 'You're sick, so I won't talk about this any further. But you'll regret how you're using our children against me. You're just a plague.'

'Get out, I'm tired of your hatred.'

Just then I felt very dizzy, and he tried to grab me. Looking into his eyes, I saw an unexpected look, something warm, but it was gone in a flash.

Khamis was strong, cunning. He'd also been infected. He was now in my hands, but I couldn't take advantage of the situation because I was so sick. My head was about to explode. I lay down on the sofa as he requested, then he disappeared to call a doctor.

I stayed where I was, thinking of how I hadn't seen this before. He'd hated me so much, so how was it now turning into love? *Can we really love something we've hated? What about me? Does that mean I actually love ev-*

erything I hate?

Oh, this pain in my throat, my head, my stomach. What does time have in store for me? I remained quiet until Khamis came back with an elderly local. I looked at him suspiciously. But I wasn't strong enough to resist. I felt nauseous again.

Maybe Khamis's weakness will be my final winning ticket. I'm not strong enough to craft any more plots. My head is on fire, and all that's left is for me to step into the maze of my subconscious.

(16)

Be ahead of all parting, as if it were
behind you like the winter passing now.
For among winters, there's one such endless winter
that your heart for all time overcomes.

- Rilke *(Translated from the German by Christianne Marks)*

The whole story is strange. I really can't believe what is happening to me. Am I pregnant, like the doctor says? Pregnant by my husband, now completely forgotten, and ravaged by this lethal, undying cough, as if this is what I need on top of war? Doesn't it all seem like a made-up tale, one the mind can't conceive, but which is happening to me? And then there's Sultan, probably laughing as he gets the news from Rabea.

'You're good at lying. The child confirms that you're a loose woman, not even marrying properly. Even with Saleh, you were the mastermind. But why with me?'

He was still drunk, and he nearly succumbed to tears of disappointment in that moment, but took control of himself in the nick of time before dragging himself to his room. *He'll leave tonight, and his tale will come to an end like all the other men in my life. I think my story is also approaching its end. I'll be buried here with my baby, whom I feel nothing for. A child by a man who came and went.*

I didn't see Khamis that day; maybe he knew of my condition.

'Why are you all looking at me like that? Like I'm dying? I'm fine, and this child to be will be my support. What's wrong with you?'

'It's not safe here. This rebellion, the revolts, and you're pregnant, Zahra. Your poor child ... Rabea says you should go back to your country.'

'Go back there so they can butcher me? Are you crazy? I'm staying right here. This is my land, and there's no place for me other than this one. You two, be quiet, I can't take your chatter anymore.'

The moment they left, I made for the mirror to get a good look at my face. Another woman was looking back, someone who wasn't me. It was as if I'd been cloned, or my likeness stolen. I heard him yelling from a distance, 'You're going to die here, they'll bury you and your damned son, you'll die from shame.' His voice grew faint, 'Speak to me. I know you completely now, so speak to me.'

Stuck in limbo between strength and weakness, I listened to all he had to say, my eyes flooded with tears. Yes, he was my favourite, and perhaps I did even love him. But, for me, the wages of love were loss.

* * *

The months passed slowly as my pregnant body, charged with emotion, grew rounder and rounder. I hated how it looked in the mirror. *This bad omen of a child has ruined my beauty. Even my face has totally changed: my nose is swollen, and it's a despicable red.* After having been proud of how aquiline it had been, I was ashamed of how it looked now.

That wasn't even to mention the dark circles under my eyes. This child was the last thing I wanted. Even my movements had become laboured, and I wasn't able to work like before. I could barely carry myself, barely walk among the workers on the farm. I was like a fat cow, they whispered and laughed. How low I had fallen. I had accepted working with locals on half of my farm's acreage. The income from selling cloves was just enough for us to live on and feed the animals.

With each day, Khamis' demands grew, fuelled by persistent threats to start a strike. He was as horrible as I had imagined. Despite all the longing looks I caught him giving me, everything went up in smoke, and he went back to waging war against me, as if I'd become his sole enemy. The situation on the island was getting more turbulent. Disquieting occurrences proliferated like the plague: unhappy workers, their rebellious dispositions, and sometimes small, actual revolts. Luckily, these were quickly nipped in the bud...since they were small, individual incidents.

'What do you mean they'll pay later?'

'Don't you know that the market is stagnant and trade is slow? They'll sell the crops with difficulty, so they need time to get the money together.'

'And what about me? How will I pay the workers' wages and buy animal feed? Should I sell myself to cater to your local friends?'

'Pay from your savings, and I promise they'll pay you at the beginning of next month.'

'Savings? Did someone tell you I'm now in possession of Qarun's treasure? I want my money now.'

'They're suffering, madam. Don't you understand?'

'Okay, they're suffering. But what about me? What should I do with all the outstretched palms aimed in my direction? Should I tell them to wait till next month?'

He forced a smile and said through gritted teeth, 'You're not penniless. You have a lot. No need to get so angry. That will only affect your health and the health of the child.'

'Do you think my pregnancy will allow you to get the upper hand? Do you think I'm weaker now?'

'Don't forget that you're sick. Calm down.'

'Hear this well. If they don't pay tonight, whatever agreement we've had goes out the window, and I'll be forced to sell directly on the open market. I think you understand very well what I'm saying. The market doesn't stay still. Even during war, people will buy to stock up.'

'Why so agitated, Zahra? Let it go. They're poor, and they need your patience and goodwill.'

'I won't change my mind.'

'You don't mean what you're saying.'

'Oh, but I do, and stop threatening to go on strike. If it does happen, I'll go to the fields myself.'

'Don't be crazy, you need to rest.'

I caught his look of longing again, so I toned it down a few notches. 'You're looking out for me, but you know this isn't in my favour. So why are you doing this? Don't I matter to you?'

He stood rooted in place. 'My people come before anyone else.'

'God damn you, get out of my face!'

Sure, my reaction was a little exaggerated. But I'm feeling the pressure from all sides. I could just surrender, but what would that get me?

*   *   *

The news had struck me like lightning. Ahmed had run toward me and whispered in my ear, 'I saw him selling weapons to them.' He was talking about Sultan on the eve of his departure.

Now, he was screaming, 'They poisoned all the animals, they killed them all!'

I trembled and leaned back in the chair in a desperate attempt to regain my lost balance.

'The drinking water had rat poison in it.'

I waited for Rabea and Hamud to arrive. I couldn't even get my tongue to work to ask about who had done it. 'Do you see, Zahra, what your stubbornness has brought down on our heads? Let's move the goods to the souk now, on our backs, our heads. Your donkeys, mules, and cows were all mercilessly executed, and we'll be next,' Hamud said.

Rabea stood frowning, facing me. He saw my miserable state. His friend kept going. 'Are you not convinced by what I'm saying? Do you give in to their demands?'

I felt like I was being strangled. Munira rushed to get me a glass of water.

'Rabea, speak,' Hamud said. 'Tell her, tell her how her dear animals were lying there. Tell her about the flies, maybe then she can picture what...'

Rabea raised his hand to silence his friend after seeing the pain on my face. I really was up against it now, the sole loser in all that, however you sliced it. And justice wouldn't come to my aid because I'd always been so harsh.

I wish I could just take a nap. I don't know how to deal with these things now. Did I spend all my savings fattening up those cows? Didn't I refuse to sell them at a good price because I was waiting for a real crisis, to sell them at an outrageous price? And now they're gone, destroyed, and the donkeys at the same time. My destiny was looking eerily similar to that of those cows in the pen.

But I couldn't just wave the white flag. I stood with my belly protruding, just like any other woman who had given in to a man she hadn't loved. I made my way outside.

My word, that cow–Maysoora, she was called–was so dear to me. I had named her after our cow back home on the mountain. Like me, she had been pregnant, and she was forever smiling. I loved her. Knowing she was gone brought tears to my eyes. *She never resisted anyone. She didn't deserve to die and, like her, neither do I.*

I threw myself on the bag of feed I had bought a few days before. I tried in vain to stem the streaming tears. I was in absolute despair. If the universe could just forgive me for my mistakes, if Sultan could forgive me. Oh, Sultan! That bastard had sold the weapons being used to fight me. Sultan, who left after sullying my slave girl. Sultan, who I still couldn't find a way to hate, despite all he did.

What was left for me to do to save myself and my dignity?

Should I go looking for Salim's wife once more, after having all but forgotten about her? Was I to sell this farm and move to an unknown place all over again? If I did, I'd be bringing my beautiful property to ruin, this place where I'd first tasted the bliss of sovereignty. *I swear, I don't deserve to die.*

After my wave of sorrow came a raging fever. I stayed in bed for a week, unable to eat or drink. I felt that I was wasting away, that the end had come, and that my child would die inside me. I didn't accept any visitors. They all pitied me, and that was the last way I wanted them to look at me. *I'm not weak, despite all their insinuations. It's just that I'm alone, and one hand can't clap on its own.* My whole core shuddered. 'Rabea, will Sultan come?'

He raised his head, looking at me sorrowfully. 'Why are you thinking of him now? Didn't you push him to leave? He's with his children now, living happily with them. What's with you, Zahra?'

'You're the one who's stood by my side, Rabea. Loyal to me no matter how I've treated you. Do you love me, Rabea?'

'You've changed.' He smiled sadly. 'Africa has changed you. You ask with no shame. Come now, get up and do some work. You can buy two donkeys with the money you saved. I know they won't be enough, but they will be enough for your pride, which will be the end of us all soon enough.'

The smell of my breath annoyed me. I hadn't eaten for such a long time, and I was crying inside for food.

'Tell me what I should do now, Rabea.'

'If I tell you, will you listen?'

'If you can convince me.'

'What if I tell you to sell your farm and go back to your country? You're in the fourth month of pregnancy, and war will break out here. Have some sense, Zahra. Think of your child. Go back, but somewhere far from your family.'

'My child isn't better than me. This is the only place I have, so my child will have to live here. And if they don't want to, I'll drown them in the nearest creek.'

'How horrid you are.'

On that day, despite the heat of the sun and the heaviness of my body, which ached all over, I drove the two donkeys. Rabea, Hamud, and Kuzi pulled carts of cloves, sugar cane, and coconut.

The sun, my cough, the dirty flies, and the lazy child inside me didn't allow my head to drop for one moment. Khamis was probably on a hill somewhere watching me suffer, and Sultan up on a mast, his eagle eyes waiting for my downfall.

Of the workers, only Kuzi stayed with me. The rest sided with Khamis, calling for chaos to reign. That was how I found myself as pregnant as a mountain, and the shocks, which came one after the other, were no longer shocks but just fleeting incidents. As for Munira, she started walking like a fool again. Sultan's departure had shocked her, and the gulf between her and Kuzi could no longer be bridged. *They meet, then don't meet, another defeat in love. And how many are those!* He would serve me absentmindedly and, if she passed by, her appearance was met by untrammelled disgust.

Munira forgot everything I had told her, and whenever she saw him, she'd break down and cry. *I wouldn't make a good referee in such matters, because I myself am terrible at mending broken hearts. In this life, love outside of marriage has always meant shame for us, and that's why I can't intervene. It's too late...and I'm a shell of myself.*

'Look, Kuzi, how will we work this land? Do we have enough hands?'

'I went to every café, the land broker's, to every other place to find workers for the land, but it was all in vain. You have a reputation for being difficult.'

'They're biting my hand. Didn't I bless these workers with food and clothing?'

'Forgive them.'

At that moment, Munira came between us and looked at me. Then she turned away.

'Why are you treating her so badly, Kuzi? Shame on you for what you're doing.'

'She let me down, the whore. The man promised her marriage and she gave herself to him. The money blinded her.'

He stung me with his words. *Poor Munira. She should be able to live out her dreams. She followed love only to chance upon an explosion of regret.*

Once upon a time, I had also fallen prey to the delusion that beguiled Munira. *Maybe...who knows. Maybe inside, I was still an ordinary woman hanging onto dreams and waiting for solace at the hands of a man who didn't fear anything, but he never showed up.* I had fallen into the same pit, but I realised that fact just before defeat.

But the poor thing, she was so young and inexperienced, and she was still in shock. Maybe she would give in to the dream, carry it in her chest, and sleep on it.

'She's not a whore. She just doesn't have much sense. The fault lies with the one who misled her. You shouldn't have told everyone, Kuzi. Even if she'd done the deed with you, you still would've dragged her name through the mud.'

'Whoever does what she did deserves to die. Her family, after finding out what she did, have rejected her.'

'How easy it is for them to do so. My family has done the same to me.'

By the time we finished packaging and cleaning the goods, the tension hanging all around had taken everything out of me. I looked weakly at the two hungry donkeys.

'We'll carry the goods in a vehicle. We'll rent one, even if it's expensive.'

* * *

The next morning, I tried to get up, but I couldn't. Too heavy, too dizzy. Munira helped me up, and I had to lean all of my weight on her. 'Put sacks in the stores. We really need to sell them. This is the last time we can harvest cloves. After this, we'll go for a long time with only coconuts and vegetables as our source of income, and that's not enough. Kuzi, why are you just standing? Don't you have school?'

'I left school.' He bowed his head for a moment and then raised it, his eyes looking to the horizon. 'I have to work night and day now, since my mother's eyesight is nearly gone. Her health isn't what it used to be. I have nine sisters and we're just trying to survive. My eldest sister is ready to be married. She needs money, as her groom is really poor. I'll work as a labourer at the port until the early hours.'

'Oh, poor Kuzi, you've got so much to worry about.'

He hung his head. He'd been obsessed with his studies. He had wanted to be a great novelist, a man of importance.

'You know, Kuzi, if we sell all of these goods, it will be enough to pay for your sister's wedding and your education.'

He was different, always showing the utmost respect. *Is it because I'm in a position of power or because this young boy has something that my brothers never did? Or maybe it's just because I've changed, and my evolution has forced others to respect me. Men are the same everywhere.*

Kuzi spent his salary that day, and I added a few rupees to it. 'Tomorrow will be better.' My money had almost run out. I'd soon be left with nothing.

I was jolted awake to the smell of smoke. I looked out through the window, my head spinning. Flames were right in front of me. The storehouse was on fire. The flames scorched my face, the storehouse on the verge of collapsing. The buckets of water that Rabea and Hamud were pouring were of no use.

Khamis and his compatriots had decided to execute me, and nothing was going to stop them. They had decided to swallow me, and I had no defence. Munira came in, terrified.

'They've drowned me, Munira. They've defeated me.'

*   *   *

Smoke in my chest, my eyes, my stomach, blinding me, pressing me down.

My brothers' heads and the farm workers, Sultan, Khamis. Smoke enveloping me. I can't get a breath. Where is it coming from? There were fires at the neighbouring farms. It was war. Slaves were charging at their masters, rage boiling over. I didn't know where to run with my swollen belly. I had tried squeezing it up against the wall to flatten it, pulled at myself, but nothing worked. It stretched out before me, stubborn and ugly.

'Madam, shame on you, what are you doing? You could die.'

'Get away from me, you bad luck woman. Go and call Khamis.'

'Khamis?

'Go, now.'

'Madam, it's war. They'll rip open your belly. Let's get away from here. Rabea and Hamud have arranged for us to escape on a boat.'

'Run away?' I felt the desire to tear myself up. 'Why don't you rip me open? Aren't you also angry? Do you also want to rebel against being a slave? Go on, go get a knife and stick it right into my belly. Maybe it will die, disappear. Or if it doesn't die, strangle him, or let me do it.'

She sat down beside me in surrender. She bowed her head and started crying. The way she had after her lover, the trader of men, had departed.

'You're crying? He left you like a bitch. He hated you, you whore. I won't run away. They'll find me here with my stomach, and they'll burn me. It's all the same to me. But this is my land. I toiled for it, and came here to live on it. Not to die, I won't die, because this belly here was lawful, believe me. I won't be cast as a slut, for I haven't done anything to bring shame...'

'Madam, the slaves are tearing apart everything they come across. They have no mercy. People are terrified. Arab bodies are hanging from tree branches everywhere. Let's leave. Zanzibar is dying. Bemba will see the same fate. Let's run.'

'Run? Take me to Khamis. Take me to him now!'

'Yes madam.' She cried bitterly.

(17)

I'm not looking at you, pharaoh;
rather, I'm looking at how
the wheel turns.

- *Unknown*

'Did you bring me here to tell me this? It's very late, madam. I've got to go, there are many other things to do.'

'But Khamis, listen. All the crops are yours from today, for any price the locals want for them. The people are poor, but just leave me this land, don't let them take it and burn it. This is my land.'

'I don't understand you. You're no different from all the other landowners. You're a tyrant, just like them. A thief, just like them. You deserve to die. I'm going.'

I grabbed him by the hands, a humiliating gesture, and saw his broken eyes. 'They're going to kill me, tear me apart. You don't want me to die. You used to want me, worry about me. You brought me a doctor that day, remember? I was kind to the thieves and gave them a job on the farm. You were happy with me then. How can you let them do this? Khamis, please.'

'I came because I respect you—'

I cut him off. 'Then marry me. Take me wherever you want. I'll do whatever you want. Just get them to leave this land alone. Leave it to me. I don't have anywhere else.'

'Now you want to marry me? What about the differences you used to rant about? Will you marry a black slave?'

'Yes, just leave the land to me.'

He shook his head, stunned. 'No, I won't marry you. There are just too many differences for me to overcome.'

'But you want me. I'm sure of it.'

'Even if I were obsessed with you, I wouldn't trade my people for any woman.'

'Is that it?'

'All I can do for you is guarantee safe passage out.'

'Out? You want me to leave here, to leave this land behind?'

'I can't do anything more, Zahra. I'm a slave to my country.'

'Damn you, you bastard! How dare you refuse me!'

'Of course.' He pulled his hands out of mine and left. I reached the house and was overcome with anxiety. I found them waiting with all their possessions, ready to go.

'Come on, Zahra, let's go,' Hamud said.

'Where's Kuzi?

'They took him with them, and he didn't resist. They were accusing him of betrayal.'

Suddenly, from far off, there came the crack of gunfire and the boom of a cannon. It was war all over again. My whole life had been lost to wars.

'You go. I'll stay here, it's more honourable for me to stay here and die.'

'For God's sake, Zahra, get up. I have children and a wife. I don't want them to see me next as a corpse.'

'You go on, Hamud. You go, all of you. I don't want to run away again. I can't.'

Hamud yelled in frustration. There was a small blast from one of the nearby farms, causing the earth to rumble.

'I'm going, I'm leaving. I don't want them to get me.' He picked up his case and started running. I looked at Rabea and Munira. They looked at Hamud's receding back, then turned to look at me.

'You two, go on,' I said. 'I won't be made to run away. Don't wait for me.'

'Madam...'

'I won't die. Don't worry.'

'Madam....' Munira was crying again. Her sobbing was soon overpowered by the staccato bursts of gunfire, which grew louder, mingled with shouts. 'Get a move on, Munira, and don't believe a word that men say.' She picked up her case left, following Hamud, who hadn't turned back once.

'And you, Rabea, why are you still standing here? Get going.'

'You're crazy. In every way possible.'

Before I could respond, I saw a shadow running toward me, carrying a rifle. I ran to the house, grabbled the rusty rifle, and aimed it out the window at the figure rapidly approaching the house. Rabea stood behind me, his hands behind his back as usual, just watching.

'Zahra!' a voice yelled out. 'It's me, Kuzi!'

'Kuzi?'

I stayed where I was, with the mouth of the rifle still aimed at the running body, even though I had heard him.

'What are you doing, Zahra? Didn't you hear him? It's Kuzi.'

'They might have sent him to kill me. To prove his loyalty to the country. You go to him and see what he wants.'

'He's not doing what you think.'

Kuzi arrived, breathlessly panting, 'I have a letter from Zanzibar. They killed the carrier at the port. A letter from Zanzibar, from Sultan.'

My pulse stopped. *Is that thief of a man still alive?*

Rabea took the letter and looked toward me, worried. 'You read it,' I said. 'I don't know how to...'

'The man said that Sultan helped him escape,' Kuzi continued, 'and pressed money into his hand to make sure the letter arrived. He also said the slaves attacked the farm and Sultan's house. They've definitely taken him prisoner this time.'

'What a stupid man. How could he listen to Sultan's promises? Read me the letter,' I demanded.

Rabea was ill at ease, nauseated by the half-dried blood on the letter.

'He wrote only two lines.'

'You're so slow; read it to me, read it.'

'It says, "Zahra, there is a European boat waiting for you at the port. Your name is on the list, and you'll be safe there. Things here are as bad as they can get. I won't run, and I don't think I will survive this time. If I do, we will certainly meet."'

'What else? What else?'

'That's all there is.'

Finally, Sultan's connections amount to something! The connections that opened all avenues to him. His dubious connections. And today, despite all that I have done to him, to his property, here he is giving a last favour from afar. He didn't forget me.

'Kuzi, how did you get here? Aren't you afraid they'll doubt your loyalty? You've been recruited by them, right?'

'Only to work at the military hospital, to protect the injured and the nurses. They won't doubt me. I'm loyal.'

'And what about us, Kuzi? Do we deserve to die like animals? Abdul Aziz, our neighbour, they killed him and sodomised him. They raped his wife, killed her, and their girls as well.' I choked up. We had come to the end of the road. 'Should I just wait here for them to rip open my belly? I don't deserve to die.'

He didn't say anything. He looked at me, his eyes heavy with pity. My head was spinning as it recounted all the moments of my life to that moment, against a backdrop of the roar of cannon and gunshots in the background.

My small village sleeping on the shoulder of the mountain, and the clay doll sprinkled with rose water, and the rooster crowing—they all haunted my insomnia.

My father with his turquoise prayer beads, my mother…the dewy dawn and the security of the mountains….

And Salim. Salim. Salim, the origin of my tragedy.

All this came to me in the humiliating period spent awaiting my impending demise. All roads to heaven were closed, and all that was left for me was to find a dignified way to die. 'Rabea, do you remember when I ran away from the vaccination needle? There was a man who loved me and hid me away. I wish he hadn't done it, otherwise I wouldn't be dying from this diseased lung today, and this horrible stomach, and these gunshots. If he hadn't done it, at least I would've been able to avoid one path to death. But Death had its doors wide open.'

'You're spitting blood.'

'To hell with it all. You know, if I went back to my country, they'd drag me by my hair and bury me. I thought I had it made out here, but I was stupid. They won't say a hero died, but a bitch, and they're the ones who di-.' My coughing cut me off, and Rabea jumped in.

'Now's not the time to be raving.'

'Are you fed up with me? Of how crazy I am? They'll save you from me soon enough. With a bullet from my furious brother for his honour, or from those rebellious slaves fighting for their freedom.' I looked to Kuzi and smiled, but he met my smile with a frown.

'Don't you know Sultan's mother, Kuzi? She's a piece of work that should be fed to the dogs. As for me, no. I told her everyone is equal and that we should all be free. All talk. I didn't believe it, and I didn't practise it, either. I knew I'd never marry a black person as that would ruin my lineage and....' I stopped once I caught Rabea shaking his head.

'You know, I think I exaggerated what I want. I know myself. I exaggerate. The truth is that I'm really quite ordinary. I complained too much. But even so, this is still my land, and I won't let them steal it in the name of freedom. I'm also here to be free.'

'Madam, there's a boat waiting for you at the port. This is not the time for all this chatter.'

'Chatter?'

'They'll come for you. Khamis won't wait long, since he harbours great hatred for you.'

'Another man who actually loves me.'

'Madam Zahra, please move. This is wartime, so no time for joking.'

'Who said I'm joking?'

I looked at the smoky courtyard and what was left after the cannon had pummelled the farm from a distance. I held my swollen belly. 'I won't die now. I won't run away.'

Kuzi flung himself in front of me while Rabea's lips widened into a cold smile meant to put me at ease. 'I always have my ways to get what I want.' Rabea played with a piece of straw between his teeth, listening to what was being said, not perturbed by the battle raging outside. 'Kuzi, there's no escape from this.' I spun full circle to face him. 'We'd just be running to something worse. I have money. I'm still beautiful. I'll happily serve your old mother and your nine sisters.' Rabea stifled a laugh, while Kuzi opened his mouth in shock.

Time was distressed, and the steadily approaching gunfire and screams presaged the naked, inevitable truth.

Sawad Hussain

Translator

Sawad Hussain is an Arabic translator and litterateur who is passionate about bringing narratives from the African continent to wider audiences. She was co-editor of the Arabic-English portion of the award-winning Oxford Arabic Dictionary (2014). Her translations have been recognised by English PEN, the Anglo-Omani Society and the Palestine Book Awards, among others. She has run workshops introducing translation to students and adults under the auspices of Shadow Heroes, Africa Writes and Shubbak Festival. She has forthcoming translations from Fitzcarraldo Editions, MacLehose Press, and Restless Books. She holds an MA in Modern Arabic Literature from SOAS. Her Twitter handle is @sawadhussain.

Badria Al Shihhi

Author

Badria Al Shihhi is a novelist, academic professor and a Deputy Chairperson of the Omani State Council, with a PhD and MSc. In Chemical Engineering from Loughborough University. She has worked in different positions and gained many experiences. Among her busy non-literary work, she has managed to fulfil her favourite hobby of writing and published three novels and many short stories at an earlier stage (started at age of 12). She is the first female novelist in Oman. Her first novel "Crossing Embers" which was first published in 1999; is considered by many critics as the birth of true Omani novel. Badria is also a mother of five children. She is a frequent traveller and plans an early retirement to spend more time on writing and exploring new places.